Benefits

Jim Arnold

For my father, James Waldron Arnold, who always encouraged his children to follow their dreams.

CHAPTER 1

It was always that damn bus that would wake me, the Muni, early morning horror, groaning its way up the hill to exit the Castro. I'd be tangled up in sheets, staring at the ceiling, awake long before the uncertain gray promise of a new day could arrive.

My stomach would twist into knots in the dark—because I sensed something must be wrong, just had that *feeling*, a vague fear that something horrible was on its way.

Back then, in that San Francisco apartment where I, Ben Schmidt, lived alone in the early aughts, that indefinable something turned out to be cancer. Prostate cancer, at that. In my tender forties!

It wasn't fair; it wasn't pleasant; it had horrible side effects; it was nearly my undoing.

Over time it was still all those things, except now it had the gauzy overlay of a bad time survived. It seemed, sometimes, that dreadfulness happened to a different person entirely. Other times my memory dictated it was, like they'd say down at Esalen, a learning experience. A dark way to find out what you're made of. An opportunity to *grow*. I felt invincible after all the treatment ended. Even that had faded; I was superman no longer.

Odd to recall that noisy bus; it had been a while. This morning I lay on my back, my fingers inching down my torso past my navel, stopping at the tight vertical ridge of flesh above my pubes that was *the scar*. The only outwardly visible evidence of the disease that had changed so much.

Nine years later I'd made it respectably past fifty. I'd moved out of that crumbling flat on Douglass Street. Jake Brosseau and I were still together—I didn't die of cancer; he didn't die of HIV. So here we were.

The Bay Area economy had gone bonkers—again—and it had been kind to us. For the moment. We put up everything we had and bought a house—exactly, we were among the fools who bought an overpriced house in shaky San Francisco—an insanely expensive pile of old redwood, fir and plaster rising out of the back side of the hill I used to live on. Now, instead of looking down into the Castro, we turned our gaze a clean one-eighty, peering into the more baby-carriage- and golden-retriever-friendly happy blocks of Noe Valley.

Since this new house was not on a bus route, I couldn't blame my insomnia on a loud motor vehicle.

Head resting on the ivory pillowcase to my left, Jake slept like the righteous hot man he was, his breath warm and sweet on my shoulder. When I looked up, I imagined no plaster, no ceiling; it was a sky full of the stars one might see out in the desert, somewhere devoid of artificial illumination, somewhere like Joshua Tree.

I'd pretend to pick out constellations—the few I knew, Orion and the Dippers, then made-up ones in the murkier parts of space. Often this activity would put me back to sleep.

But not tonight. Something happened that kept me awake, something I hadn't seen much of since the time of the Cancer Years.

In our big bedroom a pale man floated in one of the corners, like a moonlit garden statue too light for this earth. In my periphery he appeared motionless, yet I knew he was not. He stared at me.

This was no statue. This was one of my Deadboys.

He would stare at us, a middle-aged gay couple, because he so loved the idea that I was in a relationship with Jake Brosseau and had stayed in it all this time.

It was Bernard. One of many friends who died during the Plague years, the one who valued family above almost everything. It was some relief, then, to know that he stared not only at me but also at Jake. Blond Bernard, like an aged Dennis the Menace, watching over us like some patron saint, keeping us safe.

I shut my eyes tight, hoping the vision would vanish, pretending it was only a dream, reasoning it wasn't real. A mature solution. It could work—though my greatest fear was that Bernard would ruin it all by saying something.

He didn't—this time.

When I opened my eyes again he was gone, the daylight beginning to filter through the period-appropriate lace curtains Jake had made. I swung my legs over the side of the bed and grabbed the edge of our walnut Eastlake dresser to right myself—ah, the joys of living past fifty—then shambled downstairs to the kitchen to make our coffee.

Bernard's appearance wasn't random. He, and ghostly others, visited me only when shit was about to get real.

Bags under my eyes and the ever-grayer hair greeted me in the reflection from our state-of-the-art stainless Northland fridge. *Better make it a double espresso,* I thought.

You're going to need it.

* * *

Indeed, crisis made sense as the dominant operative approach at Refuge, the SoMa outlet of the office furniture chain where I'd finally found a job. Today's resident drama on Bryant Street was the delivery of unordered, unwanted merchandise. Chair sets, midcentury knock-offs, fun Saarinen-like pieces. Normally, something like this, a clerical error of some sort, was easily fixed.

Not today.

I thought they were nice, actually, nice chairs, comfortable if a bit stiff, a superb orangey-red color at a fair price point. One didn't need to exercise tech stock options to own them.

Darien Unger disagreed.

"Pieces of shit," she screamed, red hair flying, as she kicked over one of the specimens Danny Fernandez, my younger coworker, had just unwrapped. Thank the goddess she hadn't seen me lounging in the other one we'd liberated from its box.

Darien Unger, store manager and our boss, a few years younger than me, but with an astounding entrepreneurial spirit that bordered on persistent giddiness. Bordered, yes, as in borderline. Crazy.

That's what I told myself. I'd assumed she enjoyed working with someone more or less a generational peer, hence my hire. I certainly had no qualifications in the corporate décor business.

Darien turned to me. "Did you or *did you not* look at the bill of lading attached to the box before you opened it? 'Cause if you did, you would have seen this is nothing I'd *ever* want in my store." Her skin had turned an agreeable, complementary pink.

I opened my eyes wide, cocked my head slightly to the left, but didn't answer. A reply she could appreciate.

Darien drew the back of her hand across her damp forehead.

Poor Danny hadn't budged. I felt him boring holes in me to

get a clue to his next move.

"Would you like us to pack up these two chairs and have Aaron return them to the shipper?"

Focus on accommodation. This was, after all, a day when I'd already seen one ghost. Darien straightened her long charcoal skirt, which had twisted during her Olympian dropkick.

"Let me think about it a minute. Where's my pad with my clients on it, and the pieces they were jonesing for?" She snapped her fingers.

Really, Darien?

Danny went to her desk, where he studied the mound of notebooks she kept, leaning precariously, a couple of inches off the edge. These were where she wrote reminders to herself, copied phone numbers, doodled marketing strategies and other assorted work vomit.

He pretended to know what he was looking for, a performance worthy of being in front of a camera instead of doing the supporting PA work the cute cub did on the side for local fetish porn. He'd thumbed through a few pages when—

"Oh, honestly," she said. "You'll never find it there. I'm the only one who can."

If I/we could get Darien focused, even for a moment, on a new task, her volatile temperament could be handled and another ten minutes would advance on the clock. She bent over her desk in the quest for the pieces; Danny and I moved the offending chairs out of her sightline.

I'd never been a clock-watcher at work before. This sad state I'd found myself in was unique, at least in my life, to this job at Refuge. I'd been laid off two years earlier from a marketing VP slot at an app startup (Launderheaven, which promised liberation and the correct measurement of bleach, every time), a company that never quite found its niche and ended up literally shuttered—we came to work one Monday and the place had been cleared out: furniture, plants, artwork, even the exit signs on the walls were gone. No warning. A few days later a passive-aggressive "notice of termination" arrived in the mail.

Which explained the founders were broke, the VC vault was empty, there'd be no final check. Too bad and we're so very sad.

Then I couldn't find anything. Zip. The economy? My age? Some evil combination of the two? That's what I surmised, anyway. Universal forces beyond Ben Schmidt's control finally ended that nice string of executive positions.

After the unemployment checks ended we survived on Jake's job as head window designer for tony men's shop Sloane & Bradford, which over the years had morphed into full-time work. He'd also started reselling the occasional artist friend's "masterpiece" (more on that later) with surprising luck. It turned out some of his sketchy but creative lunchtime buddies from the 'Loin were the real deal.

Did I miss the corporate travel to places like Paris, New York and Tokyo? Sometimes, when the urge to spend someone else's money arose. Truth was I didn't have as much energy as I'd had. I was, after all, a cancer survivor.

Right—Cancerworld!

Not that you can't travel after treatment—au contraire. But there was, I have to admit, an internal imperative to stay close to safety. Which sometimes meant staying home, staying in San Francisco. It helped, of course, not to have gobs of money to throw around on travel anyway. (We told ourselves that we were "house poor.")

On the one hand, rumors of my imminent demise with a recurrence of the prostate cancer were greatly exaggerated. What happened was this: the rise in my PSA, which would indicate cancer growth, was a blip not found on subsequent testing.

Equipment error? Mixed-up samples? Not sure of either, though my thin trust in the medical system was shaken even more, and I sure hope there's not some poor fellow out there who doesn't know he's got cancer. And to think it made me take a trip out to the Golden Gate Bridge and— Well, I didn't do it. I didn't jump.

I shudder at the memory.

On the other hand, I still had to live with the aftermath of being a prostate cancer survivor, a survivor of the damage the surgical removal of that gland and subsequent radiation of that area created.

Welcome to life on the Double Eye Ranch—the twin joys of Impotence and Incontinence, though in the biz everyone used the more on-trend verbiage *ED*, for erectile dysfunction. Rightly so, as no one wants to be perceived as lacking in power, now, do they?

This less stressful (at least, in most areas) job at Refuge allowed me to continue making the short films I'd started back when I was first diagnosed with cancer—which was a coincidence, not the plan. *Hell for the Holidays* went around the world on the film festival circuit and I went with it—one of the only high points to an otherwise depressing period.

Since then I'd made one other short that didn't get much of a reaction from festival programmers or the audiences. It was time to get busy on another, this attempt a simple little love story set here in the City.

So I was grateful to Refuge for the opportunity and the diversion. Playing with furniture and flirty interior decorators flush with new tech money beat the old and stuffy corporate dramas that finally did me in.

Blithely happier with my Millennial coworkers Danny and our hunky, part-time delivery / odd job transman Aaron Wang, and, yes, even with Darien Unger on her good days. Which honestly outnumbered the borderlines.

Darien didn't say whether she'd found those customers who may have been in the market for the distressing unwanted and unordered chairs. She took her phone and her notebook into her office, an enclosed cubicle at the back with a big clear picture window that looked out onto the sales floor, similar to a used-car dealership.

She muttered. An even tone. We hadn't had many customers, but that wasn't unusual for a Friday.

One guy had come in, one of the regulars. He was a building manager at one of the old warehouses on our block that had been converted into office space for startups. He also sidelined as the office decorator, buying furniture for his building's tenants. Darien called him Sarge.

Weird thing about Sarge in this era of San Francisco is that he always had a wad and always paid in cash, never with a card or an app. Old-school, very. This meant he got great deals. Today he'd purchased a rolling desk chair marked at $850 for a cool $600.

"Let's put this Sarge chair against the side wall until Aaron can get it near the back for pickup," I said.

When we finished that, Danny glanced out to the street, where early Friday afternoon traffic picked up.

He winked at me. "Time for Refuge Runway, OK? OK, Ben?"

Danny pinched my long-sleeved shirt above the forearm and led me to the store windows on Bryant Street. Refuge Runway was a game we played. One of us would stand to the right of the window, the other to the left, and we'd critique the public as they passed.

It was bitchy and it was fun and it passed the time before the

Darien-mandated four p.m. latte run.

Refuge's location near Third Street was close enough to some major startups and an impressive number of destination restaurants and galleries so that the passing parade never lacked a multitude to comment on.

Danny liked the older guys, so I wasn't surprised he basically squealed when a white-bearded, perfectly coiffed man in a tailored navy suit approached.

"Let's call him London Daddy," he said. "He's got a little apartment here, but it's exquisitely appointed, probably in those way-overpriced new buildings on the Embarcadero near the Giants."

I squinted through the glass, trying to read London Daddy.

"He'd have better taste than that, don't you think? Location, location—"

"What the fuck, Ben? Those places are sweet. I've been in *several.*"

I stuck my tongue out at him. In the back, Darien continued her droning monotone on the phone, the occasional abrupt rise or fall of her voice reassuring as opposed to ominous.

Some days I hated what San Francisco had become. Relentlessly, it seemed, like those shitty Embarcadero condos rising out of the dust of their Barbary ancestors. In my mind, London Daddy was more likely the type to pay for an occasional rental suite in a staid hotel around Union Square, something like the Fairmont or the Clift. He wasn't a full-time resident.

Then along came someone who likely was. Danny was still panting on the trail of the older guy, so he didn't see our next Runway victim until he was before him in the window—this one stopping to actually look *in* our window.

Much younger, probably a techbro, and for me, at my advanced age of post-fifty, with broken gaydar, impossible to tell if he was on our team or not. Medium-length brown curls, a trim beard that had a trace of red in it, lean but not skinny. He wore those tight pants that had a tiny bit of stretch in them so they beautifully hugged his luscious calves.

All this topped by an olive print shirt and a chocolatey cardigan. He didn't seem to notice us standing at the sides of the display window staring; instead, Sweater Boy studied the sectional grouping Darien had painstakingly placed there the week before.

"Young queen with fresh money?" I asked.

Danny raised his eyebrows, but I knew he wanted to laugh.

"Not sure that he's gay—though it looks like he lives in the City, I'd bet the Mission," he said.

"I don't know about that; a nice seating orientation like the one he's looking at would never fit in one of those skinny old Victorians. He works in a SoMa loft, young man."

Sweater Boy's head jerked up suddenly, like he heard me mention SoMa, and I was sure he would next come inside to chat us up, furnish his bisexual conference room with stock option money, when the store phone rang.

When no one picked up at the central desk station by the second ring, the incoming racket was broadcast to every corner of the store. Normally benign, except when Darien was there.

"I *thought* I saw *two* of my employees here!" she screamed. "Why isn't anyone answering our *business* phone?"

I skipped past a row of occasional tables to the extension on the sales desk. Sweater Boy had indeed opened the door; he'd be Danny's customer. Damn!

"Refuge South of Market, how can I assist you today?" I whispered into the mouthpiece.

Breathlessness was sometimes a good thing, even in retail; today it wasn't even an act.

Darien stood by her cubicle door, fists on hips, glaring, as if she expected every fucking phone call that came in to be for her.

"Yes, hello, this is Mr. Reeves at the Harvey Milk School. May I speak with Benjamin Schmidt, please?"

I don't think anyone had called me "Benjamin" since the nuns in grade school—with the notable occasional exception of my mother. I winced. "Just Ben," I said. "This is Ben Schmidt here. What can I do for you?"

"I'm Brennan Reeves, assistant principal at the Harvey Milk School on Nineteenth Street. This is about our student Logan Bourne."

My stomach hit the floor. Brennan Reeves, did I know him? My eyes scanned the top of the desk for paper to write on, but there was only the company copy of Sarge's chair sale invoice for $300, nothing else.

"What's going on? Is Logan OK?"

Darien strode toward me.

"Who is that?" she asked. "Is that for me? Give me the phone, Ben." Her freckled arm with tinkling bling lunged.

I turned away and skipped toward the back. "Yes," Brennan Reeves said, "physically, Logan's fine. Bored, but fine. His mother hasn't come to get him. It's closing in on two hours now. Today was our early schedule. I can't reach her."

That was odd. I didn't talk to Glenda Bourne, Logan's mother, all that often, but one thing had always been clear. She was prompt and devoted.

Brennan Reeves said, "Bottom line, somebody has to come pick him up. You're listed as the emergency contact. Correct?"

I guess I was. I'd forgotten that she'd put me on the form. "I'll stop at the school on my way home. I'm leaving at five, so I can be there by five fifteen. Can he wait?"

"I guess he'll have to," Brennan Reeves said. "What is your relationship to Logan?"

Darien hadn't followed me into the back, though her rage hung in the air. I spoke quietly into the phone.

"Good friend of the family," I said. "Glenda Bourne and I have known each other for many years."

* * *

I lied to Mr. Reeves. My lesbian friend Glenda—*friend* might be too strong a word; let's call her my acquaintance—checked out a vial of my donated frozen sperm banked before the prostatectomy I'd had back in Cancerworld. The result turned out to be Logan Bourne.

He was my DNA-centric child. I didn't have any defined role as a secret dad, but since Glenda worked as a film editor with a sometimes wacky schedule, she'd asked if I could be listed as an emergency contact for his school.

This was an easy thing. It implied commitment, benevolent concern, but in reality, it was only on paper. Then they called. They actually called.

I'd have to take him home; I'd have to feed him something— what do you give a nine-year-old? Carrot sticks, peanut butter and jelly, potato chips and root beer? I did a quick mental scan of our kitchen geography, such as it was, but couldn't imagine we had anything much a kid would like.

*   *   *

Aaron Wang, who'd been enlisted to drive me to the school since I'd taken Muni to work, ordered me to calm down. He was so incredibly matter-of-fact, talking about how you deal with a child. I should send Logan home with him instead.

I'd panicked—the kind of panic that a parent who's not actually a parent engages in. What would Jake think? If Logan had to spend the night, where would we put him? More important, where was his mother, Glenda?

We crossed over Castro at Eighteenth, passing Daddy Coffee. The guys were already spilling out onto the sidewalk, the after-work ritual in full bloom. Seeing them relaxed me, the knowledge that at least that one thing, the daddies gathering for after-work socializing, something I'd seen (and been part of) for decades, was still going strong. There was even a new crop: cute, fey, tech-type bros (perhaps Sweater Boy among them) with their dark, short-cropped beards mingling tentatively with the wizened remnants of Castro royalty.

So much else had changed. We'd been warned: *You don't know what you got till it's gone.* Much of it was.

Aaron turned up Collingwood and zeroed in on a parking space three-quarters of the way up the block alongside the playing field. He exhaled with a whistle, parallel parking with one big flexed arm in a single smooth motion.

How does one accomplish this manliness without discernable effort, especially one whose name at birth was spelled *E-r-i-n?*

I couldn't dwell on this conundrum; *be grateful for the moral support.* No matter how old I got, there was still something creepy about a summons to the assistant principal's office.

Harvey Milk Civil Rights Academy was an elementary school, kindergarten through fifth grade, named after the legendary gay leader and county supervisor, who incidentally once owned a camera shop about a block away.

Likely an innocuous, brick, generic-type "PS" school when they built it, if San Francisco had such things. It became somewhat enchanted with its new mission and glorious name.

"This looks like the front door," I told Aaron.

"As good as any. Look, there's a buzzer. It's going to be locked."

He was right. The green door was barred and bolted, that wire diamond webbing inside the single small window providing an extra measure of security.

There was an intercom. I pushed the button and took a deep breath. Noted the fragrant eucalyptus on the wet sidewalk from the odd October rain earlier in the day. The crackly, disembodied voice inside answered right away, and I said, "Ben Schmidt here for Logan Bourne."

The voice told us to enter and turn right at the top of the stairs. There was a *click-clunk*, and before I could grab it Aaron reached behind me and opened the door wide.

I felt queasy. Schools did that to me. The soft echoes of doors closing, lockers opening. The smell of floor wax, chalk, maybe a hint of early morning vomit, never entirely gone.

They stood in the center of the hallway, like those two dead English girls in that movie. Ghosts, again. A cold shudder slipped through my ribs and out my back.

"Mr. Schmidt? Thanks so much for coming. We're fortunate to have been able to get in touch with you," Brennan Reeves said. He put his hand on Logan's shoulder, on top of the backpack strap already there.

I was surprised at how young Brennan Reeves was. It might have even been his first year out of college, though he projected a maturity beyond that. He was the assistant principal, after all. Very short cropped Afro, black horn-rims. Dusty blue button-down shirt. A gold band on the ring finger resting inches from Logan's chin.

"Yes," I said. "Logan, how are you?"

"Where's my mom?"

Had to hand it to the kid, he was direct, like his mother. Contentious editor on all three of my short films. She was also talented, so I put up with her moods.

He probably looked like me when I was his age. Going on ten. Same blue eyes, a twinge of pride. But I couldn't say that, couldn't boast about that, because she didn't want him to know who I really was, at least not till he was twelve. A better age for this revelation, she said, after he finished the science-class unit on human biology.

My main parental involvement so far had been to wank into a

plastic container while studying a dog-eared '90s porn mag at a Berkeley sperm bank. The object of my glossy lust had a blond mullet, I remember that, trailer trash in need of orthodontia wearing smudged, red-banded white knee socks.

"Let's go to my office, gentlemen. We'll try calling Logan's mom again before you all leave," Mr. Reeves said.

Logan and I sat in the chairs in front of the desk while Aaron stood behind me. The kid didn't look at me. His arms were crossed in front of his chest. The backpack made him lean forward. His trainers didn't quite touch the floor.

Mr. Reeves, after handing back my driver's license, held the receiver against his ear, planting on his face what I'm sure he figured was a reassuring smile for the time it took for Glenda's phone to ring and ring and ring and finally go to voicemail.

Logan's eyes fell to the floor when he left the *"urgent, please call me"* message for the second or third time.

"Mr. Schmidt," he said, "I've got to close up the building. I'm going to release Logan into your care. Do you have any idea where Ms. Bourne might be?"

"Are you asking me or Logan?" I leaned forward.

"Either of you," he said, even nodding to Aaron behind me, who was texting the entire time. "Anyone here who might know."

"My mom's at work," Logan said. The most obvious thing in the world.

"Well, Logan, nobody answers the phone there," Mr. Reeves said.

"Glenda freelance edits—she works at studios and post houses all over the Bay," I said. "She could be anywhere. Maybe her phone has a dead battery?"

Mr. Reeves reached around back of him to retrieve a short-brimmed gray fedora that sat on the window ledge.

"Did your teacher give you homework today, Logan?"

Oh shit. He didn't answer, but a tear made its way down the boy's cheek.

* * *

I guess I couldn't blame Reeves for wanting to get rid of Logan and me and Aaron, but then he wasn't being a stereotypical school functionary, now, was he?

Obviously, school staff can't leave kids overnight in empty buildings. This kind of thing—retrieval mishap, simple forgetfulness—must be fairly routine. But in all fairness, who am I kidding? Who fucking forgets they have a child?

Glenda!

She would never forget. She was mom of the year. I tried her cell yet one more time in the car on the way over the hill to our house. No answer, still the annoying outgoing on her voicemail.

"Sweetie, give me a call, OK?"

Aaron was delighted circumstances turned out that he could go to his gym branch in the Castro, as opposed to the Richmond, where he lived. This transition from polite Asian woman to conceited muscle queen seemingly happened overnight—though like most things, I supposed it was more complicated. He couldn't get us out of the car fast enough, even tossing Logan's 49ers backpack onto the sidewalk on Elizabeth Street.

I had no idea what to do with a nine-year-old for a few hours after school.

"Wait, Logan, before we go in—yes, this is our house right here; you've been here before, remember?—let's go to the store on the corner."

Milk and cookies could be a start. The young Italian guy at the market usually had soccer on his overhead flat-screen TV, but it was dark today and weirdly quiet.

He usually saw me only alone or with Jake in tow. *What's the story with this kid, anyway, you pervert*—it hung in the air. Or hung in my head. *Look closely, and you'll see the boy has my eyes!* I wanted to say this, but that was forbidden. Instead:

"Do you have those fresh-baked chocolate chip cookies today? I'll take a half dozen.

"Wait, make that a dozen."

Then to Logan. "What kind of milk do you drink?" The choices were legion. Full, 1 percent, 2 percent, organic, skim, chocolate, soy, coconut. A blank look, a shrug. He didn't know. I wanted chocolate but I bought organic 2 percent.

When he saw the carton, Logan said, "Mom says that cow's milk is for calves, and I'm not one."

I effortlessly switched the organic for chocolate *almond* milk.

See, being responsible wasn't so difficult.

Checked the phone. No response from Glenda. No calls from anyone, actually.

I wondered if Jake would be home. It was still early, and gallery business usually went late. I should've called him before we left Refuge. Knowing Jake, he'd have something reasonable to say, even an idea of how to find Glenda. Always levelheaded, always the one in search of a methodological solution at times of crisis. A fixer. But I expected this would resolve itself. It had to.

Logan jumped up our steps, the scarlet-and-gold San Francisco 49ers team logo on his backpack bouncing with him. He hopped from one foot to the other as I negotiated the bag of carbs and the all-ages beverage, found the key and opened the big wooden door.

Logan ran in.

"Do you remember where the bathroom is?"

CHAPTER 2

Logan clattered on down the nicely polished wood floor. "Anyone home?" I shouted. Echoey. No one was there, the only possibilities being Jake or Breezeann, our aging hippie housekeeper who usually came once a week and stayed all day, made us dinner, then hung around to eat it with us whether we invited her or not.

It wasn't her day; I knew that much.

What would I say to Jake about Logan and the missing Glenda? The last thing he'd expect to find at the end of his workday would be a kid playing video games in our living room: his secret nephew, Logan.

Jake worked such long hours now. What a reversal—that guy used to be me. Seemed like so long ago, that job at Safe Harbor, marketing enterprise software. I was the trade show king. Or queen, right; take your pick. That didn't last and nothing much happened after. I still tried and often failed to process that; didn't like to admit that I now had a job similar to the one I'd had in college, which paid for my tuition back then. If this reverse trajectory led to its logical conclusion, my future would hold a job delivering the morning paper in the dark.

But never mind: When the mighty fall, partners rise. At least they did in my house.

It started with Jake being a middleman for the sale of his 'Loin lunch buddies' artwork to clients at Sloane & Bradford. The new tech arrivals to San Francisco were practically shitting money; why not buy some nice paintings for the walls? Impress their dates and the 'rents when they drove in from places like Provo.

When his commissions rose way over the salary of the old window-dressing position, we found and leased a dusty redbrick bow-and-truss building on Utah Street near Sixteenth. Potrero Hill adjacent. Didn't even use the word "gallery." The sign simply read "Jake Brosseau."

He knew everybody, so everybody would know what it was. I had known for a long time that Jake was acquainted with every single person in the Castro; turned out he met everyone else in San Francisco, too. And sold them art. Good for him; good for us!

Except that now I didn't see him as much since he worked so hard. It was always "just this week till we get the new show up" or "we have to have these open house wine receptions in the evening, because our buyers are at work until eight *every single day*."

I was still waiting, then, for the slower times to return. To see Jake working down in his beloved garden, or to watch him paint one of his own creations. That was the image of the man I fell in love with, that indelible image of him watering his flowers in the morning, the rising sun glinting off that copper chest hair poking through the ratty old V-neck T-shirt he always wore. The turn of his head, and the subsequent smile up to me in the window.

How many cookies do you give a nine-year-old? Three, I guessed; two seemed not enough but four was way too many. The "homemade" kind, big and chunky. Started out with two and he could have another if he asked—or if his mother still wasn't here in an hour.

I poured the chocolate almond milk into a clean, clear glass. Where was that tray I used when Jake had that flu that lasted all of January? I found it, shoved into the back of a cupboard, wiped it off. *Kid gets the royal treatment, that's for sure,* I thought as I brought *master* his milk and cookies.

Except—I didn't quite get to the living room, where I could hear the explosions and screams from whatever ultraviolent enterprise Logan had found on the TV. Instead, Jake came through the front door as I was doing my best June Cleaver in the hallway.

He raised an eyebrow, then without missing a beat: "*Darling,* you shouldn't have."

I so wanted to take this credit and run with it but could not hide Logan or the noise he made.

"Take one if you want," I said. "But they're for Logan." I nodded toward the living room.

Jake slid off his leather jacket and notched it on the coat rack next to the hall table. He wore the forest-green-and-black-checked shirt I'd given him the Christmas before, so sexy paired with that reddish-brown hair he still had so much of.

"Did I forget they were coming? Dinner? I didn't bring—"

"You didn't forget anything, babe. I got a call from his school this afternoon. Glenda never showed to pick him up. I still can't reach her."

Jake pulled one of the cookies off the tray as I stepped into the living room. The din from the video game hadn't ceased, but Logan had. He lay on the sofa, passed out, one foot dangling from the cushion, a dirty tan sock half off.

"Hey, buddy—taking a nap?" No response: I left the tray on the coffee table. I felt his forehead lightly with the back of my hand; not sure what I was doing that for, but it was something my mother always did when I was his age. It felt cool, not warm. He wasn't sick.

Jake pulled me aside. "Let him sleep, for a few minutes at least," he whispered.

I turned down the volume on the TV till it became background noise. Jake and I went into the kitchen.

He put his arms around me from behind and kissed my neck right at the point where it met my shoulder—which usually turned me into a bowl of quivering Jell-O.

"Remember? We signed up to be emergency contacts for Logan."

"Hmmm—must have been something you did and I don't think you told me."

"I hope Glenda's OK. This is really weird, her not calling or answering—"

"Call her again. We've got to get him home. What are we going to do with a kid here at night?"

I fished my phone out of my front pocket, his warm breath still on my neck. Redialed Glenda's number. It rang again the requisite six times and went to her perfunctory greeting: *"You know what to do."*

* * *

It became apparent with each passing hour that we didn't know what to do.

I found a box of macaroni and cheese in back of the quinoa, the perfect item when surprise guests show up. Plus, kids always like it.

"Jake, do we still have that blow-up bed?"

I didn't want to panic. Scrolled through the numbers again.

There was Glenda; I'd called seven times. There was Brennan Reeves, assistant principal. Should I get in touch with the school again? It was almost seven thirty p.m. No one was there, probably not even the janitor.

"Did anyone go over there, to Glenda's place? Maybe she can't answer the phone, maybe she's—"

"Not so loud! I don't know, I don't think so, we hadn't gotten that far—"

"What? That's the first thing that should've been done, Ben! I'm going over. I'll drive over. In the meantime, start the macaroni and I'll bring some other food back."

Glenda had a small, drafty one-bedroom on Steiner near Waller in the Lower Haight. Like almost everyone else in San Francisco, because of rent control she could never move unless she moved out of the city. Thus, as Logan had grown, she'd curtained off the big bay window that looked west across Steiner and made it into a space for him, in other words, his bedroom, if it was only big enough for a small twin mattress at night.

I'd seen it once, and supposed he looked out at the sunset or the city lights as he fell asleep, a nice consolation prize, since he didn't get a door.

Heard Jake back out of our driveway, a ten-foot-by-eight-foot incline from the street into the cave the previous homeowner had dug out of the small hillside to make into a garage.

He'd slammed our front door on his way out. Whatever. OK— he was mad, or he had a bad day, or he didn't expect a child at home hogging the TV. I shouldn't have let him go by himself. What if something *had* happened to Glenda? What if she was there, and what if she was—unconscious, or worse—

Don't speculate. Like worrying, a useless activity. A better project would be to start dinner, to pull out that box of mac 'n' cheese and figure it out. Did we have butter and milk? Checkmark on the milk; I had just enough left over and no "calf" need be the wiser. I opened the refrigerator door to look for some butter when I caught Logan in my periphery, in the doorway.

"You had a little nap," I said. "You doing OK?"

He blinked at me. Not fully awake, probably confused, strange house and all, and now it was dark.

"Is your little dog in here?" he asked. "It ran out of the room when I looked at it."

Butter, butter, yes, there it was; back of the fridge behind the hummus. Grabbed that and the milk. An uneasiness in my guts and the familiar spark up my back.

"We don't have a dog. You must have had a late afternoon dream. They can be quite realistic, you know."

"No, Uncle Benny! It was a little brown wiener dog; it wagged its tail at me."

* * *

Jake called back right after he'd found a parking space six blocks from Glenda's and walked to her building to tell me that, no, she wasn't there.

"For sure? There's an on-site manager, correct? We should find that person and check. Something might have happened inside."

"Ahead of you, Ben. That's the guy who opened up. An older gay man, had a big hoop earring and long white hair—he could play Gandalf in another sequel. His name is Harold; radical faerie 1.0.

"And he had a passkey. We knocked, and called her again on her mobile, no answer, so he went in. No one home, all the lights out. I don't know where she is; appears it's a mystery."

"Did you look for clues? Like you didn't see anything lying around, something that might tell us what the —"

"I didn't go rummaging through all her things, or all of Logan's things. It's a mess here, if that's what you mean. I would not know where to look or what to look for. And Harold—Harold was standing there watching me the entire time anyway."

Jake was annoyed. So was I.

"It's not a crime scene," he said.

"Not yet. God, don't get me going on that—"

"I'm coming home."

"Maybe stop and bring some ice cream? What does Logan need for breakfast? Kid cereal? But make it healthy. If you can find anything like that."

He hung up. Now I'd gone and done it, conjured up breakfast the next morning by putting it out there into the multiverse. That Glenda wouldn't reveal herself at all until tomorrow, at the earliest.

That I had a child I was responsible for, that I was actually related to, who was actually my son. Though he didn't know that, so I couldn't say anything. I'd asked Glenda to come out with this information, this matter-of-fact sperm donor identification, it's all science, and isn't science great, Logan? All that.

She insisted he wasn't old enough to fully understand: "Do you truly want to have to go to the park and hit balls with him, Ben? I can see by the look on your face, you'd rather try swimming to Alcatraz. By delaying this, I'm saving you what I know to be parental grief. Trust me."

That's where we'd left it.

Now the kid was seeing imaginary dogs. Or not imagined: He was seeing ghosts, specifically, the ghost of my old dead dachshund, Connie. That's sure what it sounded like. Had he seen pictures of me and the dog that had been gone now for at least fifteen years? I couldn't remember. There was one in our bathroom upstairs. Surely, the spectral visit from my departed friend Bernard and now Logan's sighting was no coincidence.

I wonder if I gave away my fear when he blurted out that little nugget. The poor kid. All I had to offer was my once-a-year version of macaroni and cheese. Maybe what young Logan needed was a kindly female figure, a mom surrogate. Who better to fill that demanding role than my best friend, Karen Kling?

Karen, rich Karen, who was mostly successfully in pretending she wasn't a wealthy divorcée. But you know she loved the role. Of all our friends, Karen was now the one most able to navigate the new San Francisco, that new sparkly city of money and access.

Yet even though she was a bona fide millionaire several times over as a result of her divorce from Dennis, a tech entrepreneur, she kept her day job as a librarian at the San Francisco Public Library. At night and on weekends, she still looked for opportunities to produce or fund small films, an interest sparked by her role on my own first movie, *Hell for the Holidays*.

We all got older. Karen got blonder. Because of the money, it was a premier, deluxe shade of blond. Creamier. She was stunning and she smiled all the time now; she finally realized it, though it had been true the entire time. I expected she fended off fortune hunters left and right, though she never let on.

I was *so* happy she picked up to hear my pleading: "Logan's here, his mother is AWOL, can you pop over? For just a little while?

Please?"

He'd gone back into the living room, and the barrage of crashes and automatic rifle fire meant gaming was back on.

It wouldn't take Karen long. Once her divorce settlement fully funded, she bought an old house along Buena Vista Terrace, a brick-and-wood pile that had spectacular views of downtown San Francisco, the bay, Oakland and, on clear days, all the way to Mount Diablo. She lived there alone with her two cats, luxuriating in all that space, plenty of room for a girl to get situated.

I'd known that house for all the years I used to hike up to Buena Vista Park to cruise. I'd walk past, wonder who lived there, wonder what it was like inside. Funny, now I knew very well what every room looked like and what the view was. Yet I hadn't been up in the park hunting for cock in years. Some things do change; in this case, the inevitable passage of time changed so much about sex.

From Karen's house to ours, it was your basic San Francisco roller-coaster route: down one hill, up and over another. As was her custom, she rapped twice on our wooden door, two quick knocks, then turned the knob and came in, announcing herself: "I'm here."

"And I'm back *here*, in the kitchen," I yelled, hoping she'd make a beeline without stopping to question Logan. I'd rediscovered how totally simple it was to make mac 'n' cheese and was close to the final step of mixing in the package of chemical cheesy powder that came with the box.

She stopped in the doorway. Feigning shock, leaning back into the doorframe. She wore a loose sweater, something between salmon and orange, over mom jeans.

"You need an apron, honey. Look at your shirt."

She was right, there it was, milk drips, cheesy powder dust and crumbs on the black shirt I hadn't changed out of since working earlier.

Never one to wait for an invitation, Karen marched right in, opening drawers, closing drawers, taking out what she figured we'd need: silverware, napkins, an apron for me, though it was a little late for that.

I put it on anyway. The front was a cartoon of a '60s-era family barbecue, complete with the dad flipping hot dogs and the mom (wearing this very same apron) holding a tray with five martini glasses on it. Both members of this "couple" had flaming-red hair. *Could I use one of those drinks!*

But I wouldn't, and more to the point, I shouldn't. I'd held on to sobriety tentatively since the aftermath of Cancerworld and my close encounter with the outside railing on the Golden Gate Bridge.

That had been the consummate silly move, and thinking about it made my face hot with a mixture of embarrassment and horror. In a real way, the boy playing video games in the next room was as responsible for my continued presence on this rock as much as anything.

"You look tired," Karen said.

"It's been a long day," I replied. "And it's not over yet. It's not over until Glenda calls or comes home. What about her friends? Did you meet any of them? She ever bring anyone around when she was editing the movie?"

"That was years ago, Ben. There were lots of girls, many girls, with Glenda. I hardly remember faces, much less names."

My bowl of macaroni looked so boring, so yellowish white. Wasn't I reading somewhere that you should avoid white food? That it was unhealthy. Potatoes, rice, white bread, white *macaroni* . . .

"I take it there's no current girlfriend, then?" Karen lowered her voice. "Did you ask Logan? This is getting to the point where it's serious. Where you're going to have to call *somebody*."

"Do you think we should have something else for dinner, something with some color in it?"

"Fruit is good, kids like fruit. An orange or something."

"I heard my name. Is Mom here yet?"

Logan was in the doorway. His backpack dangled from one hand, like he was ready to bound out the door with it.

"We have dinner almost ready for you here, buddy. This is our friend Karen. You remember her, right?"

"Yeah, the lady with the big house"—which he said while staring directly into Karen's chest.

"Uncle Ben, I have to go home right after dinner. I have my geography project to glue together and we have a math test Monday morning. *Where's my mom?*"

Shit. He was trying hard not to cry, but his lower lip quivered.

"Logan. She'll be here any time now, she'll knock on that door. I bet she had to stay late at work, and something like her cell phone battery died. That's why she hasn't called."

"My mom doesn't forget things like that. She could use

somebody else's phone."

Just then, exhale—*saved*—by steps on the porch. The old wood boards announced visitors before they'd have a chance to knock or ring. I knew it wasn't Glenda, because I'd know Jake's stomp anywhere.

When the heavy door opened, all three of us turned to look down the hallway. It was Jake all right, but without the bag I'd hoped he'd have, the one with cereal or granola and ice cream.

"Oh, hi, Karen," was all he said.

A man bearing no gifts and with no news, good or otherwise, was not what we needed. Anticlimactic, to say the least. "You didn't stop at the store?" I asked, and he shrugged, walking past me.

"I forgot. I'll go now. I assume by the way everybody's looking at me, no one's heard from Glenda."

He turned his head toward Logan, thought better of it, and looked at me. Karen had positioned herself behind the boy. She massaged his bony shoulders through his shirt. His eyes half-closed, he had a dreamy, faraway look, as if her kneading action hypnotized him.

"Did you go somewhere else? Jake, we talked about what to pick up when you were leaving Glenda's. I don't get it. You had to drive right past the store."

Logan turned, wrapped his arms around Karen, as far as they would go, anyway, and pressed his face into her ample bosom. Sobs.

"Oh god, Logan, don't cry. I've got macaroni and cheese and oranges—and we were going to have ice cream, and that's been delayed but it will be here—and in a minute it will all be ready."

I turned to Jake: "How could you forget something so simple?"

"There's a lot on my mind, things you don't know. Things at the gallery. Ben, it's not been an easy month. Now this."

Karen: "Keep your voices down."

We caught each other's eye as our landline rang.

"That must be her, finally!" I shouted over the ringing bells and the automated Stepford voice that announced the call.

I didn't recognize the number, but it was local, in the 415. That Glenda, wherever she was in the City, we'd go get her.

The only phone on the first floor was in the hall. I got it, but before I could say "hello" or "Glenda" or anything else, I heard a breathless but familiar tone.

It wasn't Glenda.

It was the panting voice of my mother, Margaret Kanner Schmidt—who lived in Wisconsin.

"Benjamin, it's Mom. I'm around the corner on Twenty-Fourth Street and I'm coming over. I'll explain when I get there."

CHAPTER 3

Had Mom ever been in San Francisco? She must have visited, but I couldn't exactly place it. It seemed like I had always only pictured her in the big brick house with the big bay window overlooking Lake Michigan in Milwaukee, the house I grew up in.

Usually quiet, stately and solid, somewhat like her, if a house had a personality, which they do. She fit it well. Airtight, sealed right up at every possible opening, quite unlike these drafty old San Francisco places, where I suppose you could forgive the long-dead builders as the climate here was milder than Wisconsin by several orders of magnitude.

She used the bronze knocker we'd added to the wide door. Most people rang the electric doorbell; delivery guys used their knuckles as if it were the only manly way. Margaret Kanner Schmidt would know the reason for this retro piece was to use it and revel in it.

I must've said, "It's my mother, she's here in San Francisco and she's coming over *right now*," because Jake and Karen followed me, single file, as if we were in grade school, as if we were Logan's age.

I opened the door. They lined up behind me.

Mom stood about a foot from the door. Her white hair was blown out a bit by the sea breeze, not enough to be defined as messy but not like her usual presentation. She wore a knee-length gray knit sweater-type garment with a hood; all she needed was a basket of apples and this short woman could have been a more muted, geriatric version of Little Red Riding Hood. Next to the steps behind her was a short black roller case.

"Ben!" she cried, blue eyes shining, arms outstretched.

I embraced her. I picked up that mediciney essence of evergreen that usually signaled something with gin in it. "Mom! This is *quite* a surprise."

"Margaret," Jake said, "you look fantastic, like always." He moved in to hug her as well. Whatever animosity we'd broached minutes before vanished.

"I'm so relieved," she said. A beat. Just the big smile. No further elaboration.

"You remember our friend Karen, don't you?" I asked, pulling Karen closer to me, closer to Mom, ballast.

"The nice girl from the library. Of course I do," Mom said, tepidly shaking Karen's hand.

"October is probably our finest month for a visit, Margaret," Karen said, an obvious hint of a question in her voice.

I couldn't help myself. I had to know: "*What* are you doing here?"

She sighed in the way only a mother can do to indicate disapproval. A tiny shake of the head.

"Let's go in," Jake said. "I bet I can make you a drink, Margaret."

He took her by the arm and whispered to me, "Grab the bag there, OK?" indicating the roller bag.

"Sure. No problem." *Grab the bag there?* Really?

Logan blocked the open doorway, another half-eaten cookie in one hand.

"Well now, who's this?" Mom asked.

I needed to be quick. "This is Logan, the son of one of our good friends. We did her a favor and picked him up from school today."

* * *

Mom didn't know anything about my years-past sperm donation to Glenda. She most definitely did not know the result of that was playing video games in our living room, eating more of the artisanal cookies we'd gotten earlier.

She was tired. Milwaukee, where she lived, where her very large home looking out over the lake stood, was two hours ahead of San Francisco. Then the drinks began, Jake not being able to curtail his hosting instinct. We didn't have gin, so she settled on vodka, which we kept on hand. Jake would occasionally indulge, but it was mostly intended for guests.

Of course, I always knew exactly where the bottle was and how much there was left in it. This was a secret power of alcoholism, this preoccupation with available sources of intoxication. I had it and knew it would likely never go away entirely. For the most part (and more on that later) I was able to stay away from the vodka, at least if it was in our own house.

It was now past ten o'clock and Glenda had evaporated from the face of the earth. Logan was used to a bedtime of nine or nine thirty, and he told me his mom let him stay up "till whenever" on weekend nights. That might have been a fib, but, conveniently, it was Friday. Despite the protests, he was having trouble keeping his eyes open. His last words were "But where is she?" and then he was asleep, mouth open, drool glistening onto the fresh mauve accent pillow I had gotten with my deep employee discount at Refuge.

When we moved from Douglass Street we were astonished at the size of a real, bona fide middle-class house (well, what once was a middle-class house, now worth north of $1.5 million), but even we did not have a ready solution to two unannounced guests who would require separate overnight accommodations.

That my mother had no idea this kid was her grandson only gave me more agita. I would not dwell on this; I wouldn't. Mom offered only that she felt it was time for a visit, that retirement is the time to be spontaneous, because if you couldn't be impulsive then, "when would you ever be?"

I could not argue, so I left her in the kitchen with Jake and Karen and made up the bed in the home office next to our bedroom. Logan would sleep where he was, on the couch. I put a pillow under his head and a blanket over him. We'd leave the light on in the corner.

What if he woke up and didn't know where he was? Would he remember the way to the bathroom? Would Connie, my annoying, very dead dog, reappear?

It got to the point where it seemed to me that Jake was being far too calm, as if the events of the day weren't extraordinary, something any mature adult could handle with grace. Which had a way of making me feel like I was the unreasonable one. But then *I* was the one related by blood both to my mother and to Logan.

After insisting she could stay as long as we needed, even overnight if that would help, Karen went home. She'd be back in the morning, she said, "and I'll bring the carbs." Jake went up to bed, stopping to squeeze my shoulder: "You coming?"

I nodded. Even patted his hand. But I was going to sit there at our dining room table for a while, until I could sense the atmosphere in the house settle in for the night.

"Want to make sure Logan's asleep. I'll be up in a few."

After his footsteps on the stairs faded, and the only sound was the Northland humming, I went to the front door to check the lock. I opened it to get a bit of the cool night air. Our block was empty of pedestrians or traffic. Above the roofs a block away was the lingering glow of colored sign lights on Twenty-Fourth Street, and far beyond that a few twinkling streetlights of Bernal Heights. I leaned on our porch rail.

Maybe Mom would enlighten us further in the morning, i.e., explain why she was visiting us in San Francisco and how long she planned to stay. We'd need to start being "official" regarding Glenda's disappearance; I wasn't sure how to do that, but we'd find out.

The possibilities of what happened made me shudder. I wanted an innocent explanation, but with each passing hour I realized that would be more and more unlikely.

And what about Jake? I couldn't shake the feeling there was something odd about his trip to Glenda's and then his forgetting the one thing, the one simple thing, I'd asked him to do.

Claustrophobia. Tomorrow was the weekend; I wasn't scheduled to work. Back inside, I put my head down on the dining room table and shut my eyes to the world. If I couldn't sleep, at least I'd do my best not to think.

* * *

"Uncle Benny."

I was with Logan. The kid and I were walking hand in hand on the Golden Gate Bridge. A windy but sunny, cool day. The bay roiled beneath us. We could feel its power and its longing. Then Logan laughed at me. "You would never jump. You're too chicken!"

I zipped my leather jacket all the way up, the cold metal enclosure resting against my Adam's apple. "I don't know what your mother told you, but it's not nice to talk to adults, especially your parents' friends, in this way," I said.

"Uncle Benny."

He poked me in the arm, pushing me, taunting me toward the railing. Once, then several more times. Odd I could feel that, his pushy little naked finger through the leather!

Then I wasn't on the bridge at all. I was home. I opened my eyes a fraction and Logan's outline blocked the light coming from the kitchen.

"Oh. Hey, champ, I guess I fell asleep in this chair." Jake's mother's old Parisian clock on our sideboard read quarter past two.

"Can you take me home now?"

"You have to stay here tonight. All night."

"But my toothbrush is *there*. I have to brush my teeth."

"I think I have a brand-new one for you."

I stood outside the powder room door, my forehead against the old plaster. It felt cool and hard on my skin. We had painted it a shade of gray that changed color slightly throughout the course of a day. I wondered how many layers of paint there were on this one-hundred-year-old wall.

The sound of water splashing into the sink stopped and Logan opened the door. Toothpaste on his chin. I grabbed the small towel we kept in there for guests and wiped his face.

"I don't have pajamas either. How am I supposed to go to bed?"

"For tonight you can either sleep in your pants and shirt and socks or you can sleep in your underwear under the blanket. Either one is OK. We'll fix that tomorrow."

In a sense I was glad he woke me since sleeping all night at the table would be a lumbar disaster. So much for Jake checking up on me.

"You haven't had any more dreams about that dog, have you?" I asked, only because I had to know.

"No. But it wasn't a dream. It was right there. I could even smell it." He pointed to the offending corner of the living room.

I didn't turn to look; I couldn't. Chills still raced up my spine. Logan went back to the couch and was out pretty much as soon as he was horizontal.

Although sleeping with Jake was my preference, I couldn't go upstairs and leave this kid alone. I sat in one of our club chairs and put my feet up on the ottoman.

* * *

Coffee—strong, rich and dark—like the best men, I know. The aroma woke me. Normally I got up first and made our first pot. But it was Mom in the kitchen. She'd wasted no time making herself right at home. Not dressed yet but wearing a pink quilted robe tied in a bow at the neck, with matching slippers. She was trying to be quiet, and mostly succeeding, I'd give her that.

"You're up early," I said.

"Well, dear, I'm on Midwestern time, remember, two hours ahead."

Touché. So it was. I glanced at the clock, just after eight a.m.

"Since you've made the coffee, I'd like a cup."

She pulled a Russian River hairy-chested-guy "Canoe with Me" mug out of the cupboard. "I always forget if you like it black or—"

"Just pour it, hot and nothing else."

I took a deep breath. I did not want to fight with her. Besides, even if I did, it was way too early, and without caffeine—without quite a bit of it, actually—my brain wouldn't be in fighting shape.

Sleeping in my clothes—which I did rarely, if ever—brought up bittersweet memories of more youthful days when partying all night long was a common event. Back then, the buzzing afterglow would have been punctuated by a recent fuck and the remnants of whatever drugs we'd taken that night.

Now it was neutral at best, though there is always value in knowing where one is. I would go up and take these clothes off, shower and steel myself for whatever this Glenda-searching day would bring.

Mom put the steamy cup down on our shiny kitchen island. It was one of our more spectacular upgrades to the house so far— polished granite top, an additional sink in the center—and it had cost a small fortune. I loved it: loved working at it, loved leaning against it, loved looking at it and running my finger across the cool, smooth surface. I took a sip of the hot, strong coffee and asked, "What kind of person abandons their life?"

Mom smiled at me with the hint of a giggle. "Always so dramatic. You don't have to be."

"But that's what you did, right? Did you even discuss this with Vince or with Ellen? Did you even tell them?"

She shot me one of those "how dare you" looks. Too early for the low blow of bringing the siblings into this, my two siblings who lived close enough to my mother to supposedly know what she was up to.

"I may have mentioned a little trip to get some sun."

"You don't remember?"

Giant sigh, followed by dropping her own chipped "Sonoma Gay Pride" rainbow mug down onto the granite. "I couldn't stand the silence one more second, Ben. I tried and tried to hear the lake. It's right across the street and even *that* was making no sound!"

*   *   *

It was hard to miss Lake Michigan. There's a reason they call them Great Lakes—as in, you can't see across. They even have surf, though it's small. When we were kids Mom told us to pretend it was the ocean and Europe was just over there, instead of the grim reality of Grand Rapids.

I guess there comes a time when we all need a trip. Why some people automatically pair "to see my relative" with that thought doesn't follow; what happened to visiting the Eiffel Tower or the Parthenon or even farther afield, somewhere like the Taj Mahal, to get that much-needed dose of inspiration?

We'd discuss this more later, but Saturday was for finding Glenda. I'd already checked our voicemail and our cell phones and computers for a message from her in any possible way save passenger pigeon; there was nothing.

Something had happened, obviously, and she wasn't able to get in touch. Or nothing had happened and she still didn't want to get in touch. But I'd be less of a basket case and operate better with the dispassionate, Joe Friday investigative approach—*just the facts, ma'am*—if I could get it to work.

I'd start with Logan.

Karen returned, like she'd said she would, and she brought "carbs" with her, as promised. *She* didn't forget, unlike Jake. Croissants for me and Jake and, yes, my mother; Froot Loops for Logan. Froot. Loops.

As sensible as you would expect Karen Kling to be, seasoned librarian, and on top of that filthy rich because, let's face it, she married auspiciously, you would think she might know a thing or two about nutrition.

At least there was real milk, origin cow, that could go on top of it. Not that Logan seemed to detect this abomination. A pinkish "loop" slid down off his chin as I asked, "Let's go over this again. When you left your mom yesterday, did she say what she was going to do? Anything at all?"

Margaret handed him an additional napkin. "Here you go, dear."

"I don't remember. Probably she said goodbye."

Karen shot me a look, shaking her head. She mouthed a word at me, and I could tell it was the same thing over and over, the one I definitely did not want to hear: *police, police, police.*

"Come on, Logan. Go to the bathroom and wash your face while you're in there. Uncle Jake is going to take us down to your apartment."

* * *

One of the great things about the hybrid car is that it makes so little noise, including when you're inside, but this may have been one of those times a louder motor would have been welcome in the Prius. Like when you didn't want to talk to one of the occupants (Jake, the driver) and didn't know what to say to another (Logan, the child).

We dropped Karen down on Market Street, as she had to go check in at her job at the library for an oddly scheduled Saturday meeting. If it didn't last long, she'd get a ride back up to Glenda's apartment on Steiner and meet us there.

"Mom parks in the alley," Logan said, breaking the silence as we neared their block.

"When did she get a car?" I asked. This was yet another surprise. A lasting image of "Glenda, Film Editor" that I carried around in my head was of annoyed, semibutch lesbian on a scuffed-up hybrid bike—not someone behind any conventional wheel.

What would the kid say, what would he think, when we circled behind their apartment and found her car? What if her space was empty?

Jake inched through the narrow alley behind the four-story wood building. Other than a postal guy doing weekend deliveries, there were no vehicles there.

"She's not home," Logan announced.

"Which is her space?" Jake asked. "I'll park there."

* * *

Harold, the apartment manager who wore his pride on his sleeve, which today took the form of an oversize lambda letter earring, the glinting gold visible through his Jesus-length white hair, let us in. I detected a spicy marijuana odor wafting off him; Jake raised his eyebrows at me.

"There you are, Logan," Harold said. "Has your mother returned?"

I sensed the kid felt a bit calmer just by the sight of the older man. "Her car's not here so I don't think she's home."

I turned the key in the third-floor apartment door lock, then stepped aside so Harold could enter first. Jake had his hands resting on Logan's shoulders. He wasn't going to be allowed in until—until we were sure that nothing horrible had manifested overnight.

Everything was ordinary, unsettlingly common and familiar, even dusty, a normal apartment where people lived every day. No corpse, no notice propped up, no drawers rummaged through, no sinister mess of any kind.

It was a small one-bedroom with a galley kitchen. A mismatch of furniture in the living room—there was a pink-and-blue-floral couch that evoked 1985, a brown wood rocking chair with an orange throw pillow, a new, and large, flat-screen TV, all arranged around a braided oval rug.

All of which led to the heavy blue curtain, which looked like chenille, and maybe it was, maybe it was actually a bedspread or two put together, which separated the living room proper from Logan's bedroom, a nonproportional half hexagon of space for the boy in the apartment's bay window.

The curtain was pulled back, which I guessed was how it was Friday morning when Glenda and Logan left the apartment for work and school. Dirty socks and a pair of undershorts were carelessly tossed on the bare wood floor, typical nine-year-old behavior, I guessed. Logan didn't actually have a bed; it was a single narrow mattress also on the floor, semi-made-up, the light blue quilt pulled up halfway over the pillow, a face-down teddy bear resting on top like a cherry.

I followed Logan in. The view out the bay window was across Steiner to a similar apartment building, this one with a Palace Beauty Day Spa at the street level. Two young women, their dark, long-haired heads bent over their phones, waited on a bench outside, presumably for their appointments.

"Doesn't look like she's been here since our visit last night." Harold had led Jake down the short hallway to Glenda's bedroom. I turned; they stood at the doorway looking in. Jake went inside. "Do you really think you should mess with her things in there?" he added, stuck on his spot as if there was a force field keeping him out.

Logan sat on his mattress and seemed lost in a colorful textbook there. It looked like science to me: pictures of plants and the occasional mathematical formula. Didn't understand it much then; probably not now, either. When he saw Jake go into his mother's room, he slammed it shut and bolted across the floor.

"She doesn't want you in there. Uncle Jake. No." He disappeared into his mother's room. Harold leaned back against the wall, arms folded over his skinny chest.

* * *

As forecast, it started raining. I closed the living room windows, which had been propped open. We continued our search for "clues"—on and in anything we could think of, desk, kitchen counter, even refrigerator. Everything seemed so normal, not like there'd been preparations for a trip of some kind.

I asked Logan to put some of his clothes in a bag, enough for the weekend and for Monday, maybe Tuesday even, at school. Just in case he had to stay at our house a bit longer. Just in case it got colder, and just in case there was a heat wave. Indian summer in San Francisco, hey, it could well happen.

"I don't have a bag," he said, sitting on his mattress, immobile, his red eyes fixed out the window at the people, now moving quickly to minimize their time in the rain.

"Doesn't have to be a suitcase. Don't you have a backpack? Didn't I see a backpack yesterday when we picked you up at school?"

"Yeah. That is my book bag and it's full of books and it's at your house with my homework in it. Duh."

Jake stood at Logan's curtain wall, pushing it open all the way, letting more light into the main room. "Does your mom save grocery bags? There must be something here. Paper or plastic."

"Uncle Jake. We recycle. Everything."

I laughed. "Of course, Glenda Bourne recycles. There's not that much to be sure of in this world, but that—"

"This is more fun than a bunch of monkeys, boys, but can we get on with it?" Harold sat at the dining table. "I *do* have a building to maintain here." He was knitting. Sitting there in a tenant's apartment, knitting what appeared to be a scarf.

"What *is* that?" I asked.

"Christmas is not two months away," he said, dismissing me.

"Whenever she needs a bag we go see Hu at the bodega. Down the block." Logan pointed out the window.

* * *

I assumed Logan didn't know the name of the person at the bodega, and of course that was an idiot assumption, and didn't realize that Hu was not a question at all but was the name of an Asian friend of Glenda's, and of Logan's, who was both a member of the family that owned the store and an employee.

So, the mission became not only to fetch reusable plastic bags for his clothes but also to see what this Hu person might know, if indeed she was as good a pal of Glenda's as the kid said.

Bodega was probably the correct word for this place in only the most generic sense, as it was actually a small Chinese-owned grocery store, a few doors up Steiner toward Haight. The red, slightly rusty, boxy sign above said "Zhang."

Inside, an older (than us, but not by much) Asian man sat on a stool behind the counter. Football played on a flat-screen TV placed high on the wall over the front door. I couldn't immediately tell if it was one of the locals, Cal or Stanford, and wasn't going to ask. As soon as the man saw that Logan was with us, he nodded and stood, a minor stoop.

"Hello, young man," he said. I was surprised he didn't have an accent. Another stupid assumption.

"Hi, Mr. Zhang. Is Hu working today?"

A voice from somewhere I couldn't see said, "Is that my buddy Logan with the sexy Glenda?"

"No Glenda," Mr. Zhang replied. "Just the boy."

A short, thin woman emerged from the room behind the cooler stack. She wore a black buzz cut, and the dark blue end of a snake tattoo—the snake's head, with a red forked tongue reaching—emerged from her apron collar from her neck up, almost to her earlobe.

She grinned at Logan, then realized that Jake and I were with him. She cocked her head. "Where's your moms today, kid?"

I could tell Jake had had about enough of this—shuffling from one foot to another, his patience wearing thin.

"His 'moms' didn't come home from work yesterday. She's . . . gone. We were just up at the apartment to see if she'd come back. *You wouldn't happen to know where she might be, would you?*"

I was well aware that Jake sometimes suffered from the delusion that all lesbians knew each other and thus would know intimate details including someone's whereabouts.

Hu cocked her head in the other direction.

"Let me introduce us—we're Logan's 'honorary' uncles Jake and Ben," I said, extending my hand. Which she didn't take.

"You know these guys, Logan?" Hu asked, her eyes following him.

Logan worked his way through the candy bar section in front of Mr. Zhang's cash register. "They're OK," he said, without looking up.

She pulled the counter up where it was hinged and moved to our side. Effortlessly, she took a little jump and sat on it, crossing her ankles. She had other tattoos spilling out of her pants hem. Flowers. Stars.

"I haven't seen Glenda for a few days. She comes in the store a few times a week, I'd say, and—we have a few friends in common," Hu said.

"She seems to have fallen off the face of the earth," I whispered, though I was sure Logan could hear me if he put his mind to it.

"She'd never leave her kid alone, I mean, right?" Hu picked up a box of grape juice packs to the side. "I can't imagine that."

OK, so there was some concern showing through that initial gut distaste for us, because we were men, because we were gay men, because we were white gay men. *Stop judging, Ben Schmidt. You don't really know.*

"Have you called the cops?"

She uttered what we didn't want to say out loud, but someone was going to eventually, so we might as well address it.

"Not yet," Jake said. "We're waiting for Glenda to show, but that window is fast closing. It's almost twenty-four hours."

"Man, I wouldn't wait," Hu said, leaning toward me. She put her hand on my forearm and squeezed with a surprisingly crushing grip. "Something's wrong."

Logan had picked out a giant chocolate bar, something repackaged for the Halloween season, nine inches of sickly bright orange. "I'll pay for that," Jake said. "Can you give me a couple of large plastic bags? Of course, I'll pay for those, too."

Mr. Zhang took the money for the chocolate and counted out three plastic bags, which Jake tucked under his arm.

* * *

Hu walked us back to Glenda's apartment. Harold was still outside, smoking a standard tobacco cigarette. Which surprised me: Other than the pot, he struck me as a real crystals-and-granola-type guy.

Harold held the door, one more time, and he was friendly with Hu. Obviously, he knew her, probably as well as or better than the Bournes did. She would also do a once-over inside; she said she might find something we wouldn't see, the subtext being because we were less sensitive men.

Logan filled the three black plastic bags with socks, jockey shorts, toothpaste, jeans, shirts (for school), shirts (for other than school) and a sweater (brown; I told him it went with many things). He seemed motivated for this task, perhaps because I told him it was going to be like camping.

I doubt if they'd ever slept in a tent, but I knew he read books where the young heroes made forays into the great green wilderness, and there was probably a tiny part of him that saw spending a few more days in Noe Valley with a middle-aged gay couple as a big adventure. If nothing else, we did have a backyard with a few big trees.

We kept the chat to a minimum; Harold kept rebalancing himself against the wall—I think he took the opportunity to get stoned while we were at the bodega. Hu, impressively, did a thoughtful circumnavigation of the apartment. She didn't come up with anything that she shared with us; in fact, she looked confused. Like maybe items she expected to see were missing.

* * *

Something about Sergeant Erica Ybarra made me think she had kids of her own. There was that kind smile, her age, perhaps—fortyish, I guessed. Maybe it was the prejudice telling me women of that age, of that Latin background, had to be mothers.

Though I'd lived in San Francisco long enough to realize that so many people were not what you'd initially expect that there was no point in making assumptions.

She sat there, her hair preternaturally black, pulled into a small bun at the base of her neck; Sergeant Ybarra behind her gunmetal desk at the Northern District Police Station on Fillmore. Tasteful but simple gold studs as earrings.

Her cop face was mostly unreadable, but I got a sense of amusement, one moment to the next, in the slight upturn of her lip, on only one side. She was the person who took that station's missing persons reports, so the order of the day was seriousness at all times, at all costs—or so I imagined.

"I know it's hard not to worry," she said, looking back and forth between us, Jake and me, sitting on the cold folding chairs in front of her desk. "But I can tell you, the vast majority of adults who go missing the way you've described turn up unharmed within seventy-two hours."

We went over the salient details: Glenda dropped Logan off Friday morning at the Harvey Milk School. When it was time to pick him up in the afternoon, she didn't show. Repeated calls to her mobile phone went answered. After an hour, Assistant Principal Brennan Reeves called me, emergency contact, and I went to pick Logan up.

Jake went to her apartment Friday night. No one there, no calls, no answers to our calls. Logan, who, confidentially, is my biological son, stayed with me and Jake overnight. We went back to the apartment today to see if we could find any clues to her disappearance. There was nothing.

"Do you have photos?" Sergeant Ybarra asked. We did; I

pulled one out of the album I'd made for a cast screening of our movie *Hell for the Holidays* several years before. Glenda sat on top of a bar, singing into a beer bottle.

"This is all I could find, but it's a decent picture of her face," I said.

"This is OK, but see if you can find a better one." She might have wanted to giggle, but professionalism stopped her. "We'll do the standard profile and it will be in precincts and online by tomorrow, possibly later today," she said. "Have you heard back from her parents in South Africa?"

Jake and I locked eyes. "I think we're still trying to find a number. We're trying to find some friends of hers but we don't know very many," he said.

"She took that name 'Bourne' because she liked those spy novels," I said. "It's not her original family name and I don't know what is."

Sergeant Ybarra's nose scrunched up as she focused on Glenda's newly scanned face on her computer screen. "Maybe your son knows? She's his mother, right? She probably told him what their name was. I would think."

Jake and I glanced at each other again. "We didn't ask him," Jake said.

"What about films on location? Is it possible she's gone somewhere like that?"

My phone vibrated in my back pocket. It was my mother with the message: *I cannot handle this child. Come home NOW.*

* * *

Obviously, if Glenda had gone to a film location to edit on the fly, Logan would know about it, the school would know about it, we would know about it. One of them would have told us about it. Right?

I guess the police are trained to assume that a generic public is not that clever. They wanted us to do their work for them. Undoubtedly they were busy doing important and official work, solving crimes, protecting or soothing the often outraged citizenry of San Francisco.

I knew in my gut that other than posting the missing persons information about Glenda and sharing it with other law enforcement agencies, they weren't going to send detectives out to find her. That was the province of outdated Hollywood stories, and even those were likely fictional.

They were hoping she'd turn up on her own or that they'd "come across her" in some other way—what that was I didn't even want to imagine. Though I could. Her body, floating in the cold water off Fort Point, or on a Buena Vista Park hillside under freshly fallen leaves.

I shuddered.

Or maybe not quite so dramatic. I imagined sightings of the tall lesbian—hiking in Puerto Vallarta, winning at craps in Vegas, reading a book at an off–Plaza Santa Fe coffee shop. She was, perhaps, a victim of some kind of rare amnesia, again more the province of Hollywood, but, hey, this could actually *happen*.

We got through Saturday night and Sunday morning. Sugar was underappreciated: an amazing and helpful drug. Of course, I already knew this, but its effect on a kid was truly astounding. On the way back from the police station we picked up craft coconut and chocolate cupcakes and a gallon of tropical ice cream from the locally sourced dairy—the one that had a giant photo of its own happy dairy cows grazing on a green NorCal bluff overlooking the Pacific propped up behind its spotless counter.

What happened that so irritated Margaret that she insisted on our hasty return was that Logan was asking questions she could not answer:

"Where is my mother?" "Why didn't she take me with her?" "Do I have to live here now, and for how long?" "How will I get to school?" "Who is going to make me dinner?"

Who is going to take care of me?

I can't say I blamed her. He asked us the same questions. Our answer had been "She'll be back soon," with a shrug. And it had only been a day.

Certainly, a missing person and a temporarily orphaned child, a child she did not know, a child she did not realize was a blood relative of hers, who was actually her grandson, must have been the last thing Margaret Schmidt expected when she arrived for her impromptu California vacation.

Her legal name was still Margaret Kanner Schmidt, even though she'd divorced my father many years before. She liked using the Schmidt surname because the Kanner family was well-known in Wisconsin and had a bad reputation for being rich without having a social conscience of any kind.

In recent decades they'd lost most of their money. The current reality was only a bad reputation.

But no one knew any of that in San Francisco. She could discard the past as easily as the heavy burgundy winter coat with the black faux (but convincing) fur collar she left behind in her closet in Milwaukee. Here she might reinvent.

It started on Sunday afternoon with the selection of a peach blouse, short-sleeved, something that was too light for the Bay Area's autumn. This was a typical mistake people not actually familiar with the San Francisco climate made. Mom heard "California" and thought "hot and sunny." While this may have been true elsewhere, like Death Valley, it was not the case at our house.

Part-time cleaning lady Breezeann had come over for a couple of hours at Jake's pleading. "Our household has doubled in the last day," he told her. "We need you!"

She'd set up the inflatable bed in the small alcove in our living room, something a bit more permanent for Logan. He was used to not having an actual bedroom, so I didn't feel *that* awful about it—well, OK, yes, I did, but then my mother was the current occupant of our guest area in the home office upstairs—that was until Breezeann got around to cleaning out the mother-in-law unit.

Because we had one of those! Off the garage, kind of burrowed into the small hill there. Not finished, certainly not "legal." At times like this it would come in handy—if it wasn't so dirty and full of junk.

Enter Breezeann Jasczek. She still favored faded blue jeans with a slight flare and peasant tops from oppressive regimes in Central America. She usually wore her long gray hair in a single braid down her back. Not one to talk much about her long-ago past, but whispers among our friends who also bought her maid services were that she'd been a major groupie back in the '60s.

Breezeann was soft-spoken; I figured she was often stoned but didn't care much, as she kept the place spotless. She would occasionally come up with something clever, a little whispery bit of philosophy out of nowhere, something that would go in one ear and out the other, unless someone took it seriously.

Like my mother.

All Breezeann said was, "You're going to freeze in that little shirt, dearie."

Although Mom didn't appreciate advice from strangers, I suspected it was the use of the word "dearie" that flipped the switch here.

"I'll wear what I want and what I like!" she shrieked, loud enough that I could hear her in my bedroom upstairs. In no time she was at my door, face red.

"Ben. You can't let your servant talk to me that way."

"Breezeann is the cleaning lady. 'Servant' is a little dramatic."

Mom crossed her arms and rubbed the skin beneath her shoulders, as if she was trying to warm herself. "I don't understand why you're letting her be so hateful. I'd think if anything, you would protect me."

I then did something she'd taught me when I was a boy—I counted to ten in my head.

I looked at the floor—like that child—and said, "We've got a kid whose mother fell off the face of the earth. You showed up unannounced. We're happy, of course—but cut us some slack here—*please*."

Like the angel she was, Karen rang the front doorbell and came in, like she always did, a resounding "Hellooooo" echoing up the staircase. Mom and I both turned to the sound.

"Well," I said. "A woman you actually like."

* * *

Since it didn't appear that peace could be maintained with both Breezeann and Mom in the same location, Karen—unexpectedly—stepped up. She offered to entertain Margaret for a while, show her the house and the hillside neighborhood where she lived.

"Take a sweater or jacket," I said. "No matter what you think now, it's only going to get colder."

I instructed Breezeann to clean the in-law room carefully, paying special attention to any spiders she might find under boxes or in corners, then eradicating them on sight. Mom wasn't afraid of much, but let's just say arachnids were not among her favorite creatures.

"I'll sage the space," she said. "Clear any negatives still in there, have it pristine for your mother—even if she is a bitch."

When Mom left, she kissed Jake, who had been sitting with Logan in the living room getting the nine-year-old's tutorial on how to play *World of Warcraft*. Apparently he was worthy of a kiss even if I wasn't. I told myself I shouldn't feel slighted; after all, it took her long enough to accept him as my partner. But it stung.

Later, Karen called to report that because they were having such a marvelous time, "Margaret will be staying for dinner."

I said, "You're a saint," and Karen cut me off with, "You should be nicer to her, Ben. She's lonely."

"Oh, OK."

According to Karen, she's not that bad. They were having so much fun; they had so much in common, like: succulents gardening. Margaret told her about her many trips to the Southwest, where she dug up and basically stole cacti or other protected plants from vacant lots, Native American reservations or public land.

And there was the piano. Why hadn't I told Karen that my mother could play, and play well? I didn't think of it. It's true that Karen, having come into all that money after her divorce, furnished her mansion with items that "should" be there, including a grand piano.

Then they were both film noir fans—my mother having had the benefit of seeing many of the classics as a child during their initial theatrical runs. This excited Karen no end. How lucky Margaret was to be in San Francisco, where so many of those movies were filmed and where there were retrospectives *all the time*!

So—seeing that these two were now best friends, or something, I could exhale for the first time since that phone call on Friday. The weekend was over, and my next shift at Refuge loomed.

CHAPTER 4

I opened up at ten; Danny would join me after lunch and Darien would be along shortly after, I suspected. We never really knew; she kept us on our toes that way. This past weekend included a porn-crewing gig for Danny, his moonlighting endeavor, necessary for affording San Francisco rent and with a bit of fun thrown in.

He'd be tired. The thought of all that man sex, all that lube, all that cum, all day Saturday and all day Sunday, made me horny. Even if the only thing he was doing was holding lights or covering crusty moles with body makeup, I was still jealous. I hadn't had sex with Jake in a couple of weeks—lately it had been weekends when we both could muster the energy or time—and, of course, the last couple of days were filled with both a child and a parent. Not exactly aphrodisiacs.

At the same time I didn't want to be selfish. Logan was in crisis. Mom, likewise, in some calamity of her own making. Yet we all—and I include myself—we have our *needs*.

Even cuddling with Jake, if not the possibility of morning wood—prostate cancer had pretty much eliminated that delightful phenomenon—was torpedoed by the necessity of figuring out how to get Logan off to school. All three adults were woefully unprepared.

In fact, the kid had it under control, supremely so, especially considering what had just happened. Mom was in charge of lunch (a cheese and cold cuts sandwich, an orange and one of the cookies left over from Friday night), I helped him find decent school clothes in the bags he'd brought from Glenda's, and Jake dropped him off.

We didn't want to alarm anyone at the school, so we, or rather Jake, told Assistant Principal Brennan Reeves that Glenda had gone away for a few days. End of explanation. Whatever Logan might say to his friends or teachers later on, we'd shrug or roll our eyes: *Kids, you know, those imaginations! It's Disney, 24/7!*

The early hours of this Monday morning shift were almost always quiet. The business reacted to external demands; we didn't initiate much. Thus, the wheels of commerce would have to be teed up and humming before our own phone would ring or any live customers would darken our entryway.

I hadn't forgotten Darien Unger's surly attitude from Friday even if I'd had zero time to stew over it since. As I flipped on the various accent lights throughout the store, I tried to remember when it was she'd last increased my pay. I had no idea how long we'd have two additional mouths to feed, one a growing boy and the other partial to gourmet oddities. Regardless, we'd need more money.

But that was beside the point. I deserved more, considering that I brought my executive marketing skills to this sad party as well as put up with her borderline personality.

Watch the self-righteousness, Ben. Remember that ego! Something my sober sponsor Terry would say. Check. What was objectively true, though, was that every single day, living in San Francisco got more expensive.

I walked in a deliberate, big lazy oval around the store, making sure that all the little chair-table-lamp groupings Darien had painstakingly curated had their gelled spots pointed to the exact position to show off their best features. Ending up back at our counter desk, I found the spare set of keys we kept in a drawer for emergencies.

There were keys to her office on the ring. I'd be quick—I had to check my file; it was only fair. Just check the part about my salary history. If I was going to ask for more money, I'd need these base facts imprinted in my brain.

Despite the office having that big glass window from which Darien surveilled her retail domain, it was dark in there. I checked my watch; not quite eleven. Danny would start at one. No word at all from Darien, which made me nervous, which was probably misguided: When she was noncommunicative in the mornings, it almost always meant Pilates.

I switched on her desk lamp. In the amber light, the file drawer wasn't hard to find; in fact, I knew exactly which one it was because I'd seen it before, by accident, when she'd sent me in there to find something.

Anyway, there it was—unlocked, and inside, a cluster. We each had our own folder: Darien Unger (of course *it* was empty), Danny

Fernandez, Aaron Wang, Ben Schmidt, Mehrdad Rajavi.

Wait.

Mehrdad Rajavi? Let's forget for a moment about my own salary history. How is it possible the small Refuge SoMa had an employee I was not aware of?

I raised my head for an instant to gauge the store environment: that quiet midmorning time, most workers in their offices, late stragglers occasionally loping by out front with their lattes dripping from paper cups, small trucks angling for loading zone parking. No one was looking for new office furniture on a Monday morning.

There was also an absence of the rustling and other bumps and knocks that would warn me someone was about to come in the back— the delivery and employee door.

I returned to the Mehrdad Rajavi folder. "Delivery personnel," it said—right, if so, why had I never worked with him? Start date, about ten months ago. Address—Mehrdad lived in North Beach, Pfeiffer Street. Really? And what was Darien paying this mystery guy?

Slightly less than me. OK, that part was good, so about the same as Aaron. Delivery scale, made sense. Did Darien have a third-shift employee for odd-hours deliveries? That was the only thing I could think of. And the very idea was crazy, since all office buildings were deserted by eight p.m.

I wondered if Mehrdad was a hot, swarthy Persian dude. The file didn't have a photo or even a birth date. I'd have to ask Darien; I'd have to confront her about this.

Hold on.

Maybe that wasn't the smartest idea. Not yet, not until more investigation indicated a better way forward—my reverie stopped when I felt a rush of cool air, which meant the front door had been opened. I peered out through Darien's picture window to see who'd come in.

It was one of the guys from Friday's Refuge Runway, that little store game Danny and I played when we were bored. The handsome, silver-haired man with the silver beard, the natty one Danny called London Daddy. Today he wore a hat, a brown fedora, matched to a pocket square in his sport coat. Impressive.

He stepped carefully between the high-end furniture groupings up near the front door, footwork like Astaire, working his way back like most customers did. I was going to have to actually go out there and greet this shopper.

I carefully put the employee folders, including the one for Mehrdad Rajavi, back in Darien's desk drawer.

I switched on our piped-in music, a station from the innocuous nineties, guaranteed not to excite or offend. As bland and as blond as Tipper Gore.

"Good morning!" Forced cheeriness; I was worried about this Mehrdad discovery. Was I to be fired? Would he take my place?

London Daddy turned to the sound of my voice. He smiled and took off his hat.

"It was so quiet in here I wondered if I was alone," he said, no trace of a Brit accent.

Sorry, Danny.

"Just in back cleaning up some paperwork from the weekend," I said, lying, though he'd never know or care. As I got closer I saw that London Daddy had intense blue eyes, set off nicely by his perfectly cut gray hair and beard. "How can I help you today?"

He scanned the sales floor, looking at me but beyond me as well. "It's time I got a proper desk. I've been using my dining room table, but it doesn't quite work anymore."

"Right. I get that, I do." I clasped my hands in front of my chest like I imagined a TV furniture salesman might, then glanced around till my gaze settled on a trio of desks Darien had placed against the side wall. "Let's look at these over here."

He followed me. London Daddy was a little bit taller; probably within five years of my age on either side. With the beard it was hard to tell.

"So here's three desks, one wood, one metal, one acrylic. A sample. We've got more farther back and many more we can order."

The wood desk was the nicest, a contemporary Babini design but made the old-fashioned way in Italy with real woods and care, not quickly glued together with sawdust products. It was the center choice and the one London Daddy stood next to. He pulled out all the drawers and ran his palm over the smooth, chocolatey finish.

"This one is beautiful."

"It is. How's the size? Where is your home? We deliver in the City and on the peninsula for free."

He surprised me by moving closer to where I leaned on the metal desk, my ass resting across the top. "I have a condo over on the

Embarcadero, near the ballpark," he said. "It's not far at all."

And with that his left arm reached out, his hand curving under my balls in what was a very definite and unmistakable soft crotch grab. "My name is Walter, Wally—to my friends."

I gasped, he let go of me, and Darien Unger opened the back door with her usual singsong "Good mooorninggg!"

My face tingled; I was sure it was bright red. What was this guy—who had a name like Wally—doing? Wouldn't Danny be surprised that the guy *did* in fact own a condo in SoMa. But he wasn't interested in Danny; he was interested in *me*. Age before beauty and youth? That attention came out of nowhere.

It was sexual harassment, sure, but would I ignore it? Or was this more in the category of a "confident pass"? More important, did I care?

Wally bought the Babini desk, regardless. Darien finished the sale, as was her preference, and gave him a sweet 20 percent discount on top of the free delivery.

"Will you be coming over with the furniture guys, Ben?" he asked, which got a giggle out of Darien.

I glared. Though I couldn't help but wonder what would have happened if my boss hadn't come in that exact second. Would I have returned his rude, totally inappropriate (yet thrilling) touch? What would his equipment have felt like through the expensive trouser fabric he wore?

I felt a genuine tingle down below, which, since Cancerworld, didn't amount to much without the aid of miracle ED drugs and lots of rubbing. Like Tinker Bell's blinker in *Peter Pan*, it was that weak beacon that reminded me I was indeed a sexual being but needed encouragement. Wally had just provided that.

* * *

I left work early for the scheduled reading of my new movie script, *Richmond Rack*, with the recently pulled-together cast. It had been set up prior to all the other drama that began on Friday, and I was not about to cancel something that had taken *forever* to organize.

Jake would pick Logan up from school—really, to show him how to walk over the hill to our house; it wasn't that far for a nine-year-old—and I'd be back in time for video games and bedtime, if

Glenda still hadn't materialized.

The late afternoon was clear and crisp, the fog rolling toward me from Twin Peaks to the west, the breeze on my cheeks an energy boost. I'd walk to the venue, the Springs Slog on Folsom.

The Slog, the great SoMa dive bar where I'd drowned my sorrows upon the initial news of my cancer several years before (not the wisest decision, though a colorful one), had been gentrified to be almost unrecognizable as a spa slash bar slash massage parlor slash yoga studio slash event space.

I guessed the milky glass doors and ubiquitous vanilla essence that wafted through the rooms there were somewhat reminiscent, in a metaphorical way, of all the jizz spilled in the neighborhood in the 1970s, when the area was full of gay bathhouses, cruisy alleys and mustachioed clones.

Rickie, the Slog's original owner and head bartender, was still in evidence as the general manager of the new venture. Self-gentrification, perhaps, or maybe it was merely his reluctant strategy to stay in the City.

And a good one at that. The Millennials, specifically the techbro cohort, were in evidence everywhere when I visited the place. A Warby Parker'd boy over there, brown dress shoes, no socks, sipping a mocha; in the next room another kid, looking like he stepped out of blond Minnesota, but speaking Mandarin, unfolding his yoga mat to practice.

Long gone were most of those fringe barflies I'd gotten to know, good people like Edmund, the old guy who would wear only a jockstrap in the bar. Rickie still had his beard, though—cleaned up, more precise.

The only reason I was able to use the meeting room at the Springs Slog was because it was free to the community, their way of giving back, similar places like this all over SoMa having displaced venerable arts organizations that had thrived in the converted warehouses. That, of course, and the management wanted to stay on the good side of one Jake Brosseau, trendy art gallery owner.

"Your people are in the back," Rickie said, in that expectant, excited voice he hadn't lost. "Dallas is there!"

"Just like the old days." It was weird to be nostalgic about my time with cancer and my earlier lapse with sobriety, both of which occurred in the presence of Rickie and Dallas.

"Always good to see you sloggin', Ben."

Time had served the three of us relatively well, a moderating force. We were like most people; as we plunged into middle age the partying cratered, probably one of the reasons we were still alive.

I met Dallas the day I'd started drinking again. I called her Dirty Pink Panty Girl because she kept falling on her ass and flashing her extra-special pink underpants. She turned out to be someone who shared drugs with me and had very old and very rich "boyfriends."

When I started thinking about making this new movie, another short like the others, this one a homo-inspired rom-com, I wanted to have a fantasy part to it, and a whimsical character to embody that. A being with wings, like a fairy! Like a cupid. Like Dallas, in a costume.

She wasn't an actress per se, but then her profession did require a fair amount of make-believe, though not on a traditional stage. She jumped at the chance; I think her life as the partner of a rich man up in Pacific Heights was safe but a little (or a lot) boring. There's a limit to how much one can shop and lunch, and she'd hit it fairly quickly.

The two actors having the on-screen romance, Greg Graham and Ron Frankhauser, were veterans from *Hell for the Holidays*. Ron was his old self, affable, so genuinely thrilled to be part of this or any movie, a joy to work with and comfortable to be around.

Greg Graham and I had more history. Several years earlier, when Jake and I were on the outs, the two of them had a short-lived affair. Normally that would disqualify anyone, but he was such a good actor and had such great chemistry with Ron that I'd done my best to not picture him naked and in bed with my man.

The three of them were already in the meeting room, sitting at the table, each with a to-go cup from the Springs Slog's coffeehouse room.

"Sorry," I said. "I've been running behind all day." Which was a lie, but I figured sounding breathless would work to my advantage.

The guys stood, and Dallas embraced me, mashing her considerable breasts into my chest. She still used patchouli; fine memories. "These guys bore me," she whispered. "I'm so glad you're here, Benny."

After the necessary but awkward hugs with Ron and Greg, I took the script copies out of my bag and handed them around. The movie was short, only eight pages. From somewhere else in the complex came the low and not unpleasing hum of an extended *om*, meaning a yoga class was either beginning or ending.

Everyone sat. "Before we start I have some news. Glenda Bourne, who you guys remember was the great editor on *Hell for the Holidays*, has gone missing. Disappeared, like she fell off the earth. Left her kid and everything. Gone."

Ron leaned in, narrowing his eyes. "What can we do to help?"

"I don't know. I just wanted to mention it, in case you heard something, saw something—we are the big City but we're also kind of a small town, the movie people here. It might come up."

Dallas turned to the first page of the script. "I didn't know her but maybe I'll hear something," she said. "I'm a gossip magnet."

"I bet she'll be fine, and it's not going to help to worry—now, is it?" Greg said, patting my arm, which became a rub and a squeeze.

"I suppose not," I said, pulling my arm away. "Shall we begin?"

"Wait. What is my character thinking during all this? I need to get my head into the right space," Dallas said.

I had only the vaguest idea what any internalization would be, and usually counted on my actors to invent most of it, a true collaboration.

Greg whistled. "Have you ever done *any* kind of acting before? Come on, Ben, we're not at the same level here. This is bullshit."

"Fuck you very much!" Dallas would not have any of it. She dropped her script on the table.

As I buried my face in my hands, I felt a warm, socked foot slowly caressing my calf, from ankle to knee.

CHAPTER 5

London Daddy Wally's crotch grabbing was one thing, but Greg Graham's foot pressed against my calf was the electric shock sending me back into man *hunger*, that default position of near-constant horniness I remembered from my younger life, and which now visited only occasionally—but with a usually more satisfying outcome.

I tried repeating and believing that it's "quality not quantity" for things like this but had a hard time convincing myself that this was true.

Even the idea that there's a *child staying with you whose parent has disappeared* could take a back seat to—what, an hour or two of lust, and not with one of those two men who showed me some surprising attention, but with the love of my life, Jake Brosseau.

That's what I was thinking when I left the Springs Slog and walked the few blocks toward Jake Brosseau, the gallery, in its Potrero Hill–adjacent location. He'd texted me that he was now working late, after having picked up Logan from school mid-afternoon, so I figured we could go home together in the car and I wouldn't have to take the Muni under Market Street and then that bus over the hill.

It was dark and I hurried along, even though there was plenty of traffic along Folsom and then on Ninth Street where I turned south, late commuters racing for the freeway on-ramp. Occasionally there would be a dusty tent erected, pressed tight against a building's dirty façade, temporary shelter for the night. I was simultaneously grateful and unnerved by these—likely politically incorrect—but there you are. Happy it wasn't me—yet. So, I veered off a block and walked down Utah Street, the location of the gallery in a block of mostly shuttered businesses.

Jake Brosseau gallery was in an old redbrick building that had been given new, black-trimmed, big, thick windows and the standard internal steel beam earthquake retrofit. Where those steel beams were installed on the diagonal looked like a giant *V*, which I'd joked stood for "victory in business," to which Karen Kling had replied, "With you two it *certainly* doesn't stand for 'vagina.'"

Chuckle chuckle ha ha. As I got closer I felt a weight drop, the anxiety falling, since I could tell even from a few doors down that the lights were still on inside. Funny how the dark had started making me uneasy—it wasn't that many years since I walked these streets at all hours of the night, of course, looking for *him*.

I finally found him, and he had his name over the door.

But he wasn't alone.

I stood in front of the gallery entrance on Utah Street and could see all the way into the rear of the space, where Jake's "closer" desk stood. He was back there, and so was somebody else. Jake stood in front of his desk, his back to me.

He was pulling up his pants. No, honestly, he was *pulling his pants up*. I could clearly see the smiling orange pumpkin face on the ass of the Halloween briefs I'd given him as a gag gift.

Some guy's arms were around Jake's neck. This person, obviously freshly fucked, was sitting on Jake's desk, hairy legs dangling off the edge.

I stood there in front of the door—like an idiot, not knowing what, exactly, to do next. There was that instinct that made me want to scream out, "Hey! Stop it!" but you know that would seem (and be) pathetic—a crazy middle-aged man on a deserted street ranting at a thick, locked glass door.

Whenever I'd come across sexual activity by accident in the past I'd usually make some noise: a cough, a snicker, an odd comment out of nowhere, enough to let the engaged parties know that someone else was near.

Jake moved slightly to his left and I got my first real look at the other man. He looked a bit familiar, vaguely Latino but with dark curls, a tight beard, which I had to admit was sexy, and much younger. Of course. All the young men liked daddy Jake—having a business with your big name on the outside was an aphrodisiac in a category of its own. His touch of gray didn't hurt, and he worked it.

The younger guy then stood and embraced Jake, both of them with their pants back on. I'd had enough; I was going in.

I backed up about ten feet down the block to the adjacent

storefront, took a deep breath, and made another approach.

I rattled the door handle, which I figured would be locked, and it was.

But—I had a key!

"Jakey, are you there? Lights are on," I yelled, fumbling around in my pocket for his gallery key.

Funny how the space between the two men increased by a foot or so as soon as I opened my mouth. When I looked up, Jake was halfway toward me, brow creased. The younger guy was pulling on a dark leather jacket.

I got the key in the lock, but before I could turn it Jake pushed the door open, hitting me.

"What are you doing?" he asked, breathless, annoyed.

"Hey," I said, forcing a smile, exaggerating my breath so he might think I had been walking fast. "I'm so glad you're still here, thought I'd check before walking all the way up to Muni."

The young man wrapped a paisley scarf around his neck and strolled toward the front door, toward us.

I glanced past Jake to take him in. "You're still open?"

"No. Tony works for a startup downtown. They're thinking about a corporate purchase of several works."

"Oh, I see. Private showing?"

The young man smiled broadly as he reached us at the front door. Jake had good taste; there was no denying that.

"Tony Ochoa, this is my partner, Ben Schmidt."

We shook hands. His was warm; he was glowing. He'd just had sex with my man, so of course he was. I knew what *that* felt like.

"Nice to meet you, Tony."

"Same here," he said. He glanced sideways at Jake. "I'll call you about that piece on the wall. She's gonna love the visual art from the Oregon colony. The photography, not so much. But—the boss usually makes her mind up pretty quick."

"Thank you," Jake said.

"I've got to go," Tony said, nimbly squeezing past me out onto the crumbled sidewalk. As he rushed away he twirled around and pointed at me, bro style: "Great to meet you!"

I watched him skip up the block. "Skinny jeans or skinny slacks, they make his calves look nice, don't you think?"

Jake pulled me in by my coat and closed the gallery door,

turning the lock. "I don't know. I guess."

"You *guess*? I suppose they're harder to take off when they're that *tight*."

He marched back toward the desk, switching off the various art-targeted spots with a remote. "Let me grab my bag and we can go. How was Logan's day—"

"I saw you guys through the door, Jake."

He stopped, turned around. "I know you did."

"I don't get it. Disregarding everything else, don't you think fucking a customer in your gallery is a poor business decision? *Anybody* could've come to that door."

I was remarkably calm. Reasonable, measured, a cosmopolitan gay man in the twenty-first century who had a loosely understood, monogamish relationship with his partner.

"Maybe I wanted it that way," Jake said. "Here, take these— for Logan." He thrust a bag of cookies from Anthony's at me.

"All this sugar isn't good for him."

Jake flipped the remaining lights off and opened the back door to set the alarm. "Let's go. He's a homeless child."

"We'll talk about it in the car," I said.

* * *

We didn't get far before I bailed—actually got out of Jake's car when he turned left on Dolores. One of the parrots living in the palms along the boulevard squawked when I slammed the Prius door.

He sped off, making the tires screech. *Oh, how very dramatic, Jake Brosseau.*

I couldn't handle it one moment longer. He'd started in on trying to get me to agree that our modus operandi on extracurricular activities actually *did include* dalliances with people like Tony Ochoa, and if I was disturbed or upset about it, then it was my own fault.

It was my own fault for surprising him fucking his little boyfriend in his place of business, because, well, that was inconvenient.

It had been quite a day and I wasn't having any of it. As his car—*our* black car—disappeared over the big hill, it became blissfully quiet, as it so often was on fall nights when clouds hung low over the city and no one seemed to be out.

I took the long way home. Mom had fed Logan already, like

she'd said she would. Still nothing about Glenda. I told the kid if he did a half hour of homework he could play a half hour of video games before bed.

The atmosphere in our bedroom was frigid as I climbed under the covers next to Jake. We hadn't talked since I got home, though there was a nod here, a nod there. I lay on my back, staring at our ceiling, imagining my constellations if I could just see right through it.

"How was your walk?" he asked.

"You know how I love to walk," I said, moving one inch closer.

* * *

The new day always dawned brighter—at least in my head if not in reality. After all, we lived in foggy San Francisco. But it was also a day I worked alongside Danny Fernandez, so maybe together we could get to the bottom of mystery employee Mehrdad.

That would provide enough intrigue to get through the day. I'd realized that about myself and finally accepted it—that I needed a modicum of drama to function properly. Especially at work. A character flaw most definitely, but not one I'd ever willingly change.

It was work, then a meeting at Logan's school—which I dreaded—and then a checkup with my urologist—which I dreaded even more. That was one thing I always did my best to avoid thinking about in advance; the pain and the fear Cancerworld had instilled several years before were the dark travelers who couldn't bring themselves to say goodbye, even if the cancer had.

This appointment would be a focus on the male organ itself and the nether regions around it. Was it operating appropriately, given all the awesome functions a penis heroically signed up for? Elimination—in exactly the way designed? Or did the creaky pipes leak? And what about the expected metamorphosis into a harder, thicker force to be reckoned with—was that still ready for prime time? Or was it taking a breather?

Danny had already opened up when I got there. I would *have* to tell him about London Daddy / Wally, though it was kind of gloating, and I was above that, wasn't I?

The answer was no, I wasn't above that. But I'd wait for the opportune time. It wasn't something to blurt out over our first coffee.

Danny should have lots of energy because he'd called in sick after I left for the script reading, even though Mondays were his half shift, afternoons only. Obviously whatever porn shoot he worked over the weekend was so intense he needed a long time to recover. Details needed.

"Feeling better?" I asked, hoping that would unleash the usual torrent of spicy particulars titillating both my aging existence and our dreary storefront.

(Okay, it wasn't so dreary—Darien Unger tried and succeeded in making the showroom a dream of what your office space could look like, if only you or your company possessed a fortune. But even that had limits. It was dark on cloudy days and any time before we turned on all the little lighting subgroups.)

Danny opened his eyes wide and smiled. "You're too smart to think I was sick, Ben," he said, taking an aggressive sip from his paper coffee cup, which spilled a bit of the dark liquid onto his close-cropped beard. "Sunday was electroshock-o-rama and I needed to reduce the stimulation to a work-manageable level."

Electric sex, literally. "Do tell."

"I know I should be relentlessly excited," he said. "I know I'm lucky to be around gorgeous porno stars in leather strapping who apply voltage to their cocks and nipples and buttholes, sometimes simultaneously. But like anything, you get used to it."

I wondered if the image I had in my mind, of a hot, sweaty guy in a harness—maybe Jake, maybe not, maybe someone mature and sexy like Wally—attaching electrodes to my cock, to my taint, to my nipples, even, and then turning up the dial and grinning like Dr. Frankenstein at the charge's effect on me—was something I'd like. Or get used to.

I had a hard time believing it would. "You have to let me go with you sometime. I'd bring crullers."

Danny shook his head. He walked toward the corner of the store where some boxes delivered on Monday had been piled. "You and I would be the only ones eating them. It's a strict no-carb crowd." He pulled open his pocketknife and sliced the tape along the top of the first box. "Trust me, Ben. You'd be bored."

I wanted to point out that you're only saying this, Danny, because you think I'm old and won't be turned on by that kind of thing anymore. Sure, you think that because I'm now on the north side of fifty guys don't look, or don't look as much as they used to, but I'm here to tell you that when they do, they're quality studs like Mr. London Daddy.

But I didn't say that.

Instead, I asked, "Does Darien have any other men who work for her besides you and me and Aaron?"

He'd opened up the box, and more than a few pieces of that ghastly popcorn padding had dropped to the floor. Inside were artisanal birch lamps from upstate New York, the Niagara brand. Woodsy and popular.

He cocked his head at me. "I thought we were talking porn."

"I shifted."

"You've worked here longer than me. If anybody would know the answer to that, it would be you."

A motor rumbled behind us, outside the back door, which usually meant that someone—likely Darien—had parked and would enter at any second.

We froze. Then nothing. False alarm? "There's some paperwork; I saw a folder. Somebody named 'Mehrdad.'"

Danny gingerly removed the bubble wrap from one of the birch lamps. "You went through her things? God, Ben. That takes some balls. I bet she dusts those for fingerprints."

A chill moved through me. I wasn't much for conspiracy theories, but even I'd sometimes wonder about those trails in the sky and try to remember if I'd seen them as a kid. Darien was nothing if not a total control freak.

But never mind. Even if she fired me we'd be OK due to Jake's work at the gallery. For a while, anyway. I didn't want to dwell on the possibility of him being my sole support. Not today.

I'd tempt Danny: "Do you want to see it?"

A minute later we were both in her darkened office poring over Mehrdad Rajavi's file. As Danny read it, I kept my eyes on the front of the store, hoping we'd have a few minutes without either a customer or Darien.

"I don't have a fucking clue who this is," he said finally. "There's a phone number. We could call."

"He'd see caller ID."

"We could use a pay phone. If we can find one. Or—we could just ask Darien."

I picked up the folder and looked at it closely. There was an address—that's right, this "Mehrdad" lived in North Beach. "No, we can't do that; she'd know we were poking around. But we could check out his place."

Danny grabbed the folder from me, closed it, put it back in the drawer and kicked the drawer shut with his foot. "And for what, exactly? What do you hope to get out of this, Ben? Do you like this job? Is it good for you? I can tell you right now if you go down this road, it's not going to end well."

He pushed me out of her office, just in time for the back door to open. It was Darien.

"Good mooorninggg, boys!" she chirped.

Danny leaned into me and whispered, "You'll have to go over there by yourself. Count me out."

* * *

I had arranged with the boss to leave early for my doctor appointment. I hadn't mentioned that my first stop would be at Harvey Milk Academy for the update I needed to give to Assistant Principal Brennan Reeves.

In fact, there was no indication of any kind that I was in my fifth day as a surrogate parent / guardian / emergency contact. She'd have questions; they would be weird. It was always a little strange with Darien, and I didn't trust her. Come to think of it, what kind of supervisor calls her fifty-three-year-old, highly experienced employee "boy," anyway?

I stood on Nineteenth Street admiring the colorful glass mosaic on the outside of the school building waiting for someone to open the locked door. After I buzzed a second time (after explaining who I was *again* through their voice intercom), Logan pushed the door open himself.

"I'm surprised they allow you to let people in," I said.

"I got bored waiting for you. Mr. Reeves will be coming."

"You could start your homework. Don't you have a book or something?"

He rolled his little nine-year-old eyes at me.

"We have a library full of books." It was Brennan Reeves, standing, commanding, at the top of the short flight of stairs. "In fact,

Logan, why don't you go to the media center and discover something remarkable so I can talk to Mr. Schmidt in my office?"

I hadn't noticed how striking Brennan was, or maybe it was simply that Friday was so confusing with Glenda missing and concern for the kid that his amazing, model-worthy bone structure didn't register. The broad shoulders. The impeccable style. Now, *that* must be hard to achieve on a school salary, I thought.

Sure, let's go to your office.

"I'll see you in a few minutes," I said to Logan, and he did as he was told and walked down the hallway to the left, to what I assumed was the library, the media center, whatever, the quiet room with desks and stacks.

Brennan and I went in the other direction. I followed slightly behind him, noting that his olive green corduroys were tailored perfectly to show off his legs and a glorious backside. He topped it off with a navy print shirt and a dark brown vest, the overall effect stunning.

Or it wasn't and I was just horny. Horny and angry. Angry at Jake, for his stupid workplace dalliance with Tony Ochoa in the middle of the various crises with Glenda, Logan and my mother. Angry and jealous of Danny, who I visualized attaching electrodes to hot, naked, agreeable porn studs all weekend long.

I projected this crappy mood onto the interaction with Logan's school, and this was not the grown-up, mature thing to model for the kid—I was sure of that. But he wouldn't know, right? If Jake could do this, then why not me?

"Must be fun, working in the *Castro* five days a week?" I began, my attempt to draw out a bit of Brennan data.

He opened the door to his office, an old style with the translucent glass panel that let the light from the windows out into the school hallway. I entered first; he left the door open.

"I consider myself extremely fortunate to work at the Harvey Milk School," he said. "It's quite the journey on BART and Muni, but worth it." He moved around his desk and sat there, shuffling some loose papers and adding them to a stack of more orderly folders.

I sat down in front of the desk, the same spot as the other day. Had I noticed a wedding ring then? If so, Brennan wore no jewelry at all today.

"His mother. Any word from Logan's mother?"

"Honestly—I don't know what to tell you. It's been five days; she hasn't turned up. We filed the missing persons report over the weekend, so the police know." I sat back and crossed my legs. "The officer *did* send me an e-mail to let us know there weren't any unaccounted-for Jane Does who jumped off the Golden Gate, which I didn't find all that reassuring. We've started contacting friends of hers in South Africa—but again, we're working with old information and most of those numbers don't go anywhere."

Brennan took off his glasses and rubbed his eyes. He didn't look tired to me; if anything, more handsome. "Logan's teacher—Ms. Carini—told me that yesterday and today he seems tired, a little quiet. She also thought that he'd been crying a couple of times."

"Can you blame him?" I wasn't sure if this was merely a statement of the obvious or if we were being subtly accused of bad babysitting. "I'm sure he's had some trouble sleeping—we've had to move people around a bit as my mother happens to be visiting—so it's crowded."

It appeared my defensiveness was not lost on Brennan, as he smiled broadly—the first time I'd seen that. He clasped his hands together on the top of his desk. "It sounds like he might be staying with you for a while. Is there a quiet place for him to study and do homework?"

The tone was calm and soothing. I could feel myself relax some, and sink into the chair. He was obviously good with both kids *and* adults. "Yes. Part of our living room is perfect for that, and it's far enough away from the rest of the house to be a good place for that."

He nodded. "Good to hear. Hopefully it's a very short time and Ms. Bourne will be back and Logan will be home."

"That's what we're *all* hoping, of course." The afternoon light coming in from the west window behind him accentuated the round contours of his shoulders, making me wonder what he looked like shirtless. Pretty good, I surmised—his pecs also pressed against his shirtfront enough to indicate that he worked out. I imagined buttery, cocoa skin and a pair of dark, luscious nipples—

He opened his desk drawer and pulled out a small card, which he handed to me. "Here's my number and e-mail. If we can ever help or offer any advice, referrals—don't hesitate." Then he stood.

And I stood. He came around the desk and held out his hand. I took it and squeezed—and then I did that little thing with my thumb, that little thumb rub over the back of his hand, that thing you do when you're interested and want to show it in a flirty way.

I regretted this immediately, if not actually while in the process. Brennan's dark eyes opened wide, and he smiled, though perhaps from surprise or shock.

"Can we go home now?"

Logan was in the doorway. Mr. Reeves let go of my hand. "Did you find something astounding in the library, Logan?"

"I didn't look. I'm too hungry to read."

This made me laugh. I looked at the floor—scuffed linoleum—instead of Brennan. "Then let's go get you a snack."

He followed us to the doorway and put his hand on Logan's shoulder, a gentle push into the hall. "We'll be in touch," he said. "Please let us know if anything changes."

After nodding a quick thanks, I followed the kid out. Absolutely, my face was bright red. I couldn't get out of there fast enough.

* * *

At least there was the additional distraction (and impending humiliation) of the appointment with my urologist, Dr. Irving Kim. Logan and I hiked over the hill; I told him it was good for his quads and glutes (as it was for mine, for different reasons); then I got him set up with a fresh supply of cookies and (non-cow) milk and left for the doctor.

Prostate cancer had not killed me, but the effects of the treatment lurked like an old suit taking up precious space in a closet desperate to see some new fashion.

Those effects were the things we became focused on, as it became more and more certain the cancer was gone for good and I'd likely live a normal life span as a survivor. Sexual response was and would be forever different, like the jerry-rigged plumbing you so often see on the outside of San Francisco houses built before the advent of indoor bathrooms.

I was a man with plumbing problems. Solutions possible, yes, brief fixes, most definitely—yet something was undeniably broken.

I exited the cab on Geary in front of the Presidio HMO building, the site of so many memories, not all of them great. I'd always felt a little queasy on my way up to Urology, and today was no different.

Severely blond Soren was still Dr. Kim's right hand. He was unpredictable but usually funny, and I enjoyed our interactions and felt he genuinely cared about his boss's patients.

"If it isn't the Schmidster," he said, feigning surprise when I walked in the door. "I've been counting the minutes till you got here. Now my day is complete."

The waiting room held its usual cohort of worried-looking middle-aged men of all colors and sizes. A few had a worried-looking woman sitting close by; most did not.

"I always think one of them is about to get that 'I'm sorry, but you have cancer' announcement," I whispered to him. "That dread."

Soren raised his eyebrows. "Well. You got that and here you are, it's how many *years* later? So it's not all disaster. Do me a favor and sit down and shut up."

Chastised—of course he was right. Still, I felt bad and was happy to be quickly called into the examining room—for another wait.

I'd long ago memorized the cutaway posters of the sad, misty, yet wistful men and their reproductive innards: the pink tubes, rosy prostates, red and blue labels on seminal vesicles, the dissected penises, the empty bladders. I knew where each item was, or was supposed to be, now that I no longer passed the standard finger-up-the-butt exam since there was nothing there to poke or prod.

I didn't have to look at it for long. Dr. Kim was on time.

"Ben Schmidt! So good to see you," the doctor said, this man who actually knew what I was like on the inside, more than any lover ever could.

"Thanks, Dr. Kim. Likewise, but I have to admit I'm always nervous when I come down here."

He sat across from me at his little cart on wheels, sliding back and forth across the hard, shiny floor. He shook his head and opened my folder.

"You crack me up. Let's look at the test results here." Was his brow furrowed with worry? Or was it just a busy day, late in the afternoon, the stress having accumulated through the hours?

Must have been the busyness.

"PSA is still undetectable—that's the way we want it to stay."

I exhaled. The result was as I expected—but you never really know until they tell you. Today was not a good day to die.

He tossed the file onto the counter. "How's urination? The flow? The continence?"

I shrugged. "I'll never piss like a racehorse again—not that I ever did. I still use the thin pads when I leave the house."

"Good idea," he said. "Drop your shorts and I'll take a look."

Always dreaded this part, but I did what he asked. While Dr. Kim coldly assessed my genitalia (*he's going to notice that I shaved my balls!*), I looked out the window, straight ahead to where I could see the flat sliver of gray that was the Pacific.

It didn't take long. "You can zip up," he said, as he peeled off the green plastic gloves. "Viagra still working?"

It was always awkward trying to be businesslike as I put my underwear on in full view of another man. I suppose that for Kim, who had been in this situation thousands of times, it was about as exciting as a piece of dry white toast.

"I like the Cialis a little better. Affords some spontaneity, since it lasts so long. But yeah, all those drugs work. The body aches are worth the price."

He touched me on the arm on his way out, the way a straight man does to a gay man he wants to comfort, but not too much. That light touch. He left, and the door drifted closed.

I inhaled deeply. I'd been through a lot in this room; in fact, I was pretty sure this was where the biopsy—that speargun up my ass— took place. Something was different, though. Maybe they painted.

CHAPTER 6

Karen's house was roughly halfway between Presidio HMO and our place in Noe Valley.

I was walking and the rain started; I hadn't brought my umbrella. It would make sense to stop at Karen's for a quick visit and to borrow one of hers. Yet across Divisadero, the red neon of the Waller Liquor Bar sign felt warm. The windows facing the street were clouded with steam, giving the place an air of mystery and offering me an irresistible invitation.

Inside was what real estate people might call "cozy." I texted Karen with a link to the bar's address and said, *I'm here, come have a drink with me.* Then I ordered a Blood and Sand, a bourbon-based craft cocktail with orange juice.

I wasn't supposed to drink; the last time I was tempted was, again, when I'd received erroneous news about the cancer doing the unwanted encore. This time I hadn't worn sobriety on my sleeve—I went to twelve-step meetings but didn't talk about it much (or at all) with Jake or Karen or Danny or anybody who wasn't already involved.

That was a lie. I did have a drink on occasion, and so far it hadn't ruined me. I didn't share that information because whose business was it but my own? Just a little something to take the edge off the worry about Logan and the worry about Jake's affair.

I sat at a small red banquette facing the door. Other than the bartender, who was a young, dark-haired woman in a tailored gray tuxedo, there were only a handful of other patrons, mercifully quiet and lurking in shadows so I needn't interact with them.

Karen entered and made the mistake of trying to close her umbrella while still in the door, the result being that it got caught, blocking her. Rain flew through the opening, getting the floor and the closest table wet, sending a gust of cool, humid air toward me.

The bartender rushed to help, grabbing the offending umbrella and shaking it out behind the bar. "Thank you, thank you, what a mess!" Karen gushed, then saw me, eyeballed my drink and walked over to the banquette.

"The mark of a true star—that entrance," I said, raising my glass in a toast. "I need to take lessons."

She took her coat off and laid it on the seat, and sat down. "I'm pretty sure you know exactly what you're doing," she said. The bartender was right behind.

"Your umbrella is against the front wall," she said. "What can I get you?"

"Something good for rainy weather, maybe a house merlot?"

"I've got a Duckhorn you're going to die for. And you, sir? How is the Blood and Sand?"

I hadn't drunk much of it at all. "Not ready for another, but it's great, a good choice, thanks."

The bartender left and Karen took off the purple scarf she had wound around her neck. "I guess I'm surprised you called me to come down here. Don't you have a kid who needs dinner?"

I took a sip of my drink. The orange juice was a bit tart. "One advantage to having Mom here," I said. "She'll take him down to Twenty-Fourth Street for something."

"She's probably a great cook," Karen said. "Better than you, anyway."

We could go on and on avoiding the real things, like Glenda, like the alcohol, for a good long time, but then that was the one thing about Karen: She did not suffer fools.

She pointed at my Blood and Sand. "So what is this? I thought you weren't supposed to drink, or stopped drinking, or whatever. I can't keep up, Ben, but *come on*."

How to spin it. That *was*, after all, my previous career, was it not? Marketing, the selling and biased interpretation of high-tech software. If I could get through that, I could get through this.

"Sort of, but I have one occasionally. It's a coping mechanism," I said. "Right now it's mainly Logan. So, I thought—actually, I knew—that bourbon would help."

Karen put her hand over mine, where she still wore that big diamond engagement ring from her long-gone marriage. She loved the beautiful piece; she refused to return it to Dennis, but she paid him off.

Karen's merlot arrived. As the bartender walked away I said, "Actually it was a good doctor visit. I'm still cancer-free."

She squeezed my hand and took a sip of the wine. "I'm not surprised but I am happy. I'd always assumed it *will* end great, cause it's worked out so far. And, quite frankly, self-pity's not a good look on you. Now—let me taste that drink of yours."

She liked it, drank the rest of her merlot, and then we both had another Blood and Sand. Which was another great thing about Karen: She enjoyed getting a buzz on as much as anyone.

If only she'd stop talking about my mother! Peppering me with questions about our family's past, my childhood, my mother's own childhood (which I knew little about, except that they'd been rich).

"It's like *Dynasty*," she said. I got a mental image of Mom in big '80s hair, when she'd gone through an auburn phase.

"It's nothing at all like television!" Some of the precious blood liquid—I figured the bourbon was the blood, the OJ was the sand— dribbled down my chin. "It's sad when you're from a well-known family but the money's all been literally pissed away."

"All of it?" she asked.

"Most." Throughout the Northern states, anytime you went into an old bathroom there'd be a reminder: a Kanner urinal here, a Kanner sink over there, Kanner toilets pretty much everywhere. All installed before 1980, when things began to unravel.

"I bet you don't know the whole story."

Maybe she was right. It's not something I thought about much. I knew I'd never be an heir to plumbing; it was unlikely there'd ever even be a retail discount.

That warm glow I'd craved and needed arrived. The bar was filling up, even appearing crowded, because it was so small. Karen moved slightly to her right to grab that scarf she'd taken off before— and I saw him.

My Deadboy Mark was in the house, sitting on a stool by himself near the front door.

Mark was a photojournalist friend who died during the Plague. His hair had that same silver shimmer he'd presented with the last time I'd had a "visitation." My eyes immediately went to the floor around the stool, expecting I'd see Connie there with him, the ghost dog who presented herself to Logan at home. But no, and of course, they didn't allow dogs in bars like this one.

"Are you drunk?" Karen asked, looping the scarf around her neck. "You have this un-Ben-like kind of faraway look."

Mark smiled. He nodded and waved to me. I laughed.

"It's been a long time since I had cocktails. Good thing I'm walking home."

She stood, adjusting her coat. "The worst you can do is fret—about Logan, Glenda, the cancer. It won't help, so just don't, OK?"

"Yes, Mom." She kissed the top of my head and turned toward the door. She picked her umbrella up from where the bartender had put it—which happened to be only inches from where Mark sat. She didn't and couldn't acknowledge his presence. I knew he was invisible to her.

I squeezed my eyes shut for what seemed like a minute, hoping he would disappear. When I opened them Mark was sitting in the place vacated by Karen.

So much for wishful thinking.

He looked around. "I like this place, Ben. Bars have gotten so much nicer since I've been gone." He leaned over to sniff Karen's empty cocktail glass. "Oh, what I wouldn't give—"

The bartender appeared and snatched the glass away. "How you doing on that BS?" She chuckled. "Time for another?"

I nodded, a little shrug, what the hell, I wouldn't have to finish it if I didn't want to. Plus, I had new company. It would be rude to do otherwise.

Mark's silver hair—a departure from the alternating unreal shades of red he'd favored in life—glowed with a definable halo. He was about ten years my senior, yet his skin had no wrinkles, blemish-free, perfectly smooth.

"Haven't seen you for a while," I whispered, not wanting the other bar patrons to think I was talking to myself. "Usually it's Connie. She's been around, you know. That dog has shown herself to my son."

"Your son!" He laughed. "Who would ever have believed that?" He reached over the table with his ghost arm and caressed my cheek, which felt like a puff of cool air. "Unintended benefits of the Big C."

"I saw Bernard as well. In our house. I don't like this. Why are you guys back? The last time I was seeing Deadboys around was not a great period in my life, *if you remember*, Mark."

He was silent. So different from life, where he offered a strong, often sarcastic opinion on everything. He grinned, even if it was indulgent. Already he was starting to fade.

"The new movie is a good step, Ben. There must be a reason you survived. Why did you?"

His words hung over the table until they were cut by the thud of the new drink in front of me. "You were saying something?" the bartender asked. "Is that an echolalia thing you've got?"

* * *

I wasn't sure if I knew the answer to what Mark was asking, but I was certain that one of the benefits of cancer survival was to get grabbed in the crotch and then follow up for the sex that was promised.

Hence Wally. I thought of him instantly when I first noticed that Waller Liquor Bar neon, and even as Karen and I drank he wasn't far from my consciousness. I'd done what normally I would frown upon if someone like, say, Danny Fernandez or Aaron Wang did it: I copied down a customer's home address and phone number and e-mail. In this case, Walter Whitney: London Daddy.

That's how I found myself down on the Embarcadero nearly under the Bay Bridge. Bourbon and Deadboy Mark were to blame.

Wally's reinforced redbrick building fronted Townsend. The "reason" I'd give for showing up at eight p.m. on a weeknight would be to check on customer satisfaction, that is, his new desk, its placement, was it working to his satisfaction, et cetera. We at Refuge SoMa provided that extra touch! Something like that. He'd realize it was just to get in the door.

Anyway, he started it.

"Imagine that," he said, opening the door wide, gesturing for me to come in from the dark. The twinkling night lights and the dull roar from the bridge above, punctuated by the occasional and random foghorn, were a piece of romantic San Francisco that never got old and were additionally apropos for this particular endeavor.

You'd think I'd be tired or freaked-out after drinking and conversing with a ghost in a bar—strangely, it had the cumulative effect of making me want to immerse myself in lust.

As I walked into his hallway and past Wally, I touched his arm.

"I'm here to see how the desk works."

"Of course you are. They delivered it this morning." He took my hand and led me into his living room and through a double doorway to an office alcove.

Wally's apartment was every bit as precise and intentional as his sartorial sense was. Jake and I would never be able to come close to this kind of presentation, no matter how much money we might make. It was, ultimately, a question of personality.

The place had high ceilings already, and Wally accentuated their stature with a few large paintings reaching upward, as well as hanging the drapes at ceiling level. He was a minimalist, I could tell, but the pieces he did have—a silver art deco daybed, a beautifully polished ebony baby grand among them—were stunning. Just like he was.

Wally had placed the Refuge desk under a window that looked out onto a small airshaft or building courtyard. It was still so new he hadn't put anything on top of it.

"I think you made the right decision," I said. "This one is perfect right here."

His hand had moved to my ass and then around me. He pulled me in closer and whispered, "It's absolutely what this room needed, don't you think?"

"Without a doubt."

We kissed. I liked the feel of his beard on my face. Jake often had stubble (like every man in San Francisco), but Wally's beard was softer.

"You had a cocktail?" Wally smiled. Hard to hide that. I'd had three Blood and Sands. The minimum requirement for activity of this sort. "I have some Skywalker Kush. It's very strong but I'd like you to try it."

The next thing I knew we were naked and upstairs—Wally's place was a sweet two-story. I'd had only two hits from his bong and I was sure that I had levitated over his spotless shag rug and onto his bed. Everything was so subdued and calming—from the neutral colors and the lighting to the drugs and to Wally himself—London Daddy's nice lean yoga body did not disappoint.

I didn't have any of my ED meds on me, so the post–prostate cancer erection left some, or a lot, of hardness to be desired. Wally didn't seem to mind and put his hand over my mouth—and slipped a couple of fingers inside—when I tried to explain.

"No talking, sexy man," he said.

He rolled me onto my back and I was staring up at his perfect, crack-free ceiling, my legs over his shoulders. For a few minutes, I felt like I was the center of someone's universe. Regret might come later—then again, it might not.

* * *

As it was, I floated home. It felt good to walk, and to be honest there was that certain something about getting fucked in the ass that raised my level of well-being to an almost cosmic level, though I'm sure the Kush helped.

A walk of shame, yes, but the middle-aged variety, so it wasn't overly furtive or shambling and it also occurred at the mostly civilized hour of eleven p.m. I told Jake that I was spending some quality friend time with Karen, which was true. I did. I merely left out the part about after.

In recent years, with the ever-increasing gentrification, even walking through the Mission at night was safe. Though I didn't linger, did not stop for street-made artisanal tacos or a mojito or anything else. It was drizzling again, but it was refreshing rather than annoying.

Halfway across the city yet less than four miles, an hour and some change. Only one hill, though it was big: good for the lower bod. I needed the time to think about Jake, what I had done with Wally and how to talk about it—or not talk about it. In theory, the open-relationship thing was all civilized and reasonable, but I didn't like mulling over these dalliances with Jake, particularly when I'd been the one stepping out. It was always much easier to confront him on a Tony Ochoa or someone else.

We'd initially made a pact to share all information about boys on the side. This was supposed to have a dual purpose: as titillation fodder for our sex life together and as insurance that neither of us would develop deep *feelings* for another man. Good idea, perhaps, but then what about when one of us disregarded the entire playbook? What then?

Did I want to tell Jake about Walter Whitney? Or did I want to play out a bit of the affair first? After all: He had Tony Ochoa. Wally came with access to primo marijuana. If I could convince myself that

Jake had started it, withholding would be easier.

One of Jake's many fine attributes was that he was a sound sleeper, recipient of the sleep of the just, both admirable and deserved. When I'd first met him this alien quality did not compute—after all, I was the one with insomnia or ghostly visitations (often both on the same night). As the years passed, other advantages emerged, including tonight's ability to slip into our bed without waking him up.

* * *

The bright, windy morning was cloudless, a clarity so striking it could make you weep. When I first noticed her, it was because of the orange and yellow spandex jogging outfit, blinding on a day that did not need more illumination. Finally, she was back home, or on the bridge, anyway, so not far. What a relief!

"Glenda, where have you been? I'm running out of school-appropriate clothes for Logan! I don't know what to make him wear. You *have* to take him home, OK?"

She slowed her run so much it was like she was moving through water toward me, an enormous smile on her face, fitting since she'd been gone so long.

"Didn't know you were coming to meet me here, sport! Come on," she said, grabbing my hand. "Let's get up on the rail. We can jump together!"

"But—I was just taking in the air! I'm not here to run. I'm *definitely* not here to jump!"

"Oh, come on, Ben, you know you want to!"

She wouldn't let go of my arm. I could see whitecaps in the bay. She was up on the rail already and pulling me up after her, with a strength that was remarkable. "Let go, Glenda, let go!"

She smiled and she did. Then she fell back, out of sight—

"Uncle Benny! Wake up, it's late, the old lady with the braid is making you cereal."

I opened my eyes and it was *Logan* pulling on my arm. The sun was in my face, and I felt that familiar if awful feeling of slight headache and nausea. Lovely, a hangover.

"What time is it?" I asked, not really needing an answer, already knowing it was well after my usual rising hour. Jake was gone, of course, already at work. I had the day off. I was not happy to have a hangover, though I was happy to be in my bed.

The dream disturbed me.

"Logan, why aren't you in school?"

He rolled his eyes. "It's teacher grading day. I told you yesterday!"

Teacher grading day. Good idea. I could use a furniture grading day every now and then.

I sat up; grateful there was no dizziness. Yet. "I didn't know Breezeann knew how to make cereal. I'll be right down."

I felt much better after splashing water on my face and having a cup of hot coffee shoved into my hand (thank you, Breezeann, who then pointed out the bright red flyer attached to the refrigerator announcing the bit about Logan's day off from school). It was there for all to see; her intimation was that I was a dummy for not knowing, for not remembering.

There was a bowl of flakes on the counter with a carton of nonfat milk standing nearby. "This is for me, I take it," I said, sniffing the flakes. "Where's Mom?"

"Goodness, Ben, that's right, Margaret *is* still here. Somewhere in this city. I haven't seen her today; perhaps she's gone out. You know I have my own key. Jake gave me one."

After their fight, we'd insisted on a truce, if not for our sake then for Logan's. It was good that Mom had gone someplace; it was a bad idea to leave Breezeann here alone with her.

"I was surprised to see the boy was still here," she said. "He is bored all cooped up in this house. You should take him somewhere on his day off."

Nothing like advice from the help, who, by the way, wore a granny dress today, bell-bottoms likely in the wash. It was a nice sunny day, we lived in a much better neighborhood than Glenda did, might as well show him around, no telling how long . . . though the slightest notion that this situation would drag on made my head throb more than it already did.

Fresh air, then, would do us both good. The familiar sounds of explosions and the pitiful screams of the dying emanated from the living room as I walked down the hall with my bowl of soggy flakes.

I turned into the doorway, where I expected to see Logan on the couch with his back to me, the video-game carnage splashed on our big screen in front of him. There, in the middle of the floor between me and the couch was Connie, dead dachshund, ghost dog, looking up at me, sweeping her tail slowly back and forth across the wood.

I blinked and she was gone. Would I accept that she was there, or try to blame this vision on my hangover?

"Hey, Logan," I said, "I guess we're both off today. There's a park I want to take you to."

"Or, Uncle Benny, I could stay here. I need to get my score up."

I sat down opposite him in one of our slipcovered club chairs. "This is a popular playground—Dolores Park—at least it looks popular when I go by. I haven't actually been there myself." I sipped the milk from the cereal bowl.

"Do we have to?"

What kind of kid doesn't want to go to a playground? "Yes, we have to." I stood up. "I'm going to put this in the kitchen and then we'll go. Oh—by the way, have you seen that dog in here again?"

"Yeah, but what good is it? She always runs away."

*   *   *

The immediate task was to climb over the enormous hill that separated our Noe Valley neighborhood from the Castro and, to a lesser extent, the Mission. Dolores Park was a welcome postage stamp of green situated between the two.

It was always a popular destination and more so on any sunny San Francisco day that saw temperatures north of seventy. Today would not qualify for that, but I expected a good number of kids if, indeed, all the schools had this odd holiday like Logan's did.

In its wisdom (and possibly a move to further discourage homeless encampments) the City had built this ultramodern kids' playground fairly recently.

"Glenda never takes you there?" I gasped, out of breath, at the top of the hill, as soon as the park appeared below. I took a sip from the bottle of water I'd brought along.

"No, she never did. I'd go by myself anyway. Mom doesn't have to go with me everywhere anymore."

He had a point. I was relieved to see other kids at the playground, and a few parents—or maybe they were nannies or other minders. Nobody had "nannies" when I was that age. We went to play without adults and if we hurt ourselves or got lost, then—tough. We learned from the experience.

"Bourne! I never thought I'd see *you* at this lame park," a boy shouted, seeming to appear out of nowhere. He was about Logan's age, black and a bit taller.

"Oh. Hi, Zachary," Logan said. "How come you're here if it's so shitty?"

"Hey!" I dug my finger into Logan's shoulder. "Watch the language."

"My dad thinks it's cool. Is this yours?" Zachary asked, pointing to me.

Part of me, somewhere deep inside, wanted to shout, *Yes, I am his father*—claim my biological son and take him back home like a regular dad so he could play his video games and I could take a nap.

Instead: "My name is Ben. I'm a friend of Logan's mother." I stuck out my hand and the kid knew enough to shake it.

"Well, well, who do we have here, Zachary Burns?" A thirtysomething guy, a white guy, skinny, glasses, came up and stood behind Zachary. A wide smile, something dark green stuck between his teeth, like a piece of errant arugula.

"This is my friend Logan Bourne from school. And this is Ben," he said, pointing at me.

"We were greeting young Zach," I said. "It's our first time here."

"It's Zachary, *never* Zach," the man said. He turned to the boys. "Why don't you show Logan around, then?"

The boys took off. Relieved, I'm sure, to be extricated from the old farts.

"Joshua Burns," he said, shaking hands with me. "Always Joshua, never Josh."

"Nice to meet you," I said. "Ben Schmidt. Just Ben. It's not short for anything." (I lied.)

We walked side by side down the hill on the path to the play area. "I suppose you're wondering why my son is black and I'm obviously not."

Good *lord!* Why, again, had I insisted on this outing? Oh yes—Breezeann.

"I'm sure there's a simple explanation and you're going to tell me."

A short woman sitting on a bench down ahead waved at us, or more accurately, at Joshua. He waved back. "You know Dr. Kelly? Never mind, I'll introduce you. It's like this. My husband, Marty, he works in tech, we decided to have a kid, maybe kids, though for now it's just Zachary. *So* he's adopted. *So* you're *just* a family friend?"

This was a contemporary playground, style for days, definitely not something I would have remembered from my own youth. There were only two colors playgrounds came in back then: usually flaking deep forest green and gunmetal gray—the latter being the natural color of cold swing-set poles and jungle-gym bars.

Dolores Park in the new century would have none of that. Every piece of equipment was painted a different color, all vibrant, neon even, the playground version of an inclusive rainbow flag. I supposed this was progress and a healthy use of our tax dollars. The kids were certainly entertained.

Dr. Kelly was her first name. Joshua introduced us quickly, as was his style, but I picked up that she was a dermatologist at SF General, that her kid was a bit younger than Logan and Zachary, a Tyler, a Tyler Dong-Gutierrez, in fact.

Tyler was seven years old, on the short side even for that age. Seems he adored Zachary and struggled to keep up with the two older boys as they cruised around the playground.

It was possible in this universe that these two parents might know Glenda. Joshua shook his head, but Dr. Kelly asked a few follow-ups: Where did they live? Lower Haight. What school? Harvey Milk. Where again did she work? All over, SF, East Bay, South Bay, even up in Sac, freelance, film and video editor. All of which produced a blank.

It was like Glenda was a cipher. Not actually, though: Remember Hu. That tough little Hu Zhang from the bodega. I still thought she knew more than she was telling, that she might be the clue to finding Glenda.

A shriek erupted. It was Tyler; parents descended. Site of disaster was the purple-painted seesaw. Tyler was mismatched, not with Logan or Zachary but with a girl. She pulled the classic remove yourself from the teeter-totter when it's on the ground and watch the other kid fall.

The culprit had a name: Destiny. Yet another classmate of Logan and Zachary's. She looked familiar; perhaps I'd seen her at the school or in the neighborhood somewhere.

"I told him I was getting off. It's his own fault for not listening," I heard her say, in a high, not-so-innocent voice as we approached. Dr. Kelly shook her head. Tyler was crying and trying to hold on to his mother's leg, while she looked him over quickly for injuries.

"Are you here by yourself, young lady?" she demanded.

"Yes. I came by myself today." Destiny was quiet. Skinny, black, as tall as Zachary, puberty soon but not yet visible. She probably knew she was in trouble and was trying to figure a way out.

I didn't see any blood on Tyler; his reaction seemed a bit more extreme than the actual hurt. As a rookie "parent," I didn't really know. Maybe she would take him to emergency for X-rays. She was a doctor, after all; maybe she could get it done for free.

"Oh dear, *now* what have you done?" A woman who looked like a totally grown version of Destiny, including pigtails, approached, a folded laptop under her arm. "Destiny?"

"I didn't do anything! Tyler is faking!"

A small group formed; parents, kids, the other adults. For me, this was a new world with new rules. To say I wanted to disappear disparaged invisibility.

Destiny's mother introduced herself as Belinda, Belinda Stackhouse. She was sorry, she said, she worked for the City and was trying to find a quiet corner of the park to check up on some e-mails but apparently she could not let her daughter alone for a single fucking second.

"Your daughter does not play well with the other children," Joshua offered.

"This Tyler is not your kid, is he, so maybe you should shut up," Belinda said.

Joshua grabbed Zachary by the arm and backed away. "If this is the kind of people we find here, maybe it's not the best place for our son. Come on, Zachary, we'll go somewhere else."

"Seriously, Dad?" Zachary wasn't happy. But they started to walk away.

"We're going, and remember, it's a Leave No Trace park."

Finally, Tyler stopped crying. Cookies, which Dr. Kelly happened to have a few of in her bag, helped. Even Destiny got one. So did Logan. So did I. Girl Scout Thin Mints.

"I'm so sorry," Belinda said. "Sometimes Destiny needs that extra attention. It's very hard being a divorced mom and working full-time."

Tell me about it, I thought. I could go into the Glenda saga for yet another thing that could happen to a single parent but decided to wait.

The group dispersed and the playground went back to what it had been before the seesaw incident. Destiny left with her mother and I sat on a bench with Dr. Kelly.

I told her that I was Logan's guardian, that his mother had just disappeared one day.

"That's so awful. I can't imagine it," she said, looking over to where Logan pumped himself higher and higher on a swing. "He seems to be taking it OK, at least today."

"Sometimes I catch him crying, or notice that his eyes are red," I said. "He's probably too old for *this* playground, don't you think? A lot of this stuff looks like it's for little kids or babies."

"I'm sure he'd like to be with the older boys. They always do. Let me ask you: What if Glenda never comes back? What then?"

* * *

Dr. Kelly Dong-Gutierrez had no trouble verbalizing that concern, that elephant in the room Jake and I thought about, though when we'd start to talk about it, we still couldn't—he or I would change the subject fast.

It hadn't even been a week and our lives were upended. Not just one houseguest but two, in addition to those apparitions (only I—and sometimes Logan—could see) who were not living. Affairs, that Tony Ochoa with Jake, and honestly there was no way I could claim innocence with my own dalliance with London Daddy Wally.

Is that what it was, a dalliance? I liked Walter, that old-fashioned name and the brimmed hats he wore. He lived with a certain classic style that not many from our generation still clung to. In his case, it was not only refreshing but also pointed to a sense of security lacking in the modern world.

How to reconcile my strong permanent commitment to my man Jake Brosseau and my desire to get Wally to royally fuck me again? My face felt hot when I realized my reliving of sex time with Wally coincided with my walk home with nine-year-old Logan.

He, at least, was quiet. All the running around with Zachary, Tyler and Destiny, however brief, had dissipated some of that excess energy. As soon as we walked in the door, he was back in the living room firing up *WoW*.

Breezeann called out from the kitchen. "The sheriff called. She left her number."

Due to the video-game screams and thuds, Logan didn't hear her. I hurried back to the kitchen.

"Please keep your voice down with anything regarding Glenda," I said. "I don't want him to either get his hopes up or, heaven forbid, hear bad news."

"I don't think it's bad news. I didn't sense that in her voice."

There was a "festive" arrangement of harvest-colored gourds on the kitchen island, which hadn't been there when we'd departed for Dolores Park. "That looks nice," I said, nodding to the decoration.

"The holidays are coming. *Somebody's* got to do something," she said.

I fished out Erica Ybarra's card from my wallet and dialed in. When she actually answered the phone, I was surprised: "First of all, we haven't found Glenda Bourne, to get that in there at the outset," she said. "We've had some calls, though, so I wanted to let you know."

I kicked the doorstop (actually, a ten-pound dumbbell) out of the way so that the old swinging door between the hallway and the kitchen would close. "I wanted to get back to you on that other issue, about the name. Logan looked at me like I was crazy when I suggested he might have a different *real* last name, so whatever it once was is not something he knows."

"Interesting. Understand that we're only reactive here; we don't have the personnel to go out and investigate unless there's some evidence. With Bourne, there just isn't. This is a good thing, Mr. Schmidt, as when we do have evidence it's usually in the form of a corpse."

"Then we count ourselves lucky," I whispered.

"We had one call from someone in the Russian River area who saw the missing persons flier on our website. The man insisted he saw her hiking alone up there in the redwood park."

"She *does* do things like that—the hiking, the redwoods—but still I can't imagine that she'd not tell anybody, or not take her kid with her, since he'd love that. Plus, that would be a day trip."

"I've alerted the Sonoma County sheriff just in case."

Breezeann barged through the swinging door. "When you leave this closed, your big house doesn't heat evenly, you know that, right?"

"Shhhh!" I couldn't help myself. "Not you, Officer Ybarra. There's someone here. What was the other call?"

"It was odd, because it came in on an anonymous tip line, even though that's not the norm for a missing persons case. The caller didn't leave her name or other ID and it was made on what must be one of the last pay phones in the City. She said we should be looking in South Africa, and it would be easy to find her there."

"That's very strange. Someone who knew her that well should have been in contact with us directly, I mean, if they have some real, honest information."

"That's why we wanted to alert you to this. Is it possible she's gone 'home' for a while?"

"I'm surprised there's *any* pay phones left in this town."

"This one's on the street outside a tourist motel on Lombard and Buchanan, Howard Johnson in the 94123. So again, if you can find any numbers for her or the family back in South Africa—I think it's worth pursuing."

CHAPTER 7

ONE WEEK LATER.

I was still convinced Hu Zhang knew something. Or perhaps she was just one of those mysterious people who cultivate an air of suspicion around themselves. Another trip to the bodega would have to wait.

This was the afternoon Danny Fernandez and I planned to finally find mystery employee Mehrdad Rajavi. Danny had originally told me, "No, you'll have to go over there by yourself," wanting no part of it; apparently the curiosity became too much.

I would meet him for a coffee in Union Square and we'd go from there. I sat in the window of a new, rather boho joint across from the Chinatown Dragon Gate at Grant Avenue. It was that time of the afternoon, a little after five p.m., when workers were leaving their offices, a parade of well-dressed and mostly younger tech workers, the winners in this new economy (that did not seem to value experience or maturity).

But I wouldn't go there; I wasn't going to dwell on slights, even if they were legitimate. We had our own workplace drama—not so different from when I was the marketing veep at the old place, as long as you didn't look at the paychecks.

But how could one *not* look at the paychecks? I was admiring the blue-and-gold star-shaped hanging lights, metal with little holes throughout that let the sparkling white light out, when Danny walked in.

He'd put in the nose ring, the septum thing, which he never wore at work and which I did not find attractive, but whatever. Perhaps another generational thing I didn't get. Truth was it did not seem to hamper him when it came to finding partners.

"OK, so, I'm here," he said, as he sat on the wooden stool next to me. "I can't believe you talked me into this, Ben."

"Stop. You're as curious as I am. This is going to be fun!" The place was filling up, so I lowered my voice. "Need a jolt before we head out?"

Danny nodded and left his shoulder bag and gray watch cap on the counter. I resumed my observation of the passing parade outside, determined to be judgment-free. Probably should have ordered a decaf, considering the time of day, but now I was buzzed and excited to play secret agent—when who should walk by the window but *Wally.*

My first inclination was to look away, but it was too late. He saw me. Smiled from ear to ear. Dressed in a beautiful gray suit, blue tie. Crap, he was coming in. He walked through the door behind a group of giggling Japanese schoolgirls on holiday—just as Danny returned with his drink.

They arrived at my station at the same time, nearly colliding. Wally nodded to Danny. "Sorry! Don't want to interrupt, but—I had to stop and say hello."

I knew young Danny well enough to see that look in his eyes that meant wheels were cranking behind. "Do I know you?" He was gushing. "You look so familiar, handsome!"

Damage control. "That's because he's our customer at Refuge! Danny Fernandez, meet Wally Whitney, proud owner of a beautiful new Babini desk from our store."

I could feel drops of sweat fall from my pits to my flanks, stinging me.

Wally extended his hand to Danny. "Happy to meet you. You weren't there the day I bought my desk."

They shook. "I guess you're not from London," Danny said. "I'll pretend I'm not disappointed."

Wally raised his eyebrows and glanced at me quickly. "Whatever you say." Then to me: "Thanks again for the desk, Ben. It's working out even better than I hoped." He squeezed my forearm.

"Happy to hear. We've got a store full of great things—but you know that. Hope you'll be back soon."

Wally smiled. "Like I said, didn't want to interrupt, and I have an appointment myself. Take care, guys." And he was out the door.

Danny took a sip of his coffee and winked at me. "You so totally got the D; you totally fucked that guy, didn't you, Ben?"

*   *   *

Danny knew. I couldn't lie to him; he'd see right through it. He laughed—then frowned, reminding me that it was he who "saw London Daddy first!"

Still, I knew Danny would find my extracurricular activities admirable, and he'd have my back—not that he'd ever see Jake, but he'd keep it to himself. He was a good guy that way, and men of his generation didn't seem to place much heft in strict monogamy.

However—I was still who I was and it embarrassed the crap out of me to have my coworker know about my dalliance. I kept my mouth shut, hoping he wouldn't ask for specifics.

We trudged up the hill through Chinatown. There wasn't much daylight left, so the sooner we got to North Beach, the better. Danny was distracted by the colorful overstocked store windows, by the bells and chatter, songs coming out of doorways, clouds of incense, by anything shiny hanging above.

I grabbed his arm. "Come on, don't be slow, it's getting dark."

"I don't know about this. What are we going to do once we get there?"

We easily slouched down the bayside portion of Grant and turned up Columbus, past the old "beatnik central," which was now more like "annoying tourist central."

"Are you going to talk to this guy, this Rajavi?"

"I'm not sure. Since we don't know what he looks like, it's tricky."

"What if he's an Iranian agent, or worse, a terrorist?" Danny asked, as he stopped to look at an outside menu at an Italian restaurant on Stockton Street. "Maybe when we're done with this wild-goose chase we can stop here and get some pizza. It's almost dinnertime anyway. That is—if we survive."

Just a couple of blocks farther up over broken pavement on Telegraph Hill was Pfeiffer, a short street no longer than one block. Mehrdad Rajavi's address was at the east end, butting up to the tiny Jack Early Park, a sliver of a green hillside with some stairs and enough foliage to hide behind.

We walked down the block toward the park. "We're going to pass his building and I think we should act nonchalant," I said. "We could even cross the street."

Pfeiffer was a quiet residential street with no traffic, at least at this time of the day. "How about walking up and ringing the bell? Invite him with us for the pizza?"

"What if this guy is one of Darien's friends who we know from the store, but using an alias? That's why we should watch first."

Danny grimaced, cradling his stomach with both arms. "I'm going to be starving in approximately ten minutes."

I stood behind him and literally pushed him up the first few stairs at Jack Early Park. A leafy eucalyptus appeared about halfway up the hill, roof level with Mehrdad's building across the street. "Now we wait," I said.

"Oh God. How boring is that? If you want me to wait with you, you're going to have to give me details about my London Daddy, the man you stole from me."

A middle-aged woman in black tights and pink running shoes propelled herself up the stairs just a few feet from us, not paying any mind though she could hardly *not* see us, the space was so narrow.

"I didn't steal anybody. It was all quite—spontaneous," I said, keeping my eyes focused on Mehrdad's doorway below. "What I can tell you is that he does very well for himself, but that's not surprising. His home is as well dressed as he is."

"Who cares about that shit?" Danny laughed. "I want to know about his dick and what you did with it."

No one had gone in or come out of the building, but as golden hour was upon us and the light dimmed, from a window near the front door I could see there were lamps on inside.

"Like I'm going to tell you!" On the small platform above us at the top of the tiny park, Jogging Lady was moving through a few asanas: sun salutation, up dog, down dog, plank.

"Come on, Ben, I came all the way out here for you; you could at least tell me—"

"I think we should go down there. Knock on the door, see who answers. Otherwise we'll be sitting behind this tree all night."

I'd miscalculated the length of the day. It had always confused me that in San Francisco autumn days were warmer than summer days but the daylight was less, every day. Our best chance would be to confront Rajavi before it got totally dark.

We walked back down the stairs, our running friend pushing

between us at one point, a soft "excuse me" preceding. At the bottom of the stairs on the sidewalk, she ran off. The street was empty of people, the occasional car moving by slowly, drivers looking for parking, which, like everywhere in the City, was pretty much nonexistent.

"If someone answers the door, what are you going to say?"

Good question, Danny.

"I'll be direct. I've always heard that's the best way to get an honest answer. I don't know if that's true, but it's worth a try."

Just as we crossed toward the building doorway, a deliveryman, all in brown, with dark hair and stubble, mid-thirties, I'd guess, walked out, locking the door behind him. He sure looked like he could know a Mehrdad Rajavi.

He turned and we were face-to-face. His eyes widened, our sudden appearance likely startling. "Oh, hi there—we're looking for Mehrdad Rajavi. Do you happen to know if this is the correct address?"

"What?" He blinked.

"Do you know a guy here named Rajavi?"

"Oh. I don't know," he said. "Who is asking?" He pointed a keychain at a car across the street and it chirped, lights flashing. "I'm late here."

"My name is Davis Sternberg, and this is Soren. (Danny offered up a pathetic little wave.) We're looking for the Mehrdad Rajavi who works at Refuge in SoMa."

He took a step, like he was going to blow us off and take off for the car; then he stopped. "I'm Mehrdad. This is my uniform. I'm on my way to my work now, and it's not for what you said. Understand?"

"Well—it's just that *we* work there and found out there was a guy by *your* name at *this* address who worked a different shift. We happened to be in the neighborhood so we decided to stop and say hello. To our coworker."

"Stop and say hello," he repeated. "Right." He dug into his shorts pocket and pulled out a phone. He lined up a quick shot and pushed the button. The flash blinded me.

"We don't want any trouble," I said, backing up a step.

"Now I have your picture. Stay away! Don't come back! Obviously, I don't work for your stupid company!" Mehrdad hurried to his car and opened the driver's door.

"Do you know a Darien Unger?"

Mehrdad started the engine and revved it, making a ton of noise. He opened the window halfway. "No! I don't."

"She knows you."

For a moment he looked like he was going to say something, but didn't, then peeled off toward Stockton Street.

It took a few seconds for the block to return to its previously peaceful composure. Now it really *was* dark.

"That went well," Danny said.

* * *

Jake's breath was soft and warm on my shoulder, yet I lay there, eyes wide open, staring at our dark ceiling, pondering this mystery Mehrdad Rajavi.

If he wasn't actually working at Refuge SoMa, what was his connection to Darien? What was she up to? And who was he? Intrigue! Could it be something government related? Darien didn't exactly strike me as spy material, but then if she was effective—she wouldn't.

* * *

The next morning Jake and Margaret managed to get Logan off to school. By the time I was able to drag myself into the kitchen, Mom was brewing a second pot of coffee.

"I knew you'd be down soon, so I wanted to make this fresh," she said.

There was something about that line that didn't quite ring sincere.

She poured me a cup, set it down, then put the cream carton next to it. With a clean little spoon. From Margaret Kanner Schmidt, this was the royal treatment.

I wondered what was coming. "How is that little room off the garage working out? Too cold at night?"

"It couldn't be more perfect," Mom said, pouring herself a cup. "Ben, I think this is right for me. Soon it will be the holidays and I'm not even thinking about snow or drinks around the fireplace, looking out over that frozen gray lake. I think I'm going to stay in San

Francisco."

"But—" I was going to say *at your age?* and decided against it. Instead: "What about your life in Milwaukee? What about the family, Ellen and Vince, not to mention the legacy of mighty Kanner Fixtures? Your house?"

"It can sit there for a while. It's been there for a hundred years; a couple more won't hurt it. The kids—the kids can visit."

Did this mean that Jake and I now had a new roommate? The hidden dangers of buying a home with an in-law unit already in place.

Honestly, I didn't know how I'd feel about that. I hadn't had time to process her arrival, much less her staying, what with all the activity with Logan and our other extracurriculars. It wasn't that I was against it; I just hadn't ever considered it.

"Say *something*, Ben. You're making me nervous."

I took a sip. Mom still made rich coffee. "I think it would be hard to pick up and move across the country, all by yourself."

"You did it."

True, I had, but that was so long ago I could hardly remember. Back in my adventurous youth, when the future appeared limitless. And was: "I was in college and even *I* knew how to fix a flat tire."

Add that to the list of things nobody did anymore by themselves, or that were "specialized" in our glorious service economy.

"I have the money to fix any flats. I suppose if it didn't work out I could always go back," she said.

The caffeine did its work. "If you're going to stay, you should go out—and really explore your new city."

"I'm ahead of you—Karen should be here anytime now."

* * *

If I was a little surprised that Mom had made plans with Karen—without my input or knowledge—I was more or less shocked with her news later on.

In her efforts to show Margaret around town, they stopped first in that quaint Cole Valley ravine nearby. Mom insisted the tiny, pastel morning confections on offer at the appropriately named Cakes on Cole couldn't compare to the German-inspired *Kaffeekuchen* one could find in Milwaukee—but the San Francisco scenery was better.

It might have been otherwise uneventful except for their walk after, up one side of Cole and then down the other, stopping in at this storefront and that, each one more "darling" than the one previous: a pet store with the cutest little puppies; the hole-in-the-wall that only carried natural-materials backpacks from the highlands of Honduras; the yoga studio with the SRO front room and the steamy windows where everyone was so tight "I could bounce quarters off their . . . whatever!"

Up the block a bit, though, Mom had seen the sign "Part-Time Help Wanted," red letters on white poster board, in the window of another small business. It beckoned her and Karen followed.

Bells on the doorknob, a good sign, a pleasing omen, she thought. The place was called Clean Up. They sold vitamins and supplements (probably to all the yogis from down the street) and also made juices. They were looking for someone who could be a reliable salesperson and also work the blender, follow simple formulas to make health drinks.

"I got this feeling," Mom said, "that if I asked for it they would hire me, like they'd want someone just like me. *They did.*"

She would work three afternoons a week making kale and ginger smoothies for the well-paid Millennials invested in their health. "It's a bit like *Mildred Pierce*. Kids do feel better when an actual mother makes their food."

Surprised as I was—former fixture heiress turns blender whiz in Cole Valley—it made a crazy kind of sense. The truth was, if Margaret Schmidt planned to stay in San Francisco, she'd need to do something.

"The best part is my new boss knows you! Ms. Burdette, the owner. Her first name is Dallas. A lovely young woman, even if she does have a few distracting tattoos."

* * *

Of all the people my mother could have met in San Francisco, of all the employers she could have found in the City, the last person I'd want would be Dallas.

Not because she was a lousy boss (that was a new role for her; this Clean Up outfit was new information to me) or unfair or mean or any of those things; it was because Dallas probably knew me better than any straight woman—well, other than Karen—and had seen me at a few quite awkward times. Like that ecstasy-fueled lasting-till-dawn club crawl in New York where I almost totally lost it (another story for another time).

Even Dallas would likely not blab about that; who would want to tell an older lady that sordid story anyway? No matter how close we were or weren't, I didn't want my parents to know about contraband use. As simple as that.

"News to me that Dallas has a store. She's acting in my new movie—she probably told you."

"She did, in kind of a flamboyant way. Lots of arm waving. Still, I liked her and it will certainly be a change for me."

As I tried to imagine Mom taking orders from Dallas regarding protein shake ingredients, I got a message from Hu Zhang: *Call me. I'm pretty sure I know where Glenda Bourne is.*

* * *

I told Mom it was a work-related call and went upstairs to our bedroom. Jake wasn't home yet, though I expected him soon—unless Tony Ochoa was making a gallery appearance I didn't know about. Of course, I *wouldn't* know about such a thing; that was the point.

How often were they doing it, anyway?

Would I get excited if I made Jake tell me? Maybe.

Hu's phone rang.

"Hey," she answered.

"Hi, Hu," I said, which sounded absurd. "This is Ben Schmidt, Glenda's frien—"

"I know who you are," she cut me off. "How's the kid?"

I gulped in some air. "He's fine." I guessed at this; was he in the living room post school playing his *WoW* or some other equally unfathomable-to-me game? There was suitable noise coming from that vague direction; I assumed so.

"You need to bring him down here. I miss seeing him! So does my dad."

I was tempted to say, "There's nothing I'd rather do than drop him off at his apartment on your block *permanently*," but I didn't and it wasn't true anyway, now, was it?

Instead: "Maybe this weekend. *What about Glenda?*"

Hu cleared her throat. "There's like this grapevine. Alluded to it when you were out at the store, remember? Last time she paid for something here she mistakenly pulled out a passport. I asked: 'Going somewhere, babe?' She didn't respond. Anyway—I'm told she went home to South Africa. To find herself."

I was speechless, but only for the time it took to draw in my deepest breath. So I could scream. *"What kind of a person does this?"*

"Hey. Dude. I'm like, they say, the messenger. So don't shoot me or yell at me. But listen, I got a number for you and I'll text it to you. A video call works. Remember Willow-Why is nine hours ahead of San Francisco."

"What, Willow—"

"Willow-Why is a women's spiritual retreat near Cape Town. I assume Glenda will explain more."

* * *

Jake walked in just as I was about to dial him. I waved my phone: "We know where Glenda is! I've got a number in South Africa."

I filled him in between gulps of air. "I didn't say anything to Logan or Mom, so let's keep it quiet for now."

"Why you'd think I'd blurt it out is crazy, Ben. I'm not going to say anything."

He closed the door to our room behind him.

"Just wanted to make sure."

This wasn't the time to get into it; I was in that strange space between being angry and intrigued with Tony Ochoa and yet feeling slightly guilty about my little affair-ette with Wally Whitney (if you could call it that).

Our tablet, the portal to video with South Africa, was on the dresser. It would be early morning there, but did I care if I woke Glenda up or not? She could lose a little sleep over this.

We sat on the bed together. I punched in the ID on the app that would enable the international call to Willow-Why. The tablet played an annoying little instrumental while it waited to connect at the destination.

I gasped when I looked back into the screen, because in the

interim, the camera was on us, myself and Jake—but ghostly Bernard was sitting there in back of us, on the bed, against the headboard.

"You OK?" Jake asked, perhaps annoyed.

"Sure—just realized you need a haircut kind of like yesterday."

He looked into the tablet and pushed an errant curl off his forehead. To me, Bernard was clearly there; in fact, he waved in an ethereal photo bomb. Jake didn't react.

"It's not so bad, is it? I'll go see Joe tomorrow," he said.

I slowed my breathing. Measured, deliberate, I could do this, deal with the irresponsible mother of an abandoned child and the ghost of an old friend on my bed. *No problem.* Jake didn't see him. I wondered why Logan could see ghost dog Connie; did it have to do with our shared DNA?

Our image on the tablet then dissolved, replaced by the Willow-Why logo (a big tree) with their tag line: *Your Place in the Veldt.* Underneath, a light drumming accompanied the image of a green-and-brown landscape interspersed with low, wooden cottage-like buildings.

Then even that was gone, replaced by a steaming mug. Then a hand, picking up that cup, probably coffee, probably damn good veldt-worthy coffee. Then the image of a dark young woman with dreads and a gold ring in one nostril. Somewhere inside, a rustic office. She smiled; she looked friendly.

"Hallo, Americans. You've reached Willow-Why. Do you have the correct party?" She took a sip.

"Hello," I said, leaning more into the frame, still unsure if anyone else could see Bernard. "We're looking for a friend who's staying there, Glenda Bourne. Is she there?"

"Glenda, oh yes," the woman said. "I'll get her. She arises quite early, so I believe she's around. By the way, I'm Amahle, but most English-speaking people call me Molly."

"Thanks, Molly," Jake said, and before she disappeared from view, she asked, "Who shall I say is calling?"

Before Jake could utter anything sensible, I put my mouth near the mike and said, "Tell her it's Harold from the building."

"Right," she said, her image replaced by an early morning vista through a window nearby. Jake turned to me. "Beyond weird. What are you going to say to her?"

I hadn't thought it out, exactly. "*We're* going to read her the riot act! *We're* going to find out what the fuck she thinks she's doing!

We're going to demand—"

I caught Bernard glaring at me, his arms folded over his chest, a frown, as a blurry mass of teal fabric filled the tablet screen and finally gave way to Glenda Bourne.

Glenda: woman of the hour, bags under her eyes. *Oh, sorry, did we wake you?* No makeup, of course, this tunic thing likely her nightgown.

She sighed, then pulled her ponytail tight on top of her head, though there were more than a few errant strands of brown hair.

"I knew it would be you," she said. "Harold doesn't do tech of any kind. Plus, I've had this dream during vision-questing."

She started to cry.

"If you think that's going to make us feel sorry for you—" Jake elbowed me.

Someone—assume Molly—handed Glenda a tissue. She blew her nose.

"Don't you even want to know how your kid is doing?" I could feel my neck heating up, getting itchy, getting wet.

"I know you've been taking good care of Logan," she said. "I've heard from . . . friends."

Sometimes, when I got confused or anxious or both—and this was one of those times—I'd feel both dizzy and nauseous and my head would start swimming. Or it might explode.

An odd sound came through the tablet, some kind of animal, a long, low *whoop.* Glenda reacted by looking away for an instant. "It's so beautiful here; it really is."

Was she on drugs? OK, I know my past was likewise checkered, but come on. We're in our fifties. There's a child-in-jeopardy kind of thing going on here. I cleared my throat.

"I can't believe you'd be such a cunt."

She looked directly into the camera, her lower lip quivering. "Don't call me names. Come on, you're better than that." Jake squeezed my thigh so tightly it smarted.

"Glenda, tell us what happened," Jake said. "Why did you just leave, and especially, why did you leave Logan by himself?"

She wiped her nose with the tissue. It was fully daylight there now; the occasional bright bird flew by the open window off to the side. "I can't remember that day—it's a blur. You got the note, right, sport? I was so confused. I thought about going to the bridge." She blew her nose. "Instead, I went to the airport."

I looked at Jake. His death grip on my thigh was cutting off the blood supply.

"What do you mean, *note*? What are you talking about?" I was sure my face was bright red by now.

Glenda pursed her lips. A cup of steaming something entered the frame, placed in front of her. She plopped a finger into it, stirred.

"I left a note in the apartment. I'm sure I did. You didn't find it?"

"There was no note," Jake said. "We've been over there; we turned the place upside down; we never saw anything like that."

"I'm sure I left it."

"Stop making shit up, Glenda," I said.

"How did you know where to find me if you didn't read the note?" Again, the long, drawn-out *whoop* from beyond the window—which, if anything, seemed closer this time.

"Your friend at the bodega ratted you out."

Glenda's eyes widened. She dabbed her cheeks with the tissue. Softly: "Of course. Hu."

"Yes. Thank god for her. Thank god you have friends who care about you and *your family*."

"I wouldn't just go and abandon my child."

"But that's *exactly* what you did," Jake said.

"I couldn't trust myself! I dared not take him with me, Jake! It was the best thing, really—it was."

Jake and I looked at each other again. Bernard and his blond-gray bed head were still behind me, in the periphery, still against the headboard, watching, listening.

"Enough," I said. "When are you coming back? And what, for fuck's sake, is Willow-Why?"

The camera on the South African end turned abruptly and Molly was back in view. Molly with her enormous smile. "Thanks for your question about Willow-Why! We're a licensed lesbian collective, a natural retreat out in the veldt not terribly far from Cape Town. Your visit to us can be as quiet or as social as you'd like! We have a car to collect you from the airport and all our plans include meals."

"It sounds great. You probably noticed, we're not women. Anyway. Still love to come one day. Can we have Glenda back, please?"

"Yes, she's gotten up. The restroom, I think. Can you hold?"

"Who are you talking to?" Another high voice, but this one was Logan, and he stood in our doorway. As I looked over at him, Bernard faded from view at the head of the bed.

CHAPTER 8

A WEEK LATER . . .

"B-B-B-Ben," Ron Frankhauser began, "remember, you said that we'd get paid this time around."

Never good when one of your lead actors starts the day off with a stutter. He was nervous; who could blame him? I never liked asking for money, either.

I did promise comp with this new little movie *Richmond Rack*. I'd figured that with the tiny cast of Ron and Greg and Dallas (not including bit parts or extras) it would be not only possible, but prudent, and, of course, the right thing to do.

That was before my rich ex Davis Sternberg backed out. Dr. Sternberg, successful radiologist who had treated me and fucked me back in Cancerworld, had promised a lion's share of funding for this project, but then he, too, was having "issues" with this economy, where it seemed everyone was merely trying to hold on to what they had. Regardless, the money would have to come from somewhere, which I hadn't quite figured out.

"I haven't mentioned it yet, but Lisa's pregnant," Ron said, as if he needed justification to ask about what was *my* unfulfilled promise.

"Wow! Congratulations!" Greg and Dallas—and I—cheered in chorus at this wonderful news as the four of us, along with Danny Fernandez, moved our location from a spot near the corner of Clayton and Oak in the Golden Gate Park Panhandle over to a nearby park bench under a huge eucalyptus.

News of a *baby* during test shots for *Richmond Rack*. No matter how much I would rather think about something else, it was the Bourne family who came roaring back into consciousness.

It turned out Logan had *not* heard Glenda's voice coming out of the tablet. He'd heard Amahle, Molly, who had a South African accent like his mother, and that's what he responded to.

Dodged that bullet. Glenda never came back into frame; she had fled. Which she did quite well. If it was an abrupt ending to one mystery, it did nothing to resolve the question of when—or if—she'd come home.

Which infuriated us both. If Jake and I were having difficulties managing our open relationship, this was something we could agree on.

"We have to go back there and find her note," he said, immediately after the tablet screen went dark. "We looked all over that apartment."

I agreed. While the idea gave me some hope that this whole episode was not as catastrophic as it seemed, that would hinge on finding the evidence.

Which we did not. Harold let us in the next morning, and we looked. On the desk, in the desk, behind the desk; we even picked up the rug to see if it had somehow managed to get under it. When that proved useless, we looked again in the kitchen, in Logan's alcove, in Glenda's bedroom. If there was some dusty note there, it was invisible to us.

But back to addressing Ron's concerns. "Before we start this test shot, let me say again that, yes, of course, actor pay is in the budget, and I will have a way to make sure that happens."

Ron, Dallas, and Greg sat on the park bench looking up at me hopefully. For Dallas, with the sugar daddy and her own retail business, she probably could have cared less, but it was the principle of the thing. I knew Ron's and Greg's situations well enough to know that payment meant a bit more than that.

"It's so weird I'm going to be your mom's boss," Dallas said, as Danny and I figured out where the camera would be for this shot of Cupid tempting the two men.

"Didn't you block this out before we came over here?" Danny asked, clearly frustrated I wasn't as professional as the porn directors he usually worked with.

"I had this idea that Cupid dropped in from the sky—you know, the wings and all—but since there's no budget to fly her, we have to figure another way."

Greg shook his head; mock amusement, followed by a wink. Not to me, but to Danny. Now he's flirting with my DP, my coworker, my sleuthy compatriot? Since the footsie campaign at the table read,

I'd had a couple of very hard fantasies of what sex with Greg would be like. I mean, why not?

Why not was because Greg was going cub scouting. "Why not make her a different kind of Cupid, the kind that comes from below, like a slithering thing?" Greg asked.

I think all four of us frowned. No one saw Cupid, this god of love, as something of the low earth. This little film was about men meeting in the city, but I wanted to keep it, if not lofty, well, aloft. There was a reason Cupid had wings.

"For now, let's try her entrance from the left. She'll circle around in back of the bench so the guys don't know she's coming—let's walk that one out."

*   *   *

I'd left a message for Sergeant Erica Ybarra earlier in the day but hadn't heard back—though that didn't surprise me, as her outgoing said she'd be in court all day.

As I was rushing to change into my art gallery reception and fund-raising finery for an exhibit opening later at Jake Brosseau, she called back, and I explained the situation to the best of my ability, vague though it was.

"She's at a lesbian consciousness-raising camp in South Africa," I said, and immediately regretted the snark. "I mean to say it's a retreat house out in the country, the veldt, they call it over there."

Ybarra was typing; I could hear the plastic clicks on her government-issued keyboard. "What did I tell you about her turning up? See."

I had two sport jackets left that were still semifashionable enough for this art crowd: gray and black. Black seemed so final or so terminal, and besides, it had a small stain on the lapel, so it was going to be the gray.

"She didn't say when she'd come back, so we have to get in touch again. At least we have the number and location. I think she's lost it, like, lost it in the head."

"While you were talking I've already removed her from the missing persons database. To verify, abandoning a child is a crime, though the prosecution of cases like this is murky at best."

Somewhere, I had a silky navy hoodie thing that hugged what

was left of my pecs rather nicely. If I could pair that with the jacket, it might be iconoclastic enough for SoMa.

"Oh man! Just what we don't want, Glenda in jail, meaning someone else, meaning *me* and Jake, still in parental roles we're clearly not ready for. I'd like to avoid that."

* * *

I dropped Logan off at the Dong-Gutierrez house down Elizabeth Street; turns out Dr. Kelly and her husband, Paul, were neighbors we'd never met until that day at Dolores Park. Their younger son, Tyler, was a thorn in Logan's side, but I thought it would be a good distraction—he kept *insisting* he heard his mother's voice emanating from the tablet that day of the conversation with Willow-Why, and of course he was correct inasmuch as she was on that call, and we were lying about it.

I didn't have the words to tell him that Glenda had, indeed, simply left him one day without saying anything. I didn't want him to ever believe that, even if it was true. I guess I was in the camp of those who thought it was best to protect children from what the world was actually like until that became untenable, and maybe even then.

Anyway. On to the San Francisco art world, where creative lying was a force all its own.

Jake had been stressed out for quite some time, and it definitely predated Glenda's disappearance. The recession affected more and more sectors of the economy, finally and including the fine art world, which for most people were luxury purchases only.

I'd known Jake was concerned because his way was to become more withdrawn than usual. He kept troubles close. Maybe it was the "manly" way of his French Canadian heritage or his rural gold country upbringing; certainly that strength through stillness was a factor in my initial attraction to him.

Tonight's reception was for two artists, one Jake had repped before and the other who was new to his Utah Street space: Rivers Sontag I had met once or twice, and we even had one of his small pieces hanging in our home office. The otter-like, bearded, and inscrutable Rivers lived in a "shack" at the back of a German professor's house in Berkeley, where he made multimedia representations of California's natural beauty. Things like mountains, forests, beaches, deserts; quite popular, at least when on display at Jake Brosseau.

The other artist was B.J. Thompson, a tall trans woman from Oklahoma who lived part of the year up in Sacramento. The B.J. stood for Bobbie Jo; Jake told me she used to be a Bobby Joe, back in the day, and I wasn't sure whether or not to believe that the sex change warranted only a simple spelling change—though that had seemed to work for Aaron at Refuge. B.J. was black, somebody's grandma now. Her "thing" was to make sculptures out of yarn or other fibers. Sometimes she would knit or crochet them, making unique hanging pieces Jake intuited there would be demand for.

Karen said she'd pick Mom and me up and we'd all ride together. When I came down the stairs, Margaret was already waiting in the hall. She was acclimating to San Francisco so quickly; her look struck me as something elegantly post-hippie—it was the tweed plus denim plus long strings of beads that did it. She looked happy. At least, she was smiling—but there was an anxious edge.

"Logan's all taken care of?" she asked, turning to the hallway mirror to reposition strands of her white hair.

"I took him to the sitter an hour ago."

"So, it's all taken care of."

"He's all set for tonight. Are you OK? You seem nervous."

A honk from outside; a Prius honk, which I knew since we had one of our own. Karen's was the more expensive model, of course, and it was red.

"It's my first fancy event as a *resident*," she said, then lowered her voice: "I don't want to disappoint Karen or anyone else."

What an odd thing to say, I thought, as we tumbled down the steps and got into the car, Mom in front, me in back. "Did you bring your checkbook? What would impress this crowd most would be to buy some of the art."

* * *

I waited until Karen got stopped by the first light, at Church Street—to drop the bomb on both of them that we'd located Glenda.

Good thing, too, as Karen screamed. With the car windows rolled up. That girl was unexpectedly excitable for a librarian, a perpetual and mostly entertaining source of unpredictability.

I explained the situation the best I could under the circumstances, which meant being interrupted, constantly:

"How could any mother do that?"

"Logan must be so angry—and hurt—I can't even imagine."

"Glenda was in cahoots with friends *here*? That little grocery employee is evil, if you ask me."

"Will you—or the school, or someone, *anyone*—press charges?"

The only answer I was almost 100 percent sure of was that Logan still did not know—and I made them swear to secrecy. Though kids pick things up; they know more than they let on. I had learned that much being a substitute parent.

And, of course, the one question they had to ask that there was no good answer to: "When is she coming back home?"

We parked in a lot about half a block away from Jake Brosseau; there were figures milling around the front doors of the main entrance on Utah Street, a good sign for Jake; actually, a good sign for *us*.

Subtle yet thumping EDM-type music from inside got ever louder as we crossed the street. Jake always hired a DJ for these things; he said it made them more like "events" and "hipper" for the younger crowd, what he coveted for a new customer base.

He'd say: "That's where the money is. These kids all have money. And empty walls."

Outside there were both familiar-looking faces and people I definitely knew, including Darien Unger, in dark tailored slacks and a bright red jacket no one could miss. I forgot, for half a second, that the Refuge staff got put on Jake's default guest list a while back. It made sense: We sold furniture to people with personal or company budgets for such things. We'd be likely referrals. Still, though—*Darien Unger!*

Introductions all around. That was one way to get Mom and Karen to stop the focus on Glenda for a few minutes. Darien seemed amused. Like it was odd that I'd have a mother—or a friend, for that matter.

Though she was polite. "Nice to meet you, Mrs. Schmidt," she said to Mom, who quickly corrected her, telling her to use her first name: "My dear, friends call me Margaret."

There was a clutch of bodies at the door; why was she outside, anyway? I thought Darien, like the rest of us, had given up cigarettes a long time ago. Could I come up with something witty to say about Middle Eastern men? A sly but as yet untraceable reference to Mehrdad, whom we still had to deal with?

But no—I couldn't think. Sensory overload with Karen, Mom, the crowd at this thing. There were benefits to planning in advance, especially for situations like these. Nothing was going to merely roll off my tongue, and certainly not after I saw Jake's boy toy, Tony Ochoa, through the gallery's open doors.

He was dressed to the nines in a fitted gray suit, black shirt, no tie. I had to admit that, at least from this distance, I could easily understand Jake's attraction or obsession or whatever it was.

I gently cupped my hand around Mom's thin upper arm, nudging her toward the door. Darien had waylaid Karen, who implored me with her eyes. Not likely to take excess shit from anyone, she'd have to extricate herself. "We're going in," I announced, stifling a cough.

The music was louder inside, but oddly, not irritating. The EDM played by the DJ off to the side, a young woman with purple hair in pigtails, gave the gallery a darker, sexy club vibe. I wasn't so sure about whether that made it conducive to art buying—or matched the tastes of half the crowd, rich and north of fifty—though I figured Jake knew what he was doing.

He'd rounded up some heavy hitters for this reception; early enough for a first stop on many night's itineraries. Over there were Chip Llewellyn and Diana Vandermark, staples at this sort of thing. They still hadn't married but they both still had money, something to do with boats. Deep in conversation with Rivers Sontag about one of his pieces—a good sign.

"I'm not used to this kind of thing—should we look at the artwork?" Mom asked, a bit loudly, to make sure I heard over the music.

"Yes, but very casually. It's also important to smile and to drink something and eat something; chitchat is good too, and of course, especially for you since you're that fresh face."

"The new girl in town!" It was Karen, caught up to us, no Darien alongside.

"How did you lose my boss—and where is she?" I asked, looking around, convinced that Darien knew I was on to her, whatever that was, and though I had my suspicions, nothing was certain or proven.

"Outside," Karen said. "I got the feeling she wanted to leave, so maybe she did."

I wasn't sure whether that was a good sign or not. I knew this evening did not revolve around me or Refuge's SoMa franchise, and I resolved not to let Darien's unexpected appearance derail me.

Karen hooked her arm into Mom's. "There's always some decent food and wine at these Jake events," she said. "Let's find out what they've got tonight."

That was also a diversion I looked forward to. The caterer's table was up against a far wall, so you'd have to pass all the art along the way.

We moved in that direction. Once we did, both Jake and Tony came toward us. Why not? We were all adults; this was the twenty-first century.

My stomach started to grumble.

"Margaret! This is your first time at my gallery, isn't it? What do you think?" Jake was in his finest entrepreneur mode, all smiles, all charm.

"I'm so proud of you; that's what I think." She beamed, and this admission from her was unexpected. I choked up until I remembered it was Tony Ochoa who stood a half step behind Jake.

Jake hugged her. "Thank you," he said. Then, though it had to be awkward, he turned toward Tony and made introductions: "My friend Tony Ochoa, this is my mother-in-law, Margaret, our dear friend Karen, and of course you met my partner, Ben, before."

"What's to eat?" I asked, probably louder than I should have.

* * *

Such as it was, I ended up in art-opening Siberia. I thought the others had followed me to the food and beverage table, but they had not. Jake had arranged for those tiny edible baskets of Caesar salad, which were about two bites, which I found addictive.

There were other things, notably some grilled chicken pieces with peppers, colorful and tasty, on skewers. Sonoma Valley wines, which I passed up this time, closing my eyes and holding my breath, since both the sight and scent of alcohol had that mesmerizing effect on me and one sip at an event like this would not end there and would likely spell utter disaster. (Either that, or I'd end up at yet another stranger's condo—which on second thought might not be so bad.)

While I was refilling my celadon-colored paper plate with more—after all, the owner was my husband (or the closest thing to it)—the other featured artist, B.J. Thompson, regal and imposing in a green, yellow and black tunic or caftan or whatever, floated over to the caterer's table as if adrift. She had me in her sights, so I tried to remember her background and quickly took in a couple of the larger yarn pieces to comment on.

"Delightful, isn't it," she said, more a statement than a question. She had a slight tremor, clasped her large, wrinkled brown hands together, pink nail polish, a beautiful pro manicure.

"It is," I managed, even to elaborate: "The chicken is especially tasty."

B.J. took one of the little plates. "You're Ben, aren't you? Jake's partner?"

"Yes. We haven't met before, though—"

"He pointed you out to me and Rivers when you came in. I could tell he was so happy to see you. I pick up on things like that; I'm an intuitive, you know."

Her Angela Davis–style fro was completely symmetrical and close to being all white. I wondered if she'd ever used her own hair as an art fiber—had it been me, I would have been tempted.

Still, her comment about Jake warmed me. I glanced over to where I'd last seen him, and he was still there, surrounded by a small crowd, schmoozing, and hopefully, *selling*.

"That's so nice to hear," I told B.J. "Tell me, which is your favorite piece on exhibit here?"

She whirled around, to take it all in, I assumed, but also to be able to make her garment billow. Why else wear it? As it was, at more than six feet, she dominated the room.

B.J. raised her arm and pointed with one of those sharp nails. "Over there. I call it *Railroad Town*. It's one of the Oklahoma pieces from last year."

I honestly didn't know what to say. *Railroad Town* was a yarn piece, large, hung on a wall. I could not make out a discernable structure, or shape, at least from where I was standing. But I didn't have to say anything, because—

"That *is* you, isn't it, Ben? I thought I saw you from across the way."

I should have known that Wally Whitney, of course, would have the connections and interest to be on Jake's events list. He'd had art on his walls, surely. I was too preoccupied the one time I was over there to notice much that wasn't him personally.

I didn't even worry that truths might come out now because of his proximity to Jake, to Karen, to my *mother*, even. I was happy to see him. Wait till Danny heard that he was here. I gave him a big smile.

"Wally Whitney, this is B.J. Thompson, one of the two artists featured here tonight," I said, snapping with worrisome ease back into marketing mode.

"Oh, Ben, we were talking before you got here," B.J. said, giving Wally an air-kiss.

"My company has two of B.J.'s wall pieces in our conference room," he said, winking at me. "I get to see them at least five times a week." His perfectly cut dark suit (navy or black, could not tell which in the low light) was accented by one perfect red silk scarf.

"I think you need more," I said, raising my skewered chicken to emphasize that point.

I wanted to visit Wally again, wanted to take a look at his walls with more of a focus—at least in his bedroom. I wondered if he wanted that too, and how to broach this now, when I saw that Tony was headed in our direction. Tony—by himself, no Jake-shield, just him in his suit, walking toward me with . . . purpose.

He looked great; there was no denying that. I found it hard to admit, even to myself, that I admired his confidence.

Tony raised his eyebrows before speaking. I wasn't going to bite, but he had no way to know that for sure. "I've never been to a party like this before. This is so much fun."

I could be dismissive and come off as a horrid old thing, or I could reflect his callow enthusiasm.

B.J leaned into Wally and whispered something, followed by a giggle. My cheeks were hot and my collar started to get wet where it met my neck. It was obvious that they knew about Tony and Jake; I could sense it.

"These things *are* fun," I said. "Hilarious when someone actually buys something."

B.J. hooked her arm into Wally's. "Thank you for reminding me of my true purpose here," she said, smiling at Tony. "It's to make a sale. Walter, would you introduce me around some more, to all your fancy downtown friends?"

He gave her a little theatrical bow and turned to me: "We'll catch up to you two in a bit." Wally then grabbed Tony's upper arm and squeezed.

Tony patted his damp forehead as they walked away. "I'm glad they're gone, aren't you?" he asked, smiling broadly, showing near perfect teeth.

"That's kind of an odd thing to say."

He leaned in closer. "Jake probably told you that I dig older guys. Right?"

My head was about to explode from the realization that Jake's boy toy was cruising me at *Jake's very own gallery party*, when the entire place was pitched into darkness and silence.

Tony used this amazingly lucky event to embrace me, his lips awkwardly trying to find mine, and they didn't, because I pushed him away.

There was a shred of loyalty to my man, after all—thin though it may have been.

Whose voice was the next thing I heard, to be sure. "Oh God, did I not pay the fucking electric bill?" This screeched whisper got ever closer, until Jake was at my side. Along with Tony, still.

"Fuck! Everybody's going to leave," he said.

"Wait. Roll out more drinks, stronger drinks. Do we have candles?" I hadn't been a highly regarded marketing executive (aka highly paid event planner) in another life for no reason.

"Yes. Candles," Tony said, hardly audibly, what with the rising din inside the gallery from concerned guests. "Atmosphere."

"Shit. No. Why would I have candles? Fuck! What am I going to do?"

While Jake panicked, I mentally scanned the neighborhood's business geography, or what I remembered of it. Safe Harbor Software had been located nearby; I'd spent many hours walking these streets when I should've been at my desk.

There had been a chain store that sold household goods—including a million different kinds of candles—a couple of blocks away, and it was early enough to still be open. That is, if it hadn't gone out of business in the recession.

"SoMa Life. The store. I can go there and get candles, be back in twenty minutes," I said, gearing up to save this night and, at least for a bit, to get away from these people.

"I'll go with you. We'll need a lot—more than one person can carry." I guessed Tony was right. I wasn't going to be able to get away from him.

Jake was like a deer in the headlights except there were no lights. Then he said, "Go. Hurry! Grab as many as you can and get back here."

My two-block walk/run with Tony was mostly silent, save for the occasional car horn or "urban camper" grocery cart clatter on the sidewalk. I thought I should say something but did not know what that would be, words that weren't ridiculous.

Such as: Did you think our lives were a porn film?

Such as: What, exactly, are your intentions here?

Both of which betrayed that there *was* interest on my part. I couldn't hide that, and thus it was absurd to insinuate that Tony was the bad guy.

At SoMa Life we cleared out an entire shelf of medium-sized pillar candles, four shopping bags full.

Walking quickly on the return, both of us loaded down with a full bag in each hand, we got stuck at the crosswalk at Townsend. "You have to let me kiss you before we get back," Tony said.

On the green I stepped into the street. "I'm in the awkward position of defending my cheating husband." I laughed. "That's an odd place for me to be."

Another half block, in silence. "Don't you want to touch me, too? Now it's all I can think about!"

Up ahead I could see the crowd at Jake's mingling under the streetlamps in front of the gallery. Good—they hadn't all left; he must have opened up the good booze and started pouring. We would be back there in minutes.

Tony nudged me with his shoulder, pushing me into the slightly recessed doorway of an old beauty supply store. We dropped the heavy bags of candles at our feet; then his arms were around me tight and he kissed me, deep.

I liked it. I liked his soft, short beard tickling my cheeks; I liked the taste of his big tongue in my mouth. Realizing on some level the massively consequential—and totally unwanted—complications of such a coupling, on another level I absolutely did not care. So I pushed my tongue back into his mouth and sank into his chest.

Eventually (after how long? was it minutes or mere seconds in this bliss?) a high-pitched peal of laughter from a woman down the block reminded me of our mission. I broke away from Tony and picked up my two bags.

"We have to get back before he—*we*—start losing customers."

Tony glanced around at the other buildings on the block and across the street, where Potrero Hill began its rise. "All the lights are on everywhere else. Kind of weird that the gallery went dark."

I sighed. *So young.* "Not so weird. It's what happens when you can't pay the electric bill."

We were almost back. Jake was out front now, watching us approach, his brow creased. Tony smiled at him. "I want to be with both of you," he said.

CHAPTER 9

Rarely in our relationship had I had any deep sense of guilt. Neither Jake nor I was perfect, and we'd both been responsible for our share of idiotic men-related and other dramas, all of which, so far, had passed without irreparable damage to our bond.

But now this—lying in bed Saturday morning, literally still tingling from the attentions of Tony Ochoa, Jake's boy—what was he anyway? Boyfriend? Lust object of the moment? Official *amante*? Something else entirely?

So I lay there, staring at the ceiling and, yes, tingling, something that amounted to the post–prostate cancer version of morning wood. It's not merely that he said, "I want to be with both of you," but how he said it—his warm, moist breath in my ear, the way he caught my eye directly. The almost imperceptible upturn of one corner of his mouth.

The aroma of fresh coffee wafted in. Mom was busy downstairs and I detected other vague mumbling, which had to be Logan. I reached under the quilt slowly and grabbed myself, how I imagined Tony might do it if he had the chance. Jake turned over, laid his arm over my chest and burped into my shoulder.

I still floated a quarter inch off the polished concrete floor of Refuge when I opened up an hour later. The normal morning angst I would feel about Logan and Glenda, as in, when the fuck would she return, had been replaced—at least today—by the competing visions of lust with Tony and Jake's ruin as a gallery owner.

We didn't discuss the power outage in detail after we returned with the SoMa Life candles. No, we put them out, strategically, and lit them, and the gallery was transformed into a magical place. The art was less visible, thus prospective buyers would need an additional viewing to firm up any decision to purchase.

But if the product was less obvious, the atmosphere itself was much more convivial. Alcohol helped. It seemed to me people stayed longer, the conversation louder—or maybe simply more noticeable since Anika, the DJ, had to pack up and go home—no electricity for her, either.

What was not discussed was how this came to be, how Jake could have found himself in such a situation, when not paying the electric bill would have such embarrassing and disastrous consequences. He was the opposite of absentminded. No, he hadn't forgotten. He'd likely hoped there'd be a sale before it became so bad they'd actually shut off service.

The more I thought about it, the more it became clear that the gallery, and thus we, the Brosseau-Schmidts, had some serious financial problems.

Danny arrived a bit later, but ahead of Darien. Unlike some of the other, better-heeled patrons of Jake Brosseau Gallery, Danny had not been so impressed by the candlelight and free drinks and had used the situation to decamp to the Inferno, one of the remaining SoMa leather bars nearby.

"More my idea of being in the dark, if you get my drift," he said with a wink. Of course I did. I wanted to hear about the Inferno's back room, and then I wanted to tell him about Tony Ochoa and what had happened—but hesitated. I wasn't sure what my own feelings about it were yet. There was also the part about not being 100 percent certain of Danny's loyalty, of his ability to keep his mouth shut.

I went into Darien's office to pick up an inventory sheet to begin the process of figuring out the retail prices of some new items. Danny was in the front of the store, straightening up and, yes, checking out the passersby, our store-specific art form.

Mehrdad's file—maybe I was mistaken; maybe I should check it all again. So I tried her file drawer and it was *locked*. For the first time in history. Had she somehow figured out that someone had been rummaging around in there?

Through the picture window I could see Danny walk toward me. I wasn't going to have time to find a key and didn't want him to know, anyway, since he preferred that I drop the whole thing, figuring nothing good would come of it either way.

Then the back door flew open, and in she came.

"Good morrninnnggg!" Darien trilled, and I was momentarily so happy I hadn't had anything to drink, hence no hangover, because that voice coupled with alcohol withdrawal would likely prove fatal.

"Good morning." Danny waved through the window from the sales floor.

She filled the entrance to the office door and, seeing me, cocked her head slightly. "I'm looking for that inventory sheet," I said. "That's why I'm in your office."

She dropped her bag on the desk chair. "Did you find it? I know it's on this pile somewhere. If I ever get organized, you know."

She wasn't suspicious. *Good.*

The doorway to the street opened and it was our regular customer Sarge—the old "friend" of Darien's who always paid in cash.

He hardly looked like a "Sarge"—he was short, wiry, thin though vascular arms always on view because of the short-sleeve dress shirts he favored—though he always did present with a perfect flat top. Maybe that was it.

"A fine day just got better!" Darien screeched, striding out onto the floor in his direction. As she passed him, Danny rolled his eyes for my benefit.

Sarge had a new tenant who needed a conference room setup. Table, chairs, maybe some lighting for a corner. Had to hand it to Darien—she pulled together pieces that he loved without any hesitation whatsoever, scribbling them down on her scratch pad, which later I'd be tasked with translating into an actual invoice.

He was readily agreeable. After all, it wasn't his own money he spent. They shook hands and she turned to me and said, "Two thousand cash price, that includes state tax!"

Sarge was in front of me at the desk. His tight, veiny hands counted out the two grand, twenty Benjamins. "Great deal," I said, summoning enthusiasm. "If you can hold on a minute, I'll type up a proper receipt on the computer."

He patted the top of his hair, the gray sticking straight up like a spike bed. "Not necessary. Do the usual and mail it to me—I'll give it to the tenant."

He turned and walked back toward the front of the store, back toward Darien. He asked her if Aaron was around, to "tell him how to coordinate the delivery." He wasn't in yet; Darien would have him call.

I felt the familiar whoosh of cool air off Bryant Street as the front door opened and caught a look at Sarge as he turned right on the sidewalk. Darien strode back to the sales desk.

I was about to open up a new invoice file for Sarge's purchase when she scooped up the cash he left—all $2,000 of it—and announced while hovering, "Why don't you and Danny take your latte breaks now? I'll do the Sarge paperwork *myself*."

We didn't need to think twice about the opportunity to leave the store and Darien for precious off-line caffeine moments. We sat on window stools in the Cobalt Brew down the block, both of us having triple-shot espressos, any attempt to conjure motivation.

I felt queasy, however. "She's going to make out a second invoice for much less than the two grand and she'll pocket the difference. Refuge headquarters will never know."

Danny took a big sip of his espresso. "And? What, then, exactly, are you saying? We should report her? Take photos? Make a video?" He leaned in to whisper. "They'd fire her ass and give us some fucking SOB boss *or* they'd just close down the franchise. If we were smart, we'd do the same thing."

Literally taken aback, I bumped my head up against the "chic" naked redbrick wall. Startled by the sad fact that Danny had the same idea I did—if our boss could get away with such shenanigans, probably we could, too.

White-collar crime never looked so easy or so imminent.

Did we need money that badly? Would I be willing to jeopardize my family, my future, my very freedom, for a little extra, and illegal, cash from an office furniture store?

We gulped down the last, lukewarm yet still potent drabs of espresso and headed back through the late and loud San Francisco morning. My stomach fluttered with that sense of dread Danny had unleashed merely by stating the truth.

Darien hummed to herself back in her office. I glanced at the sales desk for any evidence that Sarge had been in the store at all. She'd already taken his money; there was no paper invoice lying around.

A couple of clicks on the computer told me that she'd indeed already made one up there, a sale of $1,500 in merchandise for Sarge's new startup client. The heat rose up through my chest to my nose. Here was evidence; it seemed pointless to hold back anymore.

I found myself at her office door and asked, "So who is this Mehrdad Rajavi dude, anyway?"

*   *   *

Which turned out to be an ill-advised move. Premature. Note to future self: When going up against someone who holds all the power, best to have the plan worked out.

I didn't. I couldn't very well say, "I've been going through your desk, through your files, and I found out about this mystery employee!" without looking totally dishonest myself, so I was at a loss when she looked at me—quite innocently—and said:

"Who?"

Strands of that long red hair of hers fell over one eye and she seemed to freeze, lips parted slightly. She reminded me of a cornered jungle cat right before it would pounce: centered, tightened, focused.

I drew in a loud breath. "I wondered if someone new was starting. Hopefully, someone competent. And cute."

Darien didn't move her head or take her eyes off mine, but she did raise her pen, as if to make a point. "It's just you, Danny and Aaron. Business doesn't warrant adding anyone, especially with the economy dying all around us. Why, did you have a friend who needs a job? And *who*, by the way, is 'Baghdad'?"

* * *

I got out of it by shrugging and playing dumb, said something on the order of "Oh, I thought I heard you talking about some guy, must've been a customer," yet I knew via the interminable tension that hung in the air for the rest of that short shift that she knew exactly what I was getting at and this little Refuge drama was just beginning.

Karen did her best to follow along as I detailed the story later on in Dolores Park. Like Danny, she couldn't see why I didn't let sleeping dogs lie, so to speak, since pushing this narrative about Darien and white-collar crime would only end badly for *my* employment. "Someone has to stand up for principle," I said.

We were there with Logan at the playground he insisted was "for babies." The usual neighborhood friends were present, including Destiny Stackhouse and Tyler Dong-Gutierrez.

The modus operandi for the two older children (Logan and Destiny) was to tease and semibully the younger one (poor Tyler). I kept one eye on them from our bench a few yards away. Across the play area, Belinda Stackhouse watched us from behind dark glasses with the rim of a large paper coffee cup resting on her chin.

"That woman doesn't like me," I said, nodding in Belinda's direction. "For all I know she thinks we've kidnapped Logan."

Karen sighed. "Stop it. It's the other way around, isn't it? Come on, Ben, you don't like her, admit it. It's got to be hard being a single mother; you might give her some slack."

I moved an inch or two away from her. Enough for her to notice. "I don't want to be a bitch, but sometimes—"

"Sometimes?"

"You complain about things that aren't real problems. Like when there are *real* problems staring you in the face."

Her mouth was pinched tight, an unusual expression for her. My eyes shot to Logan, who, along with Destiny, ran around in a circular game, never allowing Tyler to get close.

"I thought you meant the kid."

"No. I meant Jake."

They'd always been friendly, but there was also a distance between them—or so I thought. Karen had been my friend from a time long before Jake, and it was like they both knew this was a foreign territory not to breach.

She grabbed my hand with both of hers and rubbed it. The fog had rolled in, daylight was going and the temperature had dropped. "Careful, Belinda will think I've turned."

"Last night—with the power being turned off and all that—it wasn't a fluke, Ben. Jake's gallery is going bankrupt."

Right then a small orange foam football hit me in the nose. "Uncle Benny, you're supposed to catch it!" Logan yelled from halfway across the "baby" play area. I couldn't throw it back since it had fallen behind the bench, so, my filter failing me, I flipped the kid off.

"You're flunking Basic Daddy 101."

"What do you mean, bankrupt? People—rich people—buy art there constantly."

"Jake told me it's not 'constantly' anymore."

I stood up to look over the bench for any indication of Logan's ball. Nothing. It had likely rolled underneath or down the hill, and the very last thing I wanted at that moment was to get on my knees and look.

"Maybe if Jake repped artists who made things people *want* to hang on their walls—not that there's anything wrong with yarn sculpture, but it's hard to dust."

"He said that even the popular artists—when he sells work, of course, a lot of it, most of it, goes to the artist, not the gallery, not to mention marketing and overhead—"

"Did I see you use an obscene gesture directed toward my child?"

I was on the ground with my head stuck under the bench, down there with the plastic bags and crumpled juice boxes and black decaying banana peels, but I knew Belinda Stackhouse when I heard her, and I knew she was going to make me pay for that slipup.

* * *

She read me the riot act for shooting Logan the bird. Though quite frankly, it was just as embarrassing to admit to her that I'd given the finger to the nine-year-old I was responsible for rather than her own kid. With a look I took as generic disgust, she turned away from us and led Destiny out of the park.

Now we were back home, with Jake, in the living room. Logan sat across from us in a chair, his feet not quite touching the vintage Persian rug that covered the planked floor. I tried imagining him disappearing, simply fading from view like the ghosts of my friends I'd see from time to time. By all rights he should be home with his mom, and I thought he would've been by now, but she had not returned and there'd been no further word from her.

It was up to us to instruct and enlighten; up to us to be parents.

The angry woman complained to Uncle Benny and Aunt Karen because she knows you're a better kid than Destiny is and that makes her mad.

Or, Ms. Stackhouse was upset because Uncle Benny, not thinking, used a crude gesture that means "fuck you." We'll explain what that means at a later date.

Of course, I chose the latter explanation. Reluctantly. The kid did not miss a beat. "I know what 'fuck you' is. Mom told me about that when I was six. It's OK. I think Destiny's mom is unhappy and that makes her mean."

Jake had turned his head to look at me, but I dared not return the look for fear that I would laugh. "Now that it's settled, you should go do your homework."

Logan stood. "We didn't get any. Uncle Benny, can we get another football, since you lost mine at the park today?"

"Go," I said. "We can probably afford a new ball."

Logan ran out of the room. It dawned on me that he never just walked out of any room, but ran, like he was always in a hurry, always on deadline.

Jake put his arm around me and nuzzled that area right under my ear, which never failed to drive me crazy. "I don't think we're very good at being dads," he whispered.

I sighed, more out of pleasure than resignation, and put my arms around him. "When were you going to tell me about the gallery?"

* * *

Jake avoided answering that question for a couple of minutes with his decision to kiss me instead of talking. Logan had gone, we were alone, perhaps Mom had decamped to the in-law unit for a bit, whatever it was—we sank back into the sofa and connected deeply in that way that had become, over the years, increasingly rare. His cashmere-sweater-covered chest pressed against me so tightly I could feel his heartbeat. The heat of his body and its luscious weight on me, which I craved but often forgot about until I got a small taste of it again.

"I was going to tell you there were problems with cash flow," he said, finally, coming up for air. "But it seemed like there was always the promise of a big sale right around the corner, which would fix everything. Something always got derailed."

Something always got derailed. Later on, in bed, with the sleeping Jake breathing softly next to me, this phrase kept repeating itself over and over in my head.

I felt the ridges of the long scar south of my navel, running the tip of my finger alongside it.

* * *

Monday morning the back door at Refuge was already open a sliver. A wave of unease washed over me but receded just as quickly when I heard Darien Unger's studied dulcet tones on the phone inside.

Why was she so early?

I entered, faking a hack so that there'd be noise and she wouldn't be startled—though it would serve her right if she was.

"Is that you, Ben?"

"Goood morninnng!" *My turn to say this for once!* "You're here early."

She was at her desk, the same messy desk that held all the suspicious receipts and bogus employee files. With each passing second my foreboding grew and my stomach sank. *Did you really have to mention Mehrdad? Why, Ben, why?*

"Paperwork! That bedevilment!" She laughed, and the front door—which apparently was also already unlocked—opened, Aaron bursting in along with the bay breeze.

"Great! Aaron, you're here. I have a pickup list for you. Later we'll have deliveries; it's one of those busy-bizzy days!"

It always amazed me how comfortably Aaron had slipped into the "strong, silent type" cliché, which seemed more acceptable now than what he was like as a she, yet another cliché, the "annoyed, unsociable lesbian." Harsh? Perhaps, but true. I'd have to ponder the inherent unfairness of these gender roles another time, however.

Aaron got points for rolling his eyes as he passed me in Darien's office doorway. He wore the work "uniform" I was most fond of, the tight black V-neck T-shirt over the snug black trousers and black trainers. This ensemble inevitably set off his short black hair and black eyebrows, which made for a stunning package, overall. Obviously, he was more successful at being male than Danny or I was.

But back to the boss. "Danny will be here soon, but I wanted to let you know before he got here," she began. "Come in, Ben, don't stand in the doorway where I have to shout."

I entered, trying my best to look unconcerned, though my eyes couldn't help but scan the desk area, particularly the file drawer. It was closed, but there was now a key in the lock where I'd never seen one before.

Darien's unmoving smile seemed plastered onto her face, no doubt obscuring bared teeth. She sighed.

"Are you happy here, Ben?" She cocked her head slightly, resumed the funhouse grin.

"The job's been a lifesaver," I said, preparing for the worst, clenching my fists behind my back.

"See—you didn't answer my question, which bolsters my

reasoning for making this little change here. I want someone who has a *passion* for this, not someone who needs lifesaving."

At that, she rolled her eyes and chuckled, though it sounded nervous.

"That was a poor choice of words. I love working here. It's a good group."

"The first thing out is always the honest response. Psych 101, right? Anyway—your job is safe. I'm making Danny the assistant manager instead of you, so now you'll report to him. It's less responsibility, but we'll leave you at the same pay, so everyone wins, right?"

I was stunned. I thought she was going to can my ass right then and there.

"Danny may love office furniture more than me—"

"Right. He does."

Darien's smile flattened out. It was like my lack of passion for desks and lamps had become a moral judgment. I knew this was a ploy to get me off the Mehrdad track, off the Sarge "fake receipts" track, off the whatever-else malfeasance track I would unearth when she wasn't around.

All of this was boiling inside and would erupt unless—unless a countervailing force entered, and he did just that. I opened my mouth right when Danny opened the back door.

Instead of accusing Darien of a crime, I said, "Oh, hi, Danny."

Which was provident. So close to sabotaging my near future, I listened to my thoughts race like a stone skipping on a calm lake, touching on only the most important items: Refuge funds the short film; Refuge buys Logan's school lunch and art supplies; WTF was in Tony Ochoa's pants, anyway, and how soon would I be seeing *that*. And what if Glenda just didn't come back?

"Congratulations," I muttered to Danny, sliding past him as I backed up out of Darien's office.

He raised his brows—puzzled, of course. She would have none of it. "Come in here, Danny, I have some good news!" she gushed.

The further I took myself out of this equation, the safer I'd be from either (1) murder or (2) implosion. I'd walk outside in front, even, pretend I was checking the window for design symmetry or dead moths. Bryant Street had that late morning lull when rush hour is done but before anyone is out for lunch. Bright and warm and windless, that part of the day was approaching perfection.

The vibrating phone in my pocket quickly put an end to that peace. It was Mom; that was weird, I thought; it was a workday for her and it was still early.

"This better be good," I said, as a grimy Muni bus flew past me.

"Is that any way to greet your mother? You're lucky to still have one, buster. Never forget that."

"I'm sorry. It's been a crappy day and I have a feeling that's not going to change now that you're calling. Please tell me it's about Glenda—as in, she's made contact?"

Margaret sighed. As only a mother can. "I wish it had been her. I *wish* it was that simple," she said. "It was the police. They came to the door."

This has something to do with the gallery, was my first thought. Jake was in deeper trouble than we knew, but—

"Not the regular police, the *school police*. They look the same, same blue uniforms, tall, scary. It's Logan, he's fine but he did something. He's in detention there at the Milk School and will only be released to a parent—or guardian, in your case—so you have to go over there."

CHAPTER 10

If nothing else, the school emergency was a convenient way for me to leave work with absolutely no promise of if or when I'd be back. That's it: *Leave Darien hanging.* Make her wonder what my next brilliant move might be. Let her stew!

Even if this fantasy was only in my head.

Mom had specified the familiar name of Brennan Reeves at the school. He was the man to see, the person holding Logan under guard until he could be delivered to someone responsible.

She had other details. The nature of the crimes included theft (of spray paint) and vandalism (using the stolen spray paint). Interestingly, there was a known accomplice: "You know, that little girl in the park, the one he plays with." There was only one I knew of, so it had to be Destiny Stackhouse.

And the scene of the crime—a newish craft store on Nineteenth and Castro, a block away from the school. I had noticed it as it was such an anomaly in this era—a storefront retail establishment, Precious and You, obviously targeting the dwindling gay presence in the area. And tourists. And, apparently, schoolchildren.

I took my time. Logan could cool his heels and contemplate his misdeeds as I walked over to the school from Muni. It was now lunch hour, and the street had filled.

A few storefronts, perhaps half a block, in front of me a reddish brown dachshund walked on its own, not trailing a leash, no master in sight. There were plenty of people to look at, even guys to cruise—so why did my attention go right to this dog?

It stopped, turned its head and looked me in the eye. Of course, I knew why. This was no ordinary dog; it was Connie, the same dead Connie Logan had seen at our house.

She would lead me to him. As soon as it registered that I looked back, she continued down the block, turning right onto Eighteenth toward the school.

The ghost dog was not catchable. She had never given me that satisfaction. Maybe she couldn't—there'd be no fur to touch, no licks to back away from. No matter how solid she looked from afar, the truth was Connie was ethereal.

I tried to ignore her as I got closer to Milk Academy (as if that would be possible) and particularly tried not to visibly react as I saw her walk right through the brick façade of the school and disappear.

Belinda Stackhouse was waiting at the school's front door when I arrived.

I exhaled. "Hello. Not sure I realized your daughter—Destiny, right?—went to this school."

Belinda gave me a tiny smile. "We talked about it at the playground, but I guess guys like you don't remember."

At that the lock buzzer went off and she opened the heavy school door, so I didn't say anything in return. But—I was speechless. *Guys like me?*

When our eyes adjusted to the darkness in the vestibule, it was a repeat of the first time I'd come to this school to get Logan. Brennan Reeves stood in the center of the hallway like before, but this time he had a kid on either side: Logan *and* Destiny. Behind them was a tall, bearded, ginger bear who did not look happy.

"Hi, Mom," Destiny said, not more than a whisper.

"Ms. Stackhouse and Mr. Schmidt, glad you're here. This is Randy Redding, owner of one of our neighborhood stores, Precious and You. It's about time for class to change, so please follow me before we're inundated with a sea of noisy students."

He didn't take us to his office. Instead, he led all of us quickly outside, to a playground that bordered the single-family houses on the block.

Both Belinda and I took in audible gasps as we saw the reason: the redbrick side of the school building there, as well as the designer gray siding paint of the closest private house to the school, was covered in spray-paint graffiti. Childish scrawls in pink, in black, and in gold glitter, using words that were either obscene or rude, depending on one's point of view.

"Don't you tell me my Destiny had anything to do with this!" Belinda screeched.

"Let's keep calm," Brennan Reeves said, raising his palms in front of his chest. "Destiny, do you have something to tell your mother?"

She twisted a bit, as if she almost wanted to hide behind Brennan or even Randy Redding (who had yet to say anything, though he looked about to erupt). "I did spray some words," she said, almost inaudibly, while looking at her shoes (pink-and-white trainers), "but it was Logan's idea and he made me do it."

I wanted to laugh and stifled a cough. But—serious parental guardian business this was. I conjured up the memory of my most earnest press spokesman voice from my former marketing career and asked: "Logan, is this true? What happened here? Why don't you explain?"

He was frightened. The kid looked at me, at Ms. Stackhouse, up at Brennan Reeves and even back at Randy Redding. He didn't dare look at Destiny.

"It was that *dog*! The one I keep seeing at your house, Uncle Benny. It led us into the store and right to the paint cabinet."

"Logan, are you saying you did this?" I pointed at the graffiti. One of them, right behind him on the gray house, said, "Fuck You Penis Pussy," in pink paint, underlined in black.

"This would have never happened if Logan wasn't the instigator," Belinda said. "Ever since he's been in the neighborhood and at this school, well, he's been a bad influence on Destiny."

"What if it's the other way around?" I'd be loyal to Logan, even if he had been a little shit.

"Let's calm down," Brennan Reeves interrupted. "Randy, do you want to tell the parents what happened on your end?"

Randy sighed, exasperated, like he was the student who finally got called on when he knew the answer all along.

"I saw the kids come in, which isn't unusual; we're right here down the block and we have art supplies and whatnot. My back was turned helping this other lady. When I turned around I saw these two right here—inside the counter where we keep the spray paint as required by law.

"So I told the *rugrats* to get out of there and they ran out the door with these cans in their arms!"

He used both of his own red, hairy arms to point at Destiny and Logan. "There was no dog," he spat. "We don't allow pet friends into Precious and You."

Brennan Reeves raised his hands once again. "It's better for everyone if we don't call people names; please remember that."

Eyeing Belinda and myself, Randy said, "I can't understand what kind of parents these little thieves must have, to allow this kind of thing to go on."

"Now, wait a minute," I said. "Nobody's 'allowing' this to go on. I think that's why we're here."

If Logan and Destiny could make themselves invisible, they would've chosen that option. In black paint on the school's wall, someone had sprayed, "You a Cunt Ms Diaz," also encircled with the accent gold glitter spray. I winced but also had an urge to giggle.

I didn't dare. Belinda did not trust me as it was; laughing would surely destroy any remaining credibility I had with her. My status with Brennan was still in question, but I suspected it was along the same lines.

"Logan's acting out to get attention; that's what it is," Belinda said. "Because his mother is gone. Anybody would understand this."

I heard her, but I was fixated on Randy Redding's fingernails, which were painted shiny black. Odd color for a bear, I thought.

Try as I might to come up with something witty yet cutting that wouldn't tar me as a complete douche, I was spared the immediacy of responding to Belinda by the church bells of Most Holy Redeemer, less than a block away.

Two peals, two p.m. I'd called Jake, left a message for him to meet me here. A united front, I suppose. Truth was, I didn't really know what to do, specifically, with this Logan problem.

Belinda was right, in a sense—his *mother* should be here, not me.

He hadn't moved much since we began the tour of the crime scene. I set my features into what I hoped read *disapproval* and looked down at him. "Logan—you *do* know why this is wrong, don't you?"

* * *

Jake never did show, and Mr. Reeves needed to leave. He gave the children a task: they were to write essays formally apologizing, explaining how they were going to make this better, pay Mr. Redding back for the stolen paint, and come up with a plan to clean/repaint the buildings.

"I want them to understand the real-world consequences of this kind of behavior," he said, clenching his fist, appearing (in some ways, sadly) more and more like the assistant principal his nameplate said he was.

I had to walk and shake off this day—the weird morning at Refuge and now this dreadful afternoon at Harvey Milk School—so Logan and I would take the big hill back to our house in Noe Valley. We'd left the others—not one more word from Belinda or Destiny Stackhouse—and headed toward Castro.

Walking slowly, silently, the main reason being I had no idea what to say. Maybe the kid would find the quiet intimidating. Maybe I'd come up with something wise. I guess we all were going to increase our knowledge of paint solvents.

There was movement behind me. Randy Redding came into my periphery. No doubt he was headed back to Precious and You down on the corner.

I grabbed Logan's hand and pulled him toward me so there was extra room for Randy to pass us if that's what he wanted. It was awkward. I nodded. "For what it's worth, congrats on the store," I said. "We've—my partner, Jake, and I—enjoyed the windows, especially at holidays."

Randy moved another foot away from us and glared down at Logan. "Thanks. It's been my dream. For years. It's always nice when people remember to respect that."

* * *

The silence with Logan did not last the entire way.

With the very top of the hill still not visible on our journey up and over: "Uncle Benny. This is a mountain. You're walking too fast."

"It's good for you. It builds the muscles in your legs, which you are going to need if you live in this city for a long time." I stopped for a breath but tried to disguise it. "It also builds character."

Saying that made me feel a bit uneasy about my searches into Darien's files, and my trip to North Beach with Danny to track down the real Mehrdad. However, we had been on a mission to uncover *someone else's* criminal activity; we weren't initiating it to cause harm.

There was a difference.

Logan was quiet for the rest of the day, not even asking Jake or me if he could turn on the *WoW*. Which almost never occurred. "He's mulling over the vandalism—and his part in it," Mom offered.

She was probably right. Either that, or he was coming down with something.

"I have to ask, though I'm sure you would've said something. Any calls from Hu? Any other message from South Africa or any indication at all that Glenda Bourne is alive?"

Mom closed her eyes, shook her head. "Should we try calling Willow-Why again?"

"And what, have her bail and run out of the room, or avoid us altogether? I don't think I can handle that. It's hard enough not letting it slip to the kid that we know where she is."

Later, in bed with Jake, a call to Glenda seemed more reasonable. If it was midnight in San Francisco, it was nine a.m. at Willow-Why. She'd be squeezing the OJ for her bush brekkie.

Jake leaned into me, kissing my shoulder. I turned my head so my lips grazed that thick French Canadian hair. "You usually sleep like a rock."

Our door was closed, the faint light from the hallway visible in a line under the door. Thankfully, we could have been alone the house was so quiet.

"Should we call Glenda? It's morning there."

"No," he said. "I don't want to ruin this otherwise sleepless night by calling that woman."

"But—he's not our kid. Until today I thought this would be like a long babysitting gig, but it's not."

"We can teach him some right from wrong."

I stiffened a bit when that registered—and not in the fun way.

"It's that little girl. Destiny. It must be—she's a bad influence. Glenda never mentioned any behavior problems with Logan. And of course, half his DNA is mine."

"Don't blame her! Ben, a little girl? What's the word? Chivalrous? That's *so* not chivalrous. She's also a nine-year-old."

"And we live in the post-chivalry world of San Francisco, so—"

"When were you going to mention Walter Whitney?"

If I stiffened before, now I just wanted to sink into the mattress, be enveloped by it and disappear, kind of like in that horror movie except without Freddie and all the blood.

Think fast. "I'm going to guess you met him at the gallery gala. Before or after the lights went out?"

"Before."

"So he blurted out that he knew me, and in *what way* he knew me? People have no tact these days."

"It was more like I put two and two together. Intuition. I figured you'd be a sucker for that lustrous gray hair."

"It *is* a nice head of hair. Have to admit that."

We didn't move farther apart at all. We lay there, both staring at the ceiling—even though it was dark, I knew his eyes were open.

"You're not perfect either, Jake!"

"Never said I was."

That was not a lie. He'd never claimed that kind of bogus high ground. What had we become now, brother-lovers from a story not yet written? I sensed a shift, not abrupt, something that had been in play for a while. But the complicating factors—Logan, my mother living with us, serious problems at both our jobs—made navigating the sex question overwhelming. Or at least it was beginning to seem that way.

"Tony likes you; he knows I know that. He knows I encourage it, actually," Jake whispered into my ear.

What happened next—a relentless stiffening, organically rare because of all the prostate cancer treatment I'd had—totally gave me and that unmistakable attraction to Tony Ochoa away. I turned on my side to press up against my man, slid my fingers along his chest; a little punctuation on the idea that his "encouragement" excited me.

It was, at the same time, both affirming and a little sad, since it had occurred not so much for Jake as for another guy.

He kissed my nose. "Talk to me about it after. I want to know every detail."

* * *

My newfound tumescence continued the next morning. I woke early, which usually happened when there was a lot on my mind—some of it good, like getting to "know" Tony better; some of it not good, like Logan and Destiny's theft and vandalism; and some of it questionable, like Darien Unger's perceived thievery.

What would happen if I was wrong about Refuge? Likely,

nothing good. But it was quite possible that nothing good would happen anyway.

Since I was up well before my start time at the store, I found myself with a hot latte and that aforementioned slight erection, back in Jack Early Park behind a tree staring down at Mehrdad's building.

A little—or a lot—pathetic. I got that. Stalking this guy, who by all appearances worked for UPS. Though that could be some elaborate ruse. I was so *confused*. What would I do if I saw him, if he came out of his house like before?

I'd follow him; that was my half-baked idea. Since I didn't have a car and he did, this was an almost certain fail. I took preemptive photos: his door on Pfeiffer, with the number; his car and the license plate, which was parked across the street like last time.

To what end, I wondered, after an hour or so of sitting there, behind the tree in Jack Early Park, the dregs of my coffee now lukewarm and unappetizing. Make-believe tradecraft; that's what this was. He hadn't appeared and I was *not* going to confront him at his door like the other time.

So, I headed into Refuge, where I had a new supervisor in Danny. I unlocked the back door, our usual method, turned off the alarm, and switched on the lights. It was that quiet, drama-free time before either customers or our dysfunctional management arrived. The reassuring, calming smell of new upholstery and wax. The door to Darien's office was closed. I casually rubbed my palm over the knob— and, voilà, it opened.

Which was a surprise. I was sure she'd start to lock it, since she had discovered I was on to her and the demotion proved it. I wonder if she just forgot.

The window of opportunity was small. I went in, checked the four corners of the ceiling—no cameras. That was probably coming but it wasn't in place yet.

I'd look for more files, more evidence. On top of Darien's desk was the Refuge "corporate" directory. It was thin, almost an afterthought, basically a family company in its first tentative growth spurt.

Staring up at me was the Western Regional Section, of which we were a part, along with all the stores in California and a few of the other Western states. We reported to the Denver office, where LeVon McDonald, Darien's on-paper boss, ruled from. The book was open to the page with his photo and contact information, as if waiting for me.

This is very convenient. Could it be a trap?

That would be paranoid. Likely Darien needed to call him about something, or did call him and left the book open. He was her boss, after all; they spoke weekly if not more often.

Mr. McDonald had visited us once or twice; not sure if I ever said more than a couple of words to him. He was affable in the sense of a detached, buttoned-up businessman. Prematurely balding, he seemed to not feel that he needed to appear at all "cool" even though he was the boss—which I thought refreshing. Also, since he was only around thirty, it was a little weird for us, both Darien and me, as oldsters reporting to someone nearly young enough to be our child.

I assumed he was as uncomfortable with that as we were. If so, maybe he'd welcome an informant who'd been around the block a few times. I suppressed a wince at the realization of how far I'd fallen in the world of work. Once marketing software on the leading edge of the Silicon Valley economy; now reduced to selling furniture (though high-end) for their conference calls and the insipid office drama that accompanied such an enterprise.

Oh, well—I was alive, survived cancer, still had my man, and those were the important things, yes? Those and another chance on another day.

I picked up the phone and dialed LeVon McDonald.

He answered right away; it was pushing lunchtime in Denver and it took him a beat to figure out who I was and where I was.

"Right," he said. "Refuge SoMa is always in our top ten, month over month. We'd be in a pinch without those California stores."

"Mr. McDonald, quite frankly I've agonized over whether to contact you or not on this. Where I come from it's practically anathema to go over your supervisor's head."

My mobile chirped with a text even as I was speaking. It was from Tony: *What are you doing later? I want to get naked. LOLOL!*

I lost my train of thought.

"Yes, are you there, Ben?"

I turned the mobile upside down on the desk and faced Darien's picture window. "Yes, sorry. I got distracted for a sec." Then I lowered my voice, even tho ugh I was still the only person in the building. "This is quite a serious charge—but I believe Darien has what is known in the lingo as a 'ghost employee.' At least one, or there's one that I know of."

I thought I heard a cough or a clearing of the throat on McDonald's end. "A ghost employee?"

"Someone on the payroll who doesn't actually work here."

"I know what a ghost employee is." Was he laughing?

My heart pounded; it was difficult to focus with the pressure in my ears. I laid my hands flat on the desktop to steady myself. "I know I'm taking a chance here, but there are other things. Faked invoices, for instance, for customers paying in cash."

Another pause; what sounded like papers shuffling by someone not paying attention.

"Hmmm." Finally, a response. Of sorts. I looked at his photo in the directory, right under the company's oddly retro motto of *We Strive for Integrity—and It Starts with You!* He looked as reasonable as I remembered, **someone** with gravitas, someone on his way up the office furniture hierarchy, someone I could trust.

"What proof do you have of this, Ben Schmidt?"

I hadn't rehearsed this call in my head, his likely questions and my not-so-ready answers. The clock on the wall told me Danny could walk in any second.

"There's a file on the employee—looks all routine and normal—but this person has never shown up and doesn't work here in any conventional sense."

"Can you make a copy of that?"

"You want me to make a copy of it and what then? Send it to you?" With every word, I felt more and more exposed, like maybe this was not the brightest idea after all.

"Can you do that? Discreetly, of course. No need to mail it; you can fax it, or you can scan it and e-mail it to me. Use your personal e-mail."

"Yes, I could do that." I felt like a robot in an old sci-fi movie.

"Obviously, I wouldn't tell Darien anything about this."

"Obviously." The back door made its ominous squeak. Danny had arrived. "Well, Mr. Sanchez, I'll shoot some chair ideas over to you before lunch. You're going to love the rich Italian leather on the ones we talked about!"

"I get that you have to go," LeVon McDonald said. "I'll be looking for your e-mail."

I put Darien's phone back into its charging station as quietly as possible. Danny stuck his head into the doorway. "Hello, hello—Jesus, Ben, you look like you're going to puke."

"That might happen." I sucked in some air. "That was Darien's boss—I told him about Mehrdad."

As Danny's jaw dropped, a new text popped up on my own phone, from Tony: *I really* wish *I could see you tonight.*

* * *

Danny, at least, did not have the poor taste to act like a supervisor to me, though technically he was. His ability to totally ignore or compartmentalize Darien's crimes was troublesome, however.

"It's just not smart to confront someone *borderline* like her over something like this—at least if you want to keep working here. Even *I* know this, and I'm half your age."

I narrowed my eyes. "Thanks for reminding me. I can't take back what I told Mr. McDonald. Let's find that folder."

Which would have been something to check on before making that call. I hadn't done that, and now the drawer, in which a key had miraculously appeared after I first mentioned Mehrdad to Darien, was locked. Tight. With no key anywhere.

"Oh man." Danny sighed. "You should've made a copy when you first found it."

Ugh. Of course. He was right. He was smarter than me.

The options dwindled. We could (1) find the key, which Darien likely had on her person, (2) break the lock on the desk, which Darien would immediately discover, (3) figure out how to jimmy the lock, or (4) forget about the whole thing.

Four was not an option. Neither was number two. Number one, finding the key, didn't seem likely. That left option three, playing secret agent safecracker.

I'd never believe a spy thriller again, where the charismatic hero or heroine pulls out their little file or pin and sticks it in the lock and presto, it clicks open. Doesn't happen. At least, it did not happen for us in the short time we had to fiddle with it, less than an hour before Darien swept in, meaning that endeavor was done for the time being.

Once she got there, she shooed both of us away from the back of the store, like we were third graders. "I don't want you hanging around back here. We need to be out in the store, ready to help people coming in," she said.

We don't need you back in my office where you may uncover evidence of more crimes—is what I'm sure she meant to say.

"The new arrangements seem to be working *so well* for you guys," she trilled, almost a question, and neither Danny nor I answered. She would take that as a yes.

Darien had a number of meetings set up with clients, luckily, so further interaction with either Danny or me was limited. One of these was Sarge, her "favorite" customer, who always paid in cash, and who, for all I knew, was in on whatever scam she was ultimately working. Whenever I'd pass them in a section of the store, they'd stop talking or take it real low. When I'd be out of earshot, there'd be a giggle or two and whispers.

As the day wore on, I could feel the gravity of the locked drawer weigh heavier and heavier, assuming that behind it, the crucial file on Mehrdad was likely missing. I'd been such a fool not to copy it; then again, at the time I didn't assume Darien was doing anything illegal.

My shift that day was short. With his persistent messages, Tony Ochoa had succeeded in getting me to agree to meet him midafternoon on the Embarcadero. We'd figure it out from there.

My head spun with this new urgency of getting the file evidence for LeVon McDonald. How would it happen, and heaven forbid, if I failed to deliver, then what?

Various scenarios, none with Darien being frog-marched out of Refuge, played like a video in my head, slowing only as I approached the pedestrian pier north of the Bay Bridge. Tony stood out at the end, watching a rusty barge float out into the bay.

He wore a dark blue sport coat, a refreshing alternative to the expected hoodie. I wondered if he usually got that dressed to go to work. It had been a while since I'd even stepped foot in a startup, but the commandment had always been to be as casual as possible.

Don't know if he heard me coming or expected me to be prompt (because I was, always—perhaps Jake told him), but he wheeled around as I walked up. Odd that it wasn't crowded, nice late autumn day that it was, sunny, no clouds, no fog yet. He held out his arms.

Obviously, not someone from my generation who still held the vestigial fear of possible homophobic violence coming from any and every direction. Mitigated somewhat by being in San Francisco, after all, but I never had let my guard down. I glanced around; no one was near, so I embraced Tony.

"You feel so good," he whispered.

"You too," I said; true enough, he felt great, even though this made me nervous.

"I want to kiss you, Ben."

We did. It was quick and I couldn't give myself over to it, could not sink into his chest and lose myself. I kept getting a mental image of callous young office workers in a high-rise behind us sharing binoculars and laughing at the fags. That fear was cellular; I'm not sure it would ever leave me completely.

Yet guys in Tony's generation weren't concerned.

"That's so nice. Even better than the other time," he said.

We looked out at the barge, now nearly under the bridge on its way south. "What now? Do you want to grab dinner somewhere?"

"Maybe after," he said.

*   *   *

We needed a place.

Our house was obviously out of the question; Tony said we could go to his shared apartment in the Mission but that his roommates would be there. That didn't seem right either: a twentysomething bringing a "daddy" back to his apartment—wasn't it supposed to be the other way around?

Of course it was, and even if it wasn't, I'd feel like a sleazebag.

So: hotel. Less dishonest, more like we'd be characters in a movie drama with good lighting and luxe set design. The few nearby that overlooked the bay were a little pricey for an afternoon assignation, no matter whom it was with. At least that was my opinion (and it was going to be on my credit card).

"Let's walk toward Union Square," I said. "We can get to know each other."

He hooked his arm into mine. "You're trying to be polite but you don't have to. You want to get naked as much as I do—I can tell."

I nodded. He was correct and not afraid to be blunt. Tony was nothing if not subsequent waves of refreshing. Each revelation took me closer, which was a little disturbing: He was Jake's "boyfriend."

And yet this "date," whatever it was, had been instigated by Jake and he was waiting at home for a report. There was that feeling of manipulation, even if it foresaw a positive outcome; with these things, circumstances could always backfire.

I tried not to feel too guilty, but it wasn't easy. For the most part, Jake never knew about my dalliances or I his. This was new. It wasn't hot but I was sweating. I wiped my forehead with my free hand.

We found a place before we got to Union Square: the Delos Hotel on Third Street, which had been recently renovated with a midcentury vibe. I hadn't been inside any of the rooms but was curious.

After the charge of $300 (plus taxes!) was paid (which I compartmentalized, since I wasn't at all sure we'd be able to pay the credit card in full by the due date), we got in the elevator and Tony pushed the eighth-floor button. The door closed, and not two seconds later he was pressed against me, his lips over mine and his tongue down my throat.

The elevator was mirrored, and our reflection—my arms around his back, his ass perfectly framed in the not-too-tight, not-too-loose gray slacks he wore—excited me even more. When we kissed it was apparent he was taller, something I didn't register from being with him face-to-face.

My hand shook so much that the keycard swipe took three tries before our door opened. Midcentury indeed—serene tones with bright color pops here or there, sculptural but uncomfortable chairs.

He closed the door with a kick of his heel. I pulled him in with two fingers around his belt buckle, managing to undo it in the process, until he pushed me back with a light shove to the chest.

"Look at this view," I said, which was awkward—because, for San Francisco, it wasn't anything spectacular: a glimpse of big buildings across Market Street and a sliver of the bay if you squinted hard.

Tony pulled the quilted duvet back on one side of the bed and I did the other. We stood there for a beat, smiling at each other, the mattress and its expensive, impossibly high-thread-count Egyptian cotton sheets between us. He undid the hook on his trousers and pulled the zipper down slow.

"I suppose it's easiest if we take our clothes off and get into bed," I whispered. He nodded.

So we did. Tony kicked his pants so deftly they landed on one of the dark orange Panton chairs on the opposite wall. His shorts were navy, a brief cut, the kind a man of his age and lean build looked great in.

In the odd pantheon of woodland creatures now analogous to gay men, Tony would be an otter: in good shape but not overdeveloped, with a pleasing amount of body hair—a tuft in the center of his chest and around his nipples. His legs were also quite hairy, which I loved.

My clothes came off: the casual, common pale blue print shirt, serviceable for work but boring; the dark jeans I liked that had 1 percent of spandex in them, a lifesaver for those times when inconvenient middle-aged bloat might happen.

Which it hadn't, today. I wore black undershorts. Those and the dark pants, because everyone knows you look slimmer, but for someone who'd had prostate cancer surgery, they were also insurance against telltale signs of the inevitable drip and trickle of incontinence.

Nothing sexy about that—but since I knew I'd be meeting Tony at some point during the day, I'd removed the light briefs Defendor pad, always used at work *just in case*, hoping it would be one of those days when there was no excess moisture.

And I'd taken the ED pill, two hours in advance as directed, which would give me even money of attaining wood, and, hopefully, Tony would be key in that process. I hated this intervention in trying to control the situation, when so much of sex was about giving up control. But I digress.

We slipped into bed at the same time from our opposite sides, both of us still wearing our underwear. Lips met, arms wrapped around backs, like we were log rolling, reminding me of what it was like to have both a strong libido and a passionate partner.

He pulled at my shorts and I got his off his ass, pulling them down his legs and tossing them over to that chair. Missing it, they hit the mirror with a *fwap*. Tony's ass was smooth and he had a small blue butterfly tattoo on his right cheek. Seeing that, I was surprised he didn't have more, considering his age; it seemed all the guys around thirty in San Francisco were full of tattoos.

I kissed it. Couldn't help myself.

"I see you found my little pet back there," he said.

"I like it. I like even more that I was surprised."

His cock was bigger than mine, and it was so hard, I had to kiss that, too. Almost inaudibly, Tony sighed, "More."

So there was. For both of us, neither of us content to be merely top or bottom, so we flipped. It was exhausting. But I emerged satisfied and spent. For a moment I didn't worry about Logan and wasn't concerned with the goings on at Refuge.

I knew this sex high, sweet as it was, wouldn't last, because they never do. Afterward, as we lay there with our arms around each other, still kissing, I wondered what this would mean for Jake and Tony, if anything, especially since this had been partly Jake's idea.

Tony read my mind. "What do you think if next time we invite Jake?" he asked.

"I guess we wouldn't have to go to a hotel—though it is a treat," I said.

My phone on the nightstand rang. Squinting, I read Mom's number.

"Have to get this, it might be about the kid that's staying with us." I wondered if he knew—did Jake talk about our home life, would he have discussed Logan or Glenda with Tony?

Still in bed, naked and damp, with Tony's hairy forearm around my waist, I turned to the wall: a mixed-media collage approaching a floral still life, as neutral as possible while still being in color. "Hi, Mom."

"Where *are* you? I thought you'd be home an hour ago."

"I had—some errands. What's—"

"It's that *bitch* of a maid you two insist on keeping. I've *had it* with Breezeann! Either she goes or I do."

*   *   *

It was damn hard to leave Tony. As well as our little room, our nest, the pricey rendezvous lair. One good reason was that it was paid for till the next morning. In theory we could have stayed all night kissing and fucking and watching television and ordering room service pizza, gloriously indulgent until eleven a.m., when housekeeping would come knocking.

I left him there. He had the room; he could stay or go. He could, if he wanted, invite someone else over. Jake, perhaps. Another guy; one we didn't know. A girlfriend. One of his bi-curious techbros from the job.

It was possible to come up with a lot of scenarios, most of which I would not like, because they would involve Tony having fun that I would not be a part of. Riding down the elevator, my mood sank, whatever oxytocin that remained from the sex returning to normal, nonecstatic levels.

Was this acute attraction because of Tony Ochoa himself? Or was it because he was Jake's boyfriend, solidly in the realm of forbidden fruit?

More important, what was next with him, with them both?

My phone came to life again as I turned the corner onto Market Street. Dallas Burdette had left a message while Tony and I were busy: "I checked your GiveMeMoney.com account for Richmond Rack, and, dude, you need a new strategy. No one is contributing. That title sounds like a gay porn film, hate to say. You and I both know the market for that is tiny. Tiny! Ron and I think you should find another rich person to fund the film if that Davis creep won't pay—and we were thinking of your friend Karen. She's got money, right? Anyway, call me back."

She was right; no one was donating. They gave to other projects, other charities, sure, but they didn't seem to like mine; I hadn't found that secret ingredient that made people open up their wallets.

And what was this "Ron and I think" business? Were they an item, were they hooking up? While Ron's wife, Lisa, out in Marin County got bigger and bigger every day with that baby on the way?

Then again, it was none of my business and I had been accused of having an overactive imagination. One thing Dallas did say was true: Karen could easily fund the film. Should I ask her? My stomach twisted at the thought. She was my best friend; I couldn't also try to turn her into my personal piggy bank.

Or could I?

On our stairs, even before I made it to the front porch, I could hear Mom's and Breezeann's raised voices coming from inside.

I opened the door and Mom's back was to me; she stood in the middle of the front hallway staring down Breezeann, who held her ground in the kitchen holding a spatula out in front of her as if it were a spear.

"Underwear and socks is *always* the top drawer! There is no

135

other way," Margaret screamed. She stamped her foot. It didn't make much of a sound in the slippers she wore, but she did it anyway.

"It serves no purpose to be so doctrinaire, missy. If you can't adapt—well, I have no advice for you. None." Breezeann put a lit blunt to her lips.

My mother turned to me and grabbed my arm, digging her nails into my skin. "She's calling me names! You heard her. And taking drugs! *Do* something about it!"

"Like what? What do you want me to do?" I nodded to Breezeann. "Stop acting like *Mean Girls*."

Breezeann took a big hit and blew it out at us. "Your mother is hopeless. It's true—you can't have two women running a house. It can only be one."

"See! See the way she insults me. Ben!"

Breezeann pulled her glasses down her nose and peered over the rims. "You're going to have to choose."

Turns out they were arguing over how to configure Logan's temporary chest of drawers: According to Mom, top drawer was underwear and socks, followed by a shirt drawer, a pants drawer, and a larger items drawer at the bottom. Breezeann disagreed, though it wasn't apparent why, other than to be contrarian.

Her top drawer would be reserved for "any items the child loves."

Right. Speaking of whom, where was he? He'd made himself scarce; I just hoped he wasn't out playing with Destiny Stackhouse.

"Logan had to get out of here because he couldn't stand listening to this old bag anymore," Breezeann said.

"Name-calling won't help—"

"You awful little bitch!" Mom spat back, picking a never-used rainbow-colored umbrella out of the hallway stand, making vague swordlike motions with it, advancing down the hall toward the kitchen and Breezeann.

Not sure how this was going to work—she tried opening it but thought better of it.

"Ben," Breezeann said, "you better stop her or someone will get hurt."

I inserted myself between them and managed to grab the umbrella's slippery fabric at one of the folds. I pulled until it flew out of Mom's hands, opening up on its own, now a thin physical barrier between us.

"What do you think you're doing?" This was a side of my mother that I wouldn't have believed had I not seen it.

Mom grabbed at the umbrella handle, thrusting the now fully open, billowy mass into my guts, poking me hard with the dime-sized metal tip. I retreated toward Breezeann.

"Stop it! You're behaving like one of Logan's little friends."

"What's the use? You always take her side. So much for family loyalty, Benjamin Kanner Schmidt!"

She dropped the umbrella, the metal spokes clattering on the hallway's wood planks.

"I should call the police, right now."

"Go ahead. I know all the cops in this precinct, and don't forget, honey, I've lived here since I was a teenager and the City *knows* me. I'm Haight royalty."

I glared at her. "Breezeann. Please. This isn't helping."

From behind Mom, down the hall near the front door, came the light touch of spectral doggie nails on hardwood. Without looking, I knew who and what this was, and when I turned again toward Mom, Connie the ghost dachshund stood at the doorway of the living room, watching us. What I didn't expect to see was Bernard, my blond ghost boy, standing with her. He pointed to our front door, indicating someone should leave that way; someone threatened the harmony of the structure.

Mom broke the spell. "You know what, little Miss Hippie Maid? You're correct, I don't belong here. You can have it and you can have—them," she said, nodding toward me. "I called Karen Kling earlier."

On cue, we all heard a thud on the porch, meaning someone was outside. The door opened, Connie and Bernard faded into nothingness, and Karen herself stepped into the hallway. Breathless.

* * *

"Of course you can stay with me, Margaret. I've got nothing if not room."

They embraced. "I can't wait to be out of this dreadful house," she said. "Won't take me long"—she turned to me—"my bag is half-packed already."

If looks could kill, I'd have been dead right there. She passed me on her way to the in-law apartment Breezeann had cleaned up *just for her.*

Karen didn't move. I wondered if I should feel something like betrayal. Then again, Mom would be close by but not living with me. Which:

Could be great. Could be the best of all worlds.

"For the record," Breezeann said, "I didn't start it. I always had an open mind when it came to your mother—she's just a confusing, difficult spirit."

"Maybe go clean something. Better yet—smoke a joint—outside, please. Then go clean something."

Breezeann shook that long gray hair, unbraided today, dismissed me, and left in the direction of the back hall.

Karen hadn't budged. "Honestly, if you want to be responsible for my mother and her life here in San Francisco, who am I to object?"

She exhaled. "This isn't the first time we talked about it. Margaret and me. I mean, she asked before, right after she saw my house and all the space."

"You seem close."

Karen walked into the kitchen, nodding, her arms crossed over her chest. "There seems to be a connection. Is that OK?"

"Of course that's OK; why wouldn't that be OK?"

She leaned back on my prized island, her butt bisected by the polished granite countertop. "I'm not sure I've ever been close with a friend's parent before."

CHAPTER 11

TWO WEEKS LATER.

Within an hour of that conversation, Mom had left with Karen for the mansion on Buena Vista Terrace. Breezeann, overjoyed: I could tell because she not only played the Crosby, Stills, Nash & Young CD *Déjà Vu* while she cleaned but also sang along: "Our house is a very, very, very fine house," ya, ya, ya, which I guess was appropriate considering where she was, though it sure didn't feel so fine right at that moment.

I left her wake of pot and patchouli so she could revel solo in the glory of enemy defeat. Mother had a history of nonconfrontation when paying her way out of a sticky situation would fix things easily. Thus, I wasn't terribly surprised she took that option when presented with Karen's offer.

In the meantime, I hadn't forgotten that I'd seen the ghosts. Two of them. I kept checking the living room's corners, where the spirits most often would be detected. Pillars of the community, holding the house up lest it fall in upon itself (which it nearly did quite literally back in Cancerworld).

Now Jake and I were together, solidly I thought, in a sturdier house that we owned. Actually, the bank owned it, but we pretended we did since we paid them and not a landlord who could and would make demands of us.

No Bernard, no Connie, so—I'd wait. I'd sleep on the couch if that's what it took. Anything to shake that persistent unnerving feeling that the foundation of our lives here was just as tenuous as my old apartment.

Breezeann had already moved a marble-top table away from its usual position in the front window. That's where the Christmas tree would go; the holidays were on the way and we had a kid with us this year who would expect fun and presents if it went on that long.

Oh god, Glenda Bourne! It was as if that computer call to South Africa's Willow-Why never happened. No follow-up, no resolution, no seeming concern for her own flesh and blood, her son. Still had trouble wrapping my head around that one—because Glenda was annoying, but never actually evil.

Time for a visit to Hu Zhang. I didn't want to go over there, but a call would be avoided or ignored, so best to confront her in person. I'd take Logan; he'd be happy to go back to the old neighborhood.

It was too late now; it had gotten dark and I was still on the couch. Was Breezeann cooking a turkey? Lying there I was sure it was a roasted bird I smelled; we'd have two more guests this year since Mom was now a San Franciscan and Logan was with us. Some years even Breezeann hung around for this event: how to finesse with her War on Mom?

I pondered the delicious pies (pumpkin, pecan, sweet potato) she would start days before when I felt downward pressure on my shoulder.

"Ben. You fell asleep. We have to figure out dinner."

Through my blurred vision in the darkened room, I made out Jake's leg in front of me and Logan sitting in one of the big chairs opposite.

* * *

Even if my stomach craved a meal, I shook off the nap as Logan stayed put, staring at me. I felt bad enough without any additional guilt, real or imagined, coming from him.

"We should go to your old neighborhood and see Hu," I said, figuring a covert trip to find Glenda could have additional benefits.

It worked. He jumped out of the chair. "Now? You mean *now*? I haven't had my dinner yet."

"We'll figure out something over there. Maybe there's a restaurant you like on that block?"

Jake agreed that it made more sense to show up in person than to call. He was behind the Prius wheel, Logan tucked in back for the short ride.

"I think we should talk about Tony," I said quietly as we rolled north through the Castro up onto Divisadero.

He smiled. "Yes—not the best time, though." He nodded back toward Logan. "It's time we talk about the gallery, too. Ben, it's not good."

Logan stuck his head between the seats.

"Can we stop at my apartment? I need my winter jacket. And—maybe Mom will be home."

Jake's eyes widened at that, more a reaction to Logan's "fantasy" than for the gallery downturn news—which I was anxious to hear, just not right this second.

"Logan. Number one—yes, we can stop there and get your coat or whatever. Number two—your mother isn't there, so don't get excited."

The kid slunk back without saying another word.

I was validated as we walked down the sidewalk toward the Zhang bodega and saw Hu inside, standing behind the counter. She saw us, too, and immediately picked up her phone.

Logan ran in. By the time Jake and I approached the checkout—piled high with bright Asian boxed products and other dusty sales cases, with a small opening for the cashier, just asking for a six-pointer or better—she was off her phone and leaning over toward the kid.

"Hey, buddy, I miss you. You don't come around here much," she said to Logan, totally ignoring us.

"They," he said, pointing at Jake and me, "won't let me come here by myself."

She rolled her eyes. "Seriously. How old are you, kid?"

"I'm still nine."

Hu smiled at us, finally, crossing her colorful arms against her white-apron-covered chest. "Oh, I guess walking a mile and a half through a totally gentrified city is much too dangerous, even for a big boy like you."

Jake thrust his chin forward, a move he rarely made unless he meant business. "We don't restrict Logan's activities in that way. He can come up here if he wants."

"I can?"

Logan was genuinely surprised. As was I. I didn't want him

running all over the City unsupervised. Gentrification or no, there was still quite a bit of nefarious activity lurking in San Francisco, and with any luck at all he'd stumble across it. Then where would we be? He was *nine*.

"You know, ask us *first*," I said, "before you go on any hikes or other trips. Please."

Hu winked at him. "Good thing that's out of the way. What can I do for you guys today?"

Jake: "What—"

I stretched my arm out in front of his chest. "Of course, there's only one big reason we'd be up here." I leaned toward her and whispered, "We never heard another *thing* after our video call to Willow-Why."

She pulled a chocolate bar out from under the counter and presented it to Logan. "How about this, kid?"

"Isn't that the multinational that makes slaves out of South American children?"

It was too late; Logan had already grabbed it and was ripping open the package.

Hu narrowed her eyes at me. "They don't advertise that. Pretty sure it's a myth."

I wasn't totally sure that Hu was harmless. To my way of thinking, she might as easily be a champion martial arts aficionado or an undercover spy from any number of not-so-friendly Asian countries. I didn't want to cross her.

Jake looked at me. Then her. "About Glenda— "

"That girl is so incompetent. Did you check the apartment?"

We looked at each other. "What do you mean?" I asked. "You mean *now*?"

* * *

Logan was bribed with a naturally sweetened soda to go with his sugary candy bar. I shuddered at the thought of what this was doing to the poor child's glucose levels and was certain the guilty parties—Jake and I—would pay in some way.

But that was later. Glenda was now.

It took us seconds to get to her building. No answer after we rang the bell twice, so we conjured up Harold, who was, as usual, both home and stoned.

Wearing a near-faded dashiki, barefoot with rings on both his big toes, it took him a minute to focus. Literally blinking at us when we asked if Glenda Bourne had returned.

"Are you cops? I have to know that," he said, tugging on a few strands of his white beard, taking a step back.

"Harold! Don't you remember us? The guys taking care of Logan. Glenda's friends."

"Oh. OK—if you're taking care of the boy, then where is he? Tell me that."

Jake attempted to step into the lobby of the building, but Harold stopped him with a bony flattened palm.

"He's at the bodega down the block talking to Hu Zhang," I said. "If Glenda's in there, you have to let us up."

Door knocks a few minutes later produced no Glenda, so out came the key ring. Harold opened the door.

"Don't even think of taking anything. I'm watching you," he said.

Lights were off inside. It appeared as if no one had been there since our last unsuccessful visit to find the note she insisted would be waiting there.

"This is like a rerun of a TV show no one likes," Jake said. "Nobody's been here since us."

I switched on the lamp in the living room. The blue chenille curtain that marked Logan's bedroom "wall" was open halfway. Had we left it like that? I couldn't remember.

Nothing else was disturbed. To me, anyway, it looked the same as it always had. Not cluttered, not minimalist, somewhere in between. The hodgepodge of someone who struggled. The truth was I didn't live there, so things may have been rearranged and I wouldn't notice. Logan should have been with us after all.

The kitchen. The lingering scent of spice, not specific. Probably came from items that sat there in racks and cupboards or that had seeped into the plaster of the old building.

Red cup in the sink with a big red *W* on it. Willow-Why? Wisconsin? Washington? Who knows. That was there before, when we came looking for the "note"—wasn't it?

I picked it up, sniffed. There had been tea in this cup, a light brown ring left inside the ceramic. That was the smell, not a spice, but chai. I doubted that aroma would linger for as long as she'd been gone. *Glenda and her chai.*

There was a stainless steel teapot on the stove. I touched the back of my hand to its side. It was warm.

"Jake. She's back—or there's ghosts boiling water in here."

* * *

Harold would not let us wait for the tea drinker to return. "I have chores to get done here. I can't have people not on the lease hanging out in a tenant's apartment," he said. "It's the law."

Kind of absurd, since he'd seen us around for years and we currently were taking care of one of the building's residents. We'd wait outside.

"What do you think is going to happen when Logan sees his mother?" Jake asked.

"Maybe he'll hug her. Maybe he'll hit her. Maybe both. How should I know?"

What I did know was that I needed to call Sergeant Erica Ybarra, tell her that Glenda had finally returned and complain that she and the entire SFPD had been less than useless in getting her back.

On second thought, why let her know? It wasn't like she was waiting at her desk for my call. They hadn't done much of anything beyond posting a missing persons report on their website and calling the morgue a couple of times to see if any Jane Does had washed up near the bridge. Since we'd told her that we'd found out Glenda had left the country, they took her off their missing persons lists and were likely uninterested.

At least, if we were going to wrap up by contacting her, I wanted to make sure we were correct and that Glenda was actually back.

Which would only happen once we confronted her. Which meant a stakeout.

"No," Jake insisted. "Hu will tell us where she is."

Back at the bodega, Logan had moved from the customer part of the store to sitting on the counter over on Hu's side. In our absence he'd gone, voluntarily I assumed, into enemy territory. She'd given him a bright green can of some other kind of drink, Korean script, so there was no way for me to tell what it was.

"That better not be loaded with sugar," I said.

"It's good for him, loaded with vitamin, pieces of grape, don't worry," she said. "I know how to take care of kids."

Jake and I exchanged a look. Did that mean we didn't?

"We're going to stay here until she comes back," he said, leaning in. "Or you can tell us where to find her right now."

This woman had the best poker face in the Haight. She nudged Logan. "Kid, go in the back and play on the computer. Remember where it is? Take your Bong Bong with you."

After he had gone and the familiar video game thuds and pops and explosions began, Hu leaned back over the counter, inches from Jake's nose.

"She wanted to get him a gift. She didn't have time to bring anything back from South Africa."

"She didn't have time? She had nothing *but* time!"

"If she sees you in here, she's going to leave. So you might as well go home or you'll wait all night. We're open till eleven thirty, but if you're such good parents I'm *sure* you'll want to put the kid to bed before then."

Frustrating—to put it mildly. I couldn't stand it, but smug Hu Zhang was right. That part of me that wanted to see Glenda do a cuffed perp walk out of her building was thwarted this time.

Logan came first. He hadn't even had a proper dinner, so we'd have to attend to that, it was pitch-dark outside—and Hu suddenly looked alarmed, like she'd seen one of my household ghosts in her little store. Blood-draining, jaw-dropping, genuinely surprised at something (which I expected didn't happen very often).

With all that I didn't even notice that the back room had gone quiet.

"Logan? You in there?" I asked.

I pulled a "scenes of Chinatown" tourist shower curtain aside to look into the storeroom. A computer screen glowed and the back door was open to the alley.

"He's gone," I said, glancing from Hu to Jake and back. "What are you not telling us?"

We both stared at her, waiting for an answer. She shrugged. "I can't leave the store. He probably ran to the apartment to find his mother."

* * *

When we got to the apartment door, it was open. Glenda and Logan were in the center of the living room, hugging. She was on her knees, holding him close, the hair from her signature top-of-head ponytail covering one side of her face. She looked more bronze than usual, more Amazonian—obviously, Willow-Why put her through some paces.

But you abandoned your child.

I thought I heard him say, "You stayed away so long."

No shit, kid.

I cleared my throat. "I'm not a violent person, Glenda, or you'd be dead already." It was the best I could come up with after a long, long day.

She stood, not releasing Logan, her arms protectively around him in front of her, as if she were using him as a human shield. She tried a tiny smile.

"It's good to be home."

Logan turned his head up to look at Glenda. "Can I come home tonight, Mom?"

"No." I had opened my mouth to say this, but Jake got it out first. "You will do no such thing. You'll be coming with us, Logan. All your stuff is at our house, your bed is there, your homework, all your books. You won't stay here . . . tonight."

"I don't know where to begin," she said.

"How could you do this?" I blurted; it was loud. "*I* don't know what to say to you, I'm so fucking angry!"

She dropped her arms away from her son and he stood in the no-man's-land between these two belligerent parties.

Harold appeared at the door. "There *are* other folks who live in this building," he said.

Jake held out his hand. "Logan, come with me."

Logan looked at Jake and me, then back at Glenda. He didn't move.

"We've only had a moment," Glenda said so quietly I could hardly make it out.

"And he's a little kid and it's past his bedtime—of anyone, you should realize that," I said, as calmly as I could, but I wasn't and it came out like a screech. I didn't want to be that guy, but I had become that guy right before my eyes.

Jake took a step toward Logan, grabbed his hand, and gently pulled.

They walked out. Logan followed Jake's lead, did not try to wrench his hand away, nothing like that. Which was a surprise. Harold was encased in his cocoon of not-quite-visible pot smoke—I took a deep breath hoping for the unlikely contact high, anything to distract from Glenda.

Who was now crying. Sitting on the floor in a heap, sobbing into her forearm.

"What the fuck did you think would happen?" I nodded to Harold, for confirmation on the consequences of her monumentally immature behavior, as I backed out into the hall.

"Ben—please don't call the police on me, *please don't*—if not for me then for Logan. Promise? At least until we talk."

I looked back at her. "I'm not promising you anything."

* * *

"Can we go to the park so I can say goodbye to Tyler and Destiny and that other kid?"

"What other kid? You mean Zach?"

"Yeah, but it's Zachary, never Zach," he said.

On the drive home from Glenda's, my head began to throb, and this litany of requests from Logan did not help.

"Logan. That playground is not far from the Haight; it's just in a different direction. You can keep your new friends when you move back to Glenda's—back *home*."

"I wonder what present she brought me from her trip. I guess Mom didn't unpack it yet."

Jake looked at me sideways. He shook his head.

"Keep your eyes on the road," I said. Then I turned around.

"I think you might be a little angry, or a little upset. I know you're happy she's back, but she left without saying a word. She didn't even say goodbye."

Jake's right hand was on my shoulder, pushing me to turn back around. I flicked it away.

"I always knew she'd come back; she said she would," Logan said, with a smile bigger than any I'd seen since that first day we picked him up at school.

My head was about to split. "What are you *even* talking about?" In my pocket, my phone vibrated. "She disappeared! How could you know that?" I turned around and fished the phone out of my pants.

It was Mom. "It's late for you to be calling. What now?"

"Hello to you too, dear."

We'd crossed all the streetcar tracks at Market and were headed up the steep hill on Noe, back to our house. "Sorry. I'm a little stressed. Glenda's back."

The windows of the corner taco joint we liked were steamed up, as usual, when we passed. The phone had gone silent.

"Mom?"

"My God, you are kidding me!" she yelled. "Son of a gun. The little bitch came back. What do you know? What does *anyone* know?"

Jake hit a bump in the cross street. Logan flew up off the cushion in back. "Fasten your seat belt," I said. "You know that's the rule here." To Mom: "It was you who said to never call people names. Although this time, maybe, I agree."

"You can tell me all about it over coffee. There's something else I want to discuss with you."

* * *

After we insisted that Logan try to get some sleep (he finally had a peanut butter and jelly sandwich) and leave the packing up for the morning—even though I had no idea if he was being "returned" to the person who'd abandoned him or not—I fell into bed and slept like a rock.

Mom's coffee planned for Monday had changed to "a nice little chat over lunch," somewhere on the same block as her job at Clean Up in Cole Valley. But lying there in bed that morning, it *was* blessed silence. Maybe too much silence. I was getting used to her noises and homey aromas wafting up from down in the kitchen. Now those had gone.

Jake had gotten Logan off to school. If there had been drama there, I slept through it. Constantly amazed the kid was not as traumatized as you would expect for someone abandoned by the one parent he did have.

How was that possible? Perhaps there was something I wasn't

seeing. Part of me felt our bonding should slide into place naturally due to our genetic connection, but then there was contrary evidence: Mom, for one. How could I expect my biological son to improve on that dismal precursor, especially when he was operating without the full information of his own origins?

After making my own cup of coffee, I stumbled back upstairs to take a shower. Home alone, I'd gone down to the kitchen shamelessly naked, and now unavoidably caught myself in the full-length mirror in our bedroom.

There I was, in all the fifty-three-year-old glory I'd become. This was the body of a man who had assiduously adhered to the gay gym requirement for a couple of decades but had fallen off that treadmill in the last couple of years. I still showed up to work out, of course—everybody did. It was now more haphazard, like when I actually had the energy or the day after a holiday when I felt particularly bloated.

That unplanned neglect showed. The pecs still popped out nicely, but the hair was white instead of black and there was less of that V-shape I'd courted for so long, the result of an awful widening at the waist. It approximated an "H-shape."

Small—too big to be called tiny and not big enough to be called saddlebags—"pouches" rested awkwardly above the hip bone. Over time, these seemed impervious to eradication.

In the center of my abdomen was the scar, of course, the red line, the ridge running from below the navel down into the mystery of the pubic hair, where it disappeared. There was my cock, which still worked, for which I was grateful; not too big and not too small—I always hoped those who had a chance to interact with it thought it was "just right."

My legs still had the same musculature and shape as they'd always had. I told myself this was because San Francisco was a walking town. With hills. I ignored the occasional evidence that the skin on my thighs might be perceived as crepey (like Grandma's upper arm, the one drenched in lilac water). Once both the calves and thighs had been uniformly hairy. Now it was more a patchwork; much of that hair had simply stopped growing in.

That's what I saw when I looked at Ben Schmidt's naked body. Overall, shows some age but still fit. Adjusting for age, maybe a six on the scale of one to ten. Some would say seven. Was that too generous?

Tony Ochoa might give it an eight. I always did score high on the charts of the younger guys who liked daddies. Along with that usually came the expectation of confidence. I winced at the thought of him knowing what actually went through my head on a daily basis—the doubts, the fears, the resentments—none of it pretty.

For Jake, I hoped the changes didn't register. They happened so slowly, after all. A glacial pace, the frog slowly boiling in the pot and all that. It was that way with my parents, Mom now here in San Fran and Dad down in Florida, well, they always looked the same to me. Although math tells me that when I was a child they were also forty years younger. I can't picture that without help, without the family photo album.

Across the room on the dresser top, a green light blinked, indicating someone had left a message. It wasn't only one. Three messages, all from Glenda, all in the last hour.

"Come on, Ben, you must call me, we have to figure this out."

"I'd appreciate it if you wouldn't judge me. No one knows the interior landscape of another, right? That's been your message in your movies, has it not? Besides, and I'm sick of saying this, I left a note.*"*

"Well, of course I'm calling, I have to get specifics on Logan coming back here."

One, two and three. *Now you're calling, Glenda, now you're letting us in on your crime!* My hand shook; I dropped the phone.

* * *

Zizzou was an unsurprising storefront restaurant on Cole Street, up the block from Clean Up. Its ordinariness belied the prices, which, like everything else in San Francisco, seemed to rise a few percentage points every time you went through their door.

Margaret was seated already. The place was faux Parisian, a common style in San Francisco. Go figure. It was small, pleasantly loud and cheerful, and it smelled great. Also, like in Paris, the tables were set too closely together. Eavesdropping was not necessary, as you could clearly hear everything being said at tables nearby.

I hoped that whatever Margaret wanted to discuss wasn't confidential. She'd chosen a table at the window, so we could watch passersby out on Cole. I liked that. I enjoyed the window cruising at Refuge and was sure there would be stellar, if unavailable, men to look at here.

Two empty chairs sat at her table instead of the one I expected. "Someone joining us?" I asked, bending to kiss her on the cheek.

"Oh—there were three places set here. I think they do that with all the tables in the window."

Sounded reasonable. I sat. She massaged her fingernails, surely a sign of unease. "Mom—you OK?"

Her pale blue eyes opened wide. "Glenda, of course! I have to find out what's happened!"

I threw up my hands and paused. Theatrical, yes, but I was honestly unsure how much to give out. "She left to find herself?" It had to be a question.

Saved by the waitress, come to take drink orders. "Can I get you one of our blended coffees, or a midday cocktail?" she asked.

"We should have a drink!" Mom gushed.

I patted the table. "Remember, I'm sober. Again. At least today, I'm not drinking."

"Sorry, dear, I forgot." To the waitress, whose eyes darted between the two of us: "I'll have a Bloody Mary. I know it's not exactly French, but it's what I need."

"Of course. For you, sir?"

I quickly ordered an expensive and fattening blended coffee, and the waitress, definitely a few pounds over her own ideal weight, bounced off.

"Glenda went to find herself. What does *that* mean? I never understood that expression."

She leaned in. "Probably the most irresponsible thing she could've ever done, don't you think? I mean, what with Logan. Left. At school like that. Not knowing where his mommy was, why she left, when she is coming back—it would be devastating to me, and I'm seventy-eight. I can't *imagine* for a child like that."

Her candor surprised me. Stating her age, out loud in a public place, surprised me. Perhaps we were headed to a new era of honesty.

"She went to find herself at a camp in the woods in South Africa. She's from there, you know that, right? A camp where lesbians run around naked."

It may have been a bit too loud, because two women at a table along the wall turned their heads to me with interest. I shrugged.

The waitress returned with our drinks. I closed both hands

around the coffee cup to warm my fingers. "I think we need a minute with the menu," I said.

"I'm sure they're not running around naked," Mom said. "They have wild predators there, for one thing."

"You're naïve. But whatever, I guess she found something and she's back. I don't know what we're going to do about Logan. But I'm here. What did you want to talk about?"

"We should probably order," she said, looking back at the menu. "Eggs are so expensive here! I guess it's the living wage they talk about paying the help."

"The *help*? These people work for a living. It's true we don't have to leave a tip. That's included."

"It's still a nice gesture. I can't get up and leave without tipping *something*."

That voice had come from above and to my right. Karen appeared out of nowhere. "And everything has a touch of cilantro. Which is nice. And how did I not see you coming?"

She nodded to Mom, took off her deep purple scarf and draped it over Chair Number Three. As she pulled it out to sit down, the legs scraped on Zizzou's nicely polished dark wood floor.

"I don't know. Maybe I'm becoming like those spirits you always tell me you're seeing."

I shook my head. *No, do not continue in this vein. Please. Like, if I have to tell my mother I occasionally see the ghosts of friends who died in the Plague or my little dog Connie—whatever. Good thing she moved. Good thing she is now your roommate.*

Mom giggled. She thought it was a personal joke, the ghost thing, or she was nervous. Maybe both.

"I didn't realize you were joining us, but it makes me happy," I said, salvaging. It was true. I always delighted in seeing Karen. I didn't want my festering resentment of Glenda and Darien to affect any of the relations with the other women in my life.

Ordering the food and a drink for Karen (odd, she had a Bloody Mary like Mom) was accomplished in short order. I filled her in on what I knew of Glenda, which wasn't much, just the outlines but not any real understanding or what the future might hold.

"I think there's something more, something she's not yet said—because who does that? Who leaves their kid?"

Which hung in the air.

"So, you wanted to talk about something. Something else?" I asked Mom.

Her drink was already mostly gone. She glanced at Karen with a tiny, shy smile. "I think we do."

Was I imagining it or was the color slowly draining from Karen's face, she who was always so hale and hearty and thrived magnificently in San Francisco's constant fifty-seven-degree temperature?

Karen put her hand over Mom's free one—the left, the one not holding on to the Bloody Mary for dear life. She squeezed it.

"It's OK, Mags, like we rehearsed, go slow."

Mags? That was a new one. Despite the caffeine in my drink, I felt the dread slip into a warm calm. This was all suddenly familiar, like on a cellular level, familiar.

Mom gave me a wide and courageous grin. "Karen and I have found that we're a couple now," she said, so softly I had to lean halfway across the table to hear her.

I sat there—not catatonic, but close—mouth hanging open.

"Did you listen to her, did you hear her, Ben?"

"Yes, I did hear her. This is my *mother*, Karen." I tried out a stone-cold glare; problematic since she was still my best friend, but teetering.

Back to Mom. "So what you're saying is you're now a lesbian, what, at eighty?"

"I'm seventy-eight, not eighty."

"Rounding up." The waitress came to abrupt silence with our food: various egg dishes with brightly colored and artfully arranged potatoes, peppers, arugula and orange sections. Carefully placed on vintage floral plates. Like what a tech kid with money might imagine a country breakfast amid the lavender looks like in Southern France.

I picked up my fork, but the appetite had gone. "I don't know where you think this will lead," I said.

"Well, *Benjamin*, I guess we'll find out." Her volume increased. "I'm confused here," she said, an orange section stuck on a fork in midair. "This is a courtesy, telling you this. Of all people, I thought *you'd* be happy."

I rubbed my eyes and looked at Karen. "I can't help but think this was all planned behind my back. It seems—like a plot, or something."

Karen had no problem digging into her food. "Hard to believe, I know, but not everything's about *you*, my dear."

"What about your ex, Dennis? Remember him, old rich Dennis? And all those other guys you've talked about over the years. What about them?"

She tore a mini baguette apart with such force I thought for sure she was going to throw it at me. "Like Margaret said, you of all people—I never thought much about it, honestly. Suddenly, there she was and that's all I could see."

Now they were holding hands. "Think of it this way, Ben. Now you have twice the reason to come over to that big house you love so much."

CHAPTER 12

Had there been clues? On some subliminal level maybe I'd noticed that Karen and Mom seemed closer than was warranted by the usual friend-to-friend's-mother relationship. Honestly, with all the Logan and Glenda drama (and with Wally and Tony and the work thing with Darien and Mehrdad), maybe I hadn't given it the consideration it deserved.

Or maybe the problem was I didn't believe it. My experience of sexuality was definitive and known early on; I always liked the other boys; no amount of wishing or trying to have an erotic connection with women ever worked in the slightest.

So perhaps it's a personal failing, not being able to readily accept bi-folk or later-in-life lesbian leanings such as these were. Goodness, my mother was close to her ninth decade and divorced. Karen was fifty-five, also divorced and old enough for the senior lunch at Denny's. I couldn't and wouldn't try to picture them together—there were still areas where ignorance was the better option.

And really, who could dote on the possibilities of these liaisons in your midst when you had a kid hanging around?

The need to dive into parenthood with holidays stacked up like Pacific storms rolling in from Japan wasn't the easiest thing—but we did it. Jake was game and Logan seemed happy enough—or, if not happy, at the very least he survived.

Left a note, left a note, left a note. These three words kept repeating in my head, like a silly pop song you woke up with and which would not leave you all day.

Glenda was such a liar! Why would she insist on something like this? So easily disproved. There was no note. We looked. Harold looked. All over her place, all of us.

There was no note.
Right?

* * *

I would lie in wait for the kid. I would make him explain to me what he meant when he said he knew she'd come back—because she said so. How *exactly*, Logan Bourne, did your mother tell you that she'd be back?

It was midafternoon when I got home from Zizzou. We had a bright southern view out the bay window in our living room; I didn't appreciate it enough. The gaily painted homes across Elizabeth Street—and since we were slightly uphill, in some instances we could see their roofs, and beyond that a sliver of the commercial area on Twenty-Fourth Street, Noe Valley's very own center of the universe.

The child would not get past me on his return from Harvey Milk Civil Rights Academy, although there was no one, no adult or kid, on the street at the moment. Deserted, like it was in the house, with just me.

I didn't like it so silent. Sometimes solitude was the ticket, but in this house it was definitely not a normal or preferred state of affairs. Jake, Logan, Mom (when she was here)—had to admit I'd gotten used to the comfort of at least *some* background noise. On cue, the refrigerator at the back of the house kicked in with its hum. I turned to the street: A young lady in fingerless gloves and a dark green knit hat with earflaps walked a curious black terrier. She wasn't paying attention to the dog; she was engrossed in the conversation on her phone.

I felt a cool breeze on my neck and put my hand over my skin. These old San Francisco houses were drafty, but we'd done a good job in sealing it up since we moved in.

I turned slowly and wasn't entirely surprised by Deadboy Bernard, flickering as he was, a specter looking for grounding, in the corner as usual.

"There you are again," I whispered, which seemed appropriate.

"I don't like that the child is going away," he said. "He looks just like you, do you know that, can you see that?"

Jake said that sometimes, Logan would move his arm in a certain way, or in a part of a facial expression, he would see Ben

Schmidt as a kid. I hadn't been aware of it. Logan was mostly an enigma, and he made me nervous.

"Wait a sec," I said. "Who said anything about Logan going away?"

I heard footsteps on the stairs outside but they were too heavy for a boy. Someone else was coming up to the door. Bernard got a stricken, alarmed look on his translucent face and then he flickered bright for a second and quickly faded. The bell rang.

I could see it was a man in a gray sport coat, no tie, shorter and younger than me but not by too much. He looked vaguely Latino and wore glasses.

I turned back one more time to check for ghosts before answering. "Yes? Can I help you?" I asked through the door.

"Steve Ramos from Noe Valley," he said, which was, at best, incomplete.

I opened the door a crack. "Can I help you?"

He smiled enough to show off preternaturally white teeth. He held out a business card.

"Steve Ramos, Noe Valley Estates, wanted to introduce myself before the pending foreclosure."

I grabbed at his card and opened the door all the way.

"The pending *what*?"

"This address? Is on the list we get, houses likely to go into foreclosure soon. May I step in?"

I moved into the doorway to fill it. "No. No, you may not 'step in.'" I glanced down at his card. "Where do you get this kind of information?"

Ramos smiled again. "I can't give out our sources; they're proprietary. I can assure you, though: They're accurate."

My head spun. Logan would be coming up the block any second.

"Our house is not going into foreclosure. That's—absurd."

He chuckled and glanced across our porch floor, evaluating. "We can help you with a sale, preserve some credit for whatever, wherever comes next." He looked back at me with raised eyebrows. "Keep the card and think it over."

He put his hand out to shake mine. Instead, I tried to give him his card back, but he swatted it and it fell to the porch floor. He turned to go down the stairs.

"We're in the book, Noe Valley Estates, Steve Ramos. Hope to hear from you."

"Asshole," I said, quietly, as he tripped up the block. On cue, Logan and Tyler Dong-Gutierrez walked up from the other direction.

Logan laughed as he bounded up the steps. Tyler, as the smaller kid, followed. "Hi, Uncle Ben," Logan said.

"Hi, Mr. Schmidt," Tyler piped in, in his high, little-kid voice. I winced.

"Tyler, you can call me Ben if you want. Since we're practically neighbors, tell your mom I said it was OK."

He looked at Logan. "That would be basic," he said.

"Huh?"

"Is my mom coming to get me? Tyler wants to meet her."

I opened the door and held it, taking in a deep breath. "No, Logan, your mother is not coming over this afternoon. But I do want to talk to you. Tyler, this isn't a great afternoon to play over here. You should go home and come back tomorrow."

Logan stomped into the house and Tyler just stood there, balancing his weight on one foot, then the other, back and forth.

"Logan will have to play with you tomorrow. He's got things to do."

At that he smiled. "OK. Ben!" He ran down the stairs to the sidewalk.

"Say hello to your parents!" I yelled, covering my ass, not wanting to appear more unsociable than I actually felt.

Logan had gone directly to the kitchen and was in the refrigerator. "I don't know why she's not coming—I'm all ready to go," he said.

"There's almond milk in there, right, and some cookies still left, unless you ate them all yesterday. You know, Logan, that woman—*your mother*—just left you without saying a word. I don't know that I'd want to rush right back."

He put the milk carton on the island top, then pulled a glass out of the dishwasher. "Those might be dirty," I said.

"It looks clean." He poured the milk into it. The cookie jar, which was a fat, dark green ceramic barrel-type thing (looking like a vat of toxic sludge, or alternatively, a grenade), was also on the island. He put his skinny little arm into it and pulled out a large but broken chocolate chip cookie. "There's a couple more in here."

"What did you mean when you said you were all ready to go? Did you pack your clothes?"

"I put most of them on my bed so I only need a bag. And she didn't just leave; she did go away, but she left me a note and said she'd be back, so I believed her."

"What are you talking about? We never found a note over there. We looked twice, me, Jake, Harold the manager, you were there, who knows who else?"

"I found it on my bed. It had my name on it so I didn't think it was anybody else's business."

I felt like I was on *Cops*, in an alternate universe where the perps always lied. "What did Uncle Jake and I tell you about lying?"

"I'm not lying! I still have it somewhere in my room. It's my private business."

I would not be played by this nine-year-old. "If you have it, then bring it to me, young man. You can eat that cookie later."

* * *

Dearest son Logan,

This is a personal letter for you. This is so hard for me to write, but it's something I have to do.

Here's what's going to happen, sport: I have to go back to South Africa for a while. Mom can't take you this time. (There will be another trip later, when we all will go.) I have some things to sort out and I can't do it at our apartment in San Francisco. I just can't!

You will stay with our friends Ben and Jake. They are your emergency guardians and I know you like them. They will take good care of you while I'm gone and I know you'll like their big house. (You've been there before, remember?) It'll be like camping.

Now, I must go. I promise you I'll be back before next year.

Don't be mad! It's something I have to do. I will explain all.

Your loving mother,

Glenda Bourne

Yes, she truly did sign her last name. Habit, I guess. Or maybe Logan knows other Glendas who might be his mother. I would take nothing for granted.

I told Logan he could have the other cookie at the bottom of the jar. I'd lost any appetite I might have had after the production of this actual letter, not to mention the visit of the strange man, Steve Ramos, who showed up out of the ether to inform me we were going to be homeless.

A giant weight on my shoulders—like a cold steel barbell as one preps to do those hateful squats—pushing me down. Why even insist that Logan put his clothes away? It wasn't going to happen; he was going home. It was only a matter of time. All that was left was the yelling to try to make a point.

"We'll talk about it when Jake gets home," I said.

* * *

"Do you really want to bring up Logan? I don't think you have any concept of what it means to be a parent, despite this more-or-less-successful trial run."

Mom's statement to me—another of the things she said at Zizzou before Karen got there—replayed over and over in my head.

Did I—did *we*—want to be parents? On the occasions the idea came up, the general consensus between Jake and me was that, no, we didn't. We're too old, for one thing, me in my fifties and Jake almost there. There was a reason nature made procreation's peak in the early twenties—those were the only people who had enough energy to chase toddlers around endlessly.

Even if Logan was far from being that young, he wouldn't be a kid with two daddies; he'd be a kid with two grandpas. I didn't think that was fair. Or was I simply overwhelmed? Lazy? Both?

See, this came up—although fleetingly—when Glenda asked for the sperm, way back when. That's why you hesitated. It was an honest pause.

When Jake got home he looked worried, which for him meant a slight increase in forehead lines and a tightening of the skin between his eyebrows. He was early, too: Almost always on Friday nights some tech big shot would want to come by for "private time at the gallery" before heading off to the weekend house in Sea Ranch.

"She's left a thousand messages; she wants to come get him," I said.

He stood in the hallway, looking through the mail, or pretending to. "I've enjoyed having him here. That sound—the noise from upstairs—giving this old place some new energy."

I moved into the hall, where I wouldn't have to shout. "Was it getting boring? I didn't know that."

"That's not what I meant." He smiled. "It's just I didn't think I was going to like having him around, but now it seems normal."

A significant crash came from above us. We both looked up. It had an electrical amplification quality to it, part of whatever game Logan was playing.

We both laughed, and fell into an embrace. The embrace led to a kiss, which lingered and only got deeper, wetter. We sank into each other like we'd always done, not holding anything back; I imagined our bodies literally melting together.

I didn't want to be the first to pull away. "We're going to have to decide about Glenda," I finally whispered.

We moved to the sofa in the living room.

I showed him her note to Logan. "She wasn't lying about that. But—she's fucking crazy," he said.

We agreed we didn't have the heart or the stomach to drag Glenda, and by extension Logan, through any kind of legal nightmare. It was also likely that we couldn't afford such a thing.

We figured we had to tell Brennan Reeves at the school. We'd also have to inform Sergeant Ybarra, let her know she could officially call off that misguided missing persons thing.

Or did we? How was that an actual requirement? It's not like the SFPD was doing anything active to find Glenda Bourne since I informed them she was at camp in South Africa.

Then again if she indeed *was* crazy—and there are varying degrees—was subjecting vulnerable Logan to her renewed care a good thing? Was she likely to disappear again, figuring we'd be able to take over as before?

"Then we'll tell him it's indeed like camping, like the note says. He'll be used to it," Jake said, which seemed to make a sort of tortured sense.

We lay on the couch, face to face. "You know he sees Connie, maybe even Bernard, from time to time. Probably a genetic thing. He doesn't like it; he doesn't want to live in a house with ghosts. He's a little boy who wants a real dog."

Close as I was, I got the full benefit of a Jake frown. "Why destroy this moment, Ben? You know how I feel about all that. You make it up. Maybe you feel guilty or something, but how come if there's ghosts all over, in all the years we've been together, I've never seen a thing?"

I pushed myself up. "Maybe you don't need to see them. Maybe I do."

He hooked his arm around my hip and rested his head against my thigh. "I didn't know them," he said. "Anyway, I'd find it scary, so I don't blame Logan at all."

I kept my eye on the corner of the room, where I thought I saw a flicker, or maybe it was something I projected as the result of expectation, or it could be a headlight passing out on the street. Honest truth was sometimes I couldn't tell. I moved back down to lie with Jake.

Change of subject: "The weirdest thing happened earlier. Some guy came up to the porch and tells me our house is going into foreclosure."

"Oh shit."

"Oh shit, what?"

Now it was Jake who sat up. "I was late on the mortgage a couple of days last month."

"You were *what?*" The lamp next to the sofa sputtered, went out, then came back on. We locked eyes and laughed. My phone buzzed in my back pocket.

It was a message from Danny: *I know tomorrow is not one of your days, but Darien wants you for a meeting with her at 10. Pls. confirm.*

* * *

A short time later I typed the response to Danny, obviously a yes. Like a lamb led to slaughter, perhaps, but what else could I do?

As far as the mortgage payment being late, Jake minimized it. "I had the actual check in the envelope in the Prius, stuck up in the sun visor, ready to mail—with a stamp and everything—and it slipped my mind." He was preoccupied, he said, with problems at the gallery. But it was taken care of. "I got it out this afternoon."

After I'd lost my old job at Safe Harbor and the other "executive marketing positions" became a thing of the past, we slid into a pattern where Jake handled most of our finances. He made more money than I did, usually quite a lot more, so it seemed to make sense.

It was weird at first, giving up that control. Later, blithely ignorant, I appreciated not having to worry about that aspect of our lives. Until now.

Upstairs, the relentless video game cacophony stopped. It was even quieter with no one in the mother-in-law suite below, no Margaret bumping into furniture, closing drawers, or emitting the occasional cussword (damnation!). We were going to be alone again, a couple, and it seemed as if it had already happened.

I looked in on Logan. His room light was still on, but he was asleep, on top of the blanket, still wearing his clothes. He should properly be under the covers, in pajamas—it was chilly, after all, and likely his last night here—but I didn't want to wake him up and have him ask me, for the zillionth time, what was happening with "going home."

Instead, I unfolded the extra blanket at the foot of the bed, the cream-colored piece with the blue cowboy scenes running along the borders, and draped it over him. It had been my blanket as a kid; I didn't remember putting it out in Logan's room.

I turned out the light and left the door open just a crack.

Kids like that, I remembered, because of the relentless threat of monsters. We had some friendly ghosts, and Logan did see them and didn't like it. With any luck, they'd keep themselves scarce for one last night.

*   *   *

I had a black cashmere pullover that I loved to wear because (a) it was soft, (b) it was black (which is slimming, you know) and (c) it did not need to be tucked into pants (see b, above). It was the perfect thing to wear to work, to wear at the occasion I hoped would culminate with Darien's downfall.

I fantasized that Mr. LeVon McDonald, our regional vice president, would show up in person, all the way from Denver, even though I still had not come through with the proof, that paper listing Mehrdad as a Refuge employee. Whatever, it was good to have something to distract me from our task later on, which was to take Logan "home." Which I dreaded. Dreaded both having to confront Glenda again face-to-face, and then returning to a home now quiet because there was no kid present.

Since it wasn't an actual workday for me, I entered through

Refuge's front door on Bryant Street. Shoppers were out—and the few I saw looked determined, on a mission—or maybe it was simply that hurry to get out of the annoying and ubiquitous drizzle.

Refuge was empty of customers and cold—seeing it this way, the initial impression our clients got. That was intentional, most likely, our preferred shopper being the business buyer. No one expected oatmeal raisin cookies or vanilla candles. Clean lines, subdued color palette, elegance at a price. There'd be a deal if you paid in cash, and the manager would pocket some of it!

I caught myself smirking in one of the industrial beveled mirrors that lined the right wall. *Wipe that smile off your face.* This meeting would demand the utmost in seriousness.

Aaron was in back boxing up one of the Niagara lamps. He wore a bright blue tank top, not unusual for him, even though it was, at the warmest, midfifties outside. He had big muscles, and he liked to show them off. We didn't complain—he'd probably wanted to look like this his whole life, and now he did, so, yes, good for him.

Danny stuck his head out of the doorway to the back and nodded to me. What was odd: his dress. He wore a dark gray shirt with a collar and he had a tie on. A *necktie.* Underground-porn-production cub was wearing a shimmery blue-green necktie. Both were things I'd never seen—neither that color nor Danny dressed like that. My immediate thought was that my daydream was indeed manifesting— LeVon McDonald *was* going to be part of this meeting!

Danny walked toward me; Aaron didn't stop what he was doing. "Thanks so much for coming in, Ben," Danny said. "We know it's your day off and that you're a team player."

We? Who, exactly, was *we*?

He must have noticed my confused look as he elaborated: "Darien's bringing back coffees from South Park Brew," he said. "We're getting you a skinny latte two-shot, right?"

"Close enough," I said, still wondering who was in the back, or if it was only Aaron. "You look nice."

He coughed, turned to one of the side mirrors to check the tie. "Thanks. I don't wear these often. I guess you know that."

"Is it just Aaron and you? Trying to impress, what, because of your new position?"

He wiggled the knot up a little closer to his Adam's apple. "She suggested it. I think she was trying to be pleasant."

I laughed. "I never thought you'd go over to the dark side."

He scowled. "I don't know about you, Ben, but I've got bills to pay. John's hours were cut way back, and we have to make up that income now. What's wrong with looking professional?"

I didn't want to get into it with him, at least right then. What good was I, though, or anybody really, if it was impossible to impart the wisdom of the workplace to the next generation? Wisdom hard won, I would add. I had the psychic scars to prove it.

In the back, Aaron waved his big arms over his head. "Darien incoming! I hear the heels."

Danny started back toward the rear of the store. "But wait," I said, "isn't there someone else here? The guy from regional?"

He didn't answer me. At the same time, the back door opened. Darien swept through with a cardboard tray full of coffee drinks, her red hair swirling.

"Helloooo, I'm back with the goodies!" she trilled, landing them on part of the surface Aaron was using for his packaging project. "Oh good, Ben's arrived," she said, without looking at me.

"Boys, grab your coffees and let's go in my office for the meeting; it will be short, Aaron, as to not interfere with your deliveries this morning."

Like ducklings, we followed her into the little box office, Danny first, then me, Aaron last. Darien shook her head, an attempt to distribute hair equally on both sides after the wind had had its way with it. Miraculously, it fell into place.

I took a sip of my hot latte. We sat in a semicircle around the front of Darien's desk, and she sat facing us. I have to admit she looked the part, and she looked good: tailored olive suit, white blouse, black beaded necklace. She wore the right amount of makeup and knew how to make it work for her.

She sipped her steaming foamy drink. "Danny, that tie looks great on you!" she gushed, licking errant liquid off her lip.

He nodded; he hadn't turned so much that he needed to grovel with a thanks. At least not yet.

"Thanks for coming in, Ben! We could have had this meeting by phone, but I always feel I owe it to people to talk to them face-to-face."

"But wait—"

"Like I said, this won't take long," she interrupted me. "Ben,

I'm so sorry to tell you, but your position here has been eliminated. Part of a corporate pullback. I was told this yesterday at our monthly regional call—other stores also have layoffs."

Her words were like a fierce slap, one you hadn't steeled yourself for. She made a sad, pouty-lips-down face to punctuate, and it only made me want to hit her. I glanced around the small room. My coworkers—Darien, Danny, Aaron—all had eyes on me, expecting a reaction.

"But . . . Oh!" I kept hoping either LeVon McDonald would pop out of one of the boxes she had stacked in the corner or the phone would ring and he would demand to join the meeting, to be put on speaker and put this *bitch in her place!*

But—no. Wasn't happening.

"You've undoubtedly noticed that sales are down," she continued. "We have to cut costs and between you and Danny it's clearly a case of seniority. Obviously, Aaron's job doesn't figure in because *you* can't move furniture anyway."

Pretty sure I caught a slight twitch of Aaron's flexed biceps to my left. That was a low blow, even for Darien.

She opened the center drawer of her desk and removed an envelope with "BEN" written on it in red marker. "Here's your final check. I added in a day for the winter holidays, even though we don't as policy pay benefits to part-timers. Our way of saying thank you!"

My head was about to explode. "If this is an all-staff meeting, then where is *Mehrdad?* Where is he?"

She laughed, thrusting the envelope with the check into my face. "Take it! And leave. Before I change my mind on the extra day."

I grabbed the envelope and stood. "LeVon McDonald knows all about Mehrdad Rajavi."

A wave of emotion crossed Darien's face, first something twisted, akin to the fury of a demon, followed quickly by a giant smile suggesting hilarity.

"Who do you think it was who made the decision to fire you? Our regional manager, Mr. McDonald! Honestly, Ben, go home and let Danny and Aaron do their jobs. Please?"

Hit with a brick by corruption at the very heart of the Refuge corporation. Not that I should have been surprised. I took one last sour look at Danny, hoping my displeasure with his treason would register loud and clear.

"This isn't over," I said, hoping it sounded ominous. My footsteps on the concrete floor to the front door got louder the faster and more determined I walked.

Outside on Bryant Street, the City appeared unconcerned with any of this drama. I ripped open the envelope and took the check out, speed walking straight to the bank before Darien changed her mind.

* * *

Was the lesson that I couldn't leave well enough alone? I thought about that as I stood in the teller line at the SoMa branch of Bank of America. I didn't have to wait long; the new millennium was nothing if not efficient. Even tellers did not dawdle or make more than a couple of lines of small talk.

She was young (wasn't everyone?), Latina, cheerful. One could never be too careful: I could be a secret shopper, evaluating marks. But I wasn't. It was just as it appeared, a freshly laid-off employee desperate for that last trickle of cash before the spigot closed abruptly.

"Any particular denomination?" she asked, wetting her index finger on a sponge.

"Twenties, please." It would seem like more if there was a slight bulge in the wallet; I should've asked for fives and tens. Relief: The check cleared without incident. The bank's greeter offered me a thick warm chocolate chip cookie upon leaving (anything to keep customers), which I gladly accepted.

The route to the Muni station took me past the Springs Slog. No one would blame me if I stopped in to see Rickie, told him I was in the neighborhood so thought I'd check in on the yoga schedule, then for old times' sake lingered over one or more of his special Saturday mimosas.

After all, I'd just been fired. If not then, when?

Yet my abstention resolve took hold. I walked past, quickly and with purpose. I would not, I could not, let down Jake and of course, Logan. We'd be moving him "home" in an hour or so. I couldn't be compromised.

Still—LeVon McDonald's complicity with Darien bothered me. If he indeed had ordered the cut, specifically the elimination of *my* job, then maybe it was a lot more than what it appeared, surface-wise. Maybe it was a region-wide scam. Maybe the two of them were splitting the "Mehrdad Rajavi phantom employee" salary, as well as the proceeds from Darien's other criminal moneymaking schemes.

The Federal Building—where I knew the FBI had a local office—was in Civic Center, on the north side of Market Street. If I was going to stop anywhere it should be there, report her crooked ass before I went home.

I'd need to think out exactly what I would say, exactly how to frame this. I didn't want to get innocent bystanders, such as Danny or Aaron or, heaven forbid, myself, in trouble. I didn't trust management at Refuge Corp. but was not exactly thrilled with the feds, either.

It was all academic because the nearly empty J train arrived as soon as I stepped onto the platform. It was one of those rare days when the Muni system operated as it should, i.e., no delays, so there was no way to put off the inevitable. Logan was going home.

As I turned the corner on Elizabeth Street, a couple of children were obstructing the sidewalk in front of our house. Logan was not among them. I recognized little Tyler Dong-Gutierrez, whom I liked, and Destiny Stackhouse, whom I didn't.

"Why are you out here? Isn't Logan inside?" I asked, hoping that came off pleasantly, so that Destiny would not report me to her mother, who, I figured, thought I was racist.

"Uncle Jake told us to stay out here," Tyler said. "He says we're being disruptive."

"That's a big word," I said. To Destiny: "How are you, Destiny? Nice to see you here to play with Logan."

She giggled. Not surprising; I'd long accepted that there was something about me that frightened small children, especially girls. It was unfortunate that this superpower did not extend to certain adult women (for instance, Darien).

I started up the steps. "Ben, can Logan come back to visit us?" Tyler asked. *Kid, don't ask me things like this.*

I turned around. "Of course. It'll be up to his mom. If not here, then at that Dolores Park playground."

Jake pushed through the front door and dropped a brown cardboard box at the edge of the stairs. Logan's version of a lava lamp, which had a plastic multicolored jellyfish floating in it, poked up over the sides.

"There's a lot of stuff to take back," I said to Jake.

"Not really. Mostly his clothes and this box right here. Kid travels light."

Inside it was quiet; whatever noise Tyler and Destiny created on the sidewalk didn't follow. Logan sat on the couch in the living room. His backpack and a large black plastic bag were at his feet.

"Your friends are outside waiting, Logan. Are you going to say goodbye to them?"

He jumped up. "I already did. Besides, I see Destiny at my school and Tyler is always at that baby playground."

I wondered how our punishment and atonement plans for the Precious and You theft and vandalism shenanigans at the school would transfer to the criminal Glenda.

"You seem to have it covered, then."

In my periphery there was a slight, random flicker. I knew Bernard was in the corner and if I looked that way he'd give me his sad-sack, sour, "please fix it Ben" face. I would not go there. Not today.

*   *   *

Approaching Glenda's, we drove past her building on Steiner; Harold was out front, smoking. Jake turned onto Waller, where we found that pleasant and rare San Francisco surprise, a parking spot.

Jake turned the car off and looked at me. I couldn't help it—I silently mouthed, "I got fired today!" at him.

"What?"

"We'll talk about it later," I said, turning around to Logan in the back seat. "Right now we've got to move this young man here."

Harold winked as we walked up, and though the cigarette was gone, the veil of pot smoke remained.

"Told you she'd come back," he said, in lieu of hello. "Good to see you again, young Logan!" He coughed.

"She's home, I assume," Jake said, to which Harold, still hacking, nodded and pointed.

As we walked up, Jake carrying the box, me carrying the black plastic bag (which was heavy) and Logan toting his backpack, I felt increasingly light-headed and separate from my body, which sometimes happened during times of perplexing unease.

At the top of the stairs, Glenda's apartment door was open. We floated toward it. The first thing that struck me was that it was clean. Nothing lying around; anything that we'd upended looking for *clues* as to where the fuck she'd taken off to was restored. Glenda stood in the center of the room, hands clasped in front of her, expectant but nervous. Good—she *should* be nervous. Her kid would be justified in hating her now.

Yet he went to her, put his arms around her and buried himself in her baggy tan sweater.

"Darling boy," she whispered, though loud enough for us to hear.

She wasn't alone, either. No surprise, Hu Zhang gave her backup. She sat on the kitchen counter, colorful arms folded and feet crossed. She grinned down at Logan.

"We meet again, kid."

The curtain to Logan's "room" was pulled back and his bed made. We put the box with the lamp and the plastic bag of his other belongings on top of the blanket. I was still floating; frustration mixed with anger; helplessness at being defeated here.

What Glenda did was wrong, yet I was not about to scream at her, throw things, make a scene in front of Logan. That's why Hu was there, and also it was likely Jake would serve as the brakes for such an outburst.

But still. She'd abandoned her son. Who was also my son, or at the very least, shared my DNA.

Glenda's eyes were filled and glistening now. "Thank you for taking such good care of Logan. I'm so grateful."

Sharp inhale on my part. Jake grabbed my forearm and dug what fingernails he had into the skin.

"Sure," I said. "Just let us know, maybe in advance, the next time you plan a vacation."

Hu slid off the counter. She pushed up the sleeves of her shirt even farther, into what appeared to be a fighting stance. Which wasn't going to happen, not today.

"That's right," Jake said. "If we have advance warning, we can make sure the extra sheets are clean and ready and we have the Froot Loops he likes."

Glenda, no longer teary-eyed, looked down at Logan. "You were eating junk food for breakfast? What did we learn about that?"

"It was only once, Mom, maybe two times. That was all they had," Logan said, throwing us under the nutritional bus, not leaving his mother's side. Traitor.

A call came in on my phone, where the ID flashed "SFPD Ybarra." If I answered this, life would get immensely complicated for Glenda and, by extension, for us. For Logan. Yet the seconds I stared at the screen stretched to eternity. She deserved punishment, oh yes, she did. But, like fighting with Hu—not today.

I swiped left. My concern for Logan, as well as my concern for a return to some normalcy in my life with Jake, dictated this high road, even though every other cell in my body wanted to get back at Glenda.

As we walked to the car, Logan-less, Jake asked: "Why would he ever want to stay in that shitty apartment again after being in our nice house?"

"I don't know. Something we can't see, obviously. He loves his mother, with all her many, many, many faults."

Jake stopped walking. "In the car, earlier. Did you say you got *fired?*"

CHAPTER 13

The first few minutes of our ride back were silent. Then:

"I need to go down to the gallery to mark down artwork for the sale. Why don't you come with me? We can talk there. You're going to have to tell me, and you don't want to be home stewing about Glenda."

Indeed, it was a Breezeann day, so there wouldn't be privacy at home. Yet I didn't dare go into the rabbit hole of an explanation to include Danny and our runs to Jack Early Park to spy on the person I was convinced was the nefarious ghost employee *crook*, Mehrdad. Jake would have me committed.

"But first, I have to talk to *you* about something." He pulled into the tiny space in back of the gallery, next to the old door that had ancient iron bars across its window.

I flipped on the lights inside as Jake keyed in the code to disable the burglar alarm. It was always so pristine in the gallery, the white walls, the art placed so that it seemed sparse, though there were many pieces. But I knew they all had a specific "wall life," after which they'd move closer to the back door and the price would go down.

I noticed at once that there were still a couple of Rivers Sontag paintings as well as at least one of those ghastly B.J. Thompson yarn sculptures I hated. Maybe he could *give* that one away.

"I didn't tell you the truth about that missing mortgage payment," he said.

My consciousness had gone from feeling like I was floating above everything while at Glenda's to now feeling my stomach, as well as the rest of me, falling through the gallery floor. I had resisted thinking that the guy who showed up on our porch—that Steve

Ramos—had any kind of credibility. I backed into one of Jake's white walls.

"It wasn't only one payment. I've missed several. We're not in good shape, Ben," he continued, glancing at me only sporadically, the majority of his speech inexplicably directed toward the front door.

"And now I've lost the little income I contributed to this party," I said.

"Yeah, so—what happened there?"

"'A restructuring from regional,' or so Darien said. But—just you wait a minute, Jake. This has been going on for months; you never said anything?"

He moved behind his sales counter, like that would protect him. "I thought I'd catch up, we'd have deals that were pending here"—he swept his arm to the side in an arc—"and they'd fall through, or be delayed. I kept thinking we'd be able to pay the bill but never caught up."

"Meanwhile, there was Logan moving in with us as well as my mother. Distractions," I said, not as absolution but as some kind of explanation.

"There was that. And, of course, there was that *guy* for you, what's his name, Walter? Not to mention Tony, of course."

Jake walked along the wall, taking most pieces off, which meant they'd be marked down. He got to the last one on the particular stretch of wall and it slipped from his grasp, landing with a thud on the plank floor.

"For fuck's sake," he yelled, bending down to examine the frame. "Looks OK; a tiny nick in back, which no one will notice."

"Let's get back to the mortgage," I said. "Dalliances, or whatever you want to call them, never prevented us from paying our bills before. How serious is this?"

Before he could answer, there was an echoing bang from the front door. The glass there was opaque, revealing only the outline of a person, what appeared to be a slim male person.

"I think that might be Tony," Jake said. "He was going to be in the neighborhood today."

When was he going to tell me all this? Convenient ruse to avoid answering me, which was not going to work. "How serious is this?" I repeated, louder, as he unlocked and opened the front door.

Indeed, it was Tony Ochoa. A little shiver went up my spine;

I'll admit it. I didn't even care that this liaison, this chance "oh, I was in the neighborhood" excuse was actually planned in advance, before Jake had any inkling I would be with him. Yet he specifically *asked* me to come down, rather than drop me at home.

And truthfully, who wanted to talk about business failures, foreclosures or mothers abandoning their children when someone as glorious as Tony was in the same room? I was with Jake: *This* was much more preferable.

Sometimes you want to see yourself as if in a movie, and imagine you could behave that way. Across a crowded room, like the song says, or in one you knew you had been in, such as the many and recent art openings and galas Jake held right here. Seeing *him* at the door, and rushing into his arms. Despite all the acceptance of men like us in recent decades, such behavior still seemed relegated to women, and only in fantasy scenarios.

Yet I saw myself doing that, however briefly. I wouldn't have pushed Jake to the side at all—I would have insisted he be part of such a dream embrace.

Tony smiled at Jake and they kissed once, then settled in for that hug, and the strangest thing happened: They turned toward me and opened their arms to invite me in.

So I got to float toward the door anyway. What happened next was not something I'd ever even entertained in the private space of my own heart—perhaps I lacked imagination.

I was enfolded into a Jake-Tony sandwich, the beautiful and solid, kind of rough, French Canadian husband on the one side and the young, passionate, sexy Latino otter (who was taller than both Jake and me) feeling me up on the other.

Somehow this day continued with the detached blur I first felt earlier at Refuge, when I was fired. This was so much better!

The front door was relocked and the gallery lights dimmed. A couple of matching tufted benches Jake had for gallery viewers with chronic "museum back" were hastily shoved together, under one of B.J. Thompson's soft sculptures, this one evocative of the plains, earthy colors and all. Appropriate, secured well enough that it wouldn't fall on us if we bumped into the thin flats.

A long, intoxicating blend of positive and negative spaces followed. It was surprising how easy it was for us, us three, to slide into this. It did not require much, or any, in the way of explanation; even for us, especially for me, it was refreshingly unnecessary to use words to justify or put boundaries around what we were doing.

It was much, much easier to have sex with the overpowering lust I had for both Jake and Tony than it was to ponder why Jake had basically torpedoed our future economic security. That discussion would have to wait.

Things worth noting: As I had suspected from our earlier liaison, Tony was bigger down there than both Jake and I were; I was never a size-queen type but have to admit this big cock of his was a nice benefit. Jake, on the other hand, still held the title as the handsomest man I'd ever been with and was not likely to fall from that perch. Both were pleasantly hairy; both loved to kiss and be kissed. Jake had always amazed me as a person who never had any unpleasant or discernable body odor; Tony did have a distinctive masculine scent, which was magnificent.

The two of them had no trouble filling the gallery over and over with what might have been mistaken as a cleaning crew's chlorine smell; unfortunately being prostate-less I could not contribute seed, but they more than made up for it.

At the end, we lay there, the three of us, intertwined and perspiring, our breathing and our heartbeats synched.

"Wow, guys," I whispered. It sounded sort of lame, but I couldn't handle any continued silence. "That was nice."

Tony's eyes were closed and stayed that way, but his smile remained. "You're beautiful," he said, not apparently directed to anyone specific.

Not only sweet and sexy; he was also smart. From the pile of clothing came the obnoxious intrusion of dueling buzz sounds indicating what someone hoped was an urgent message.

I turned to Jake and he turned to me. "Is that your phone?" we asked, at the same time.

"Someone has to check," he said, meaning me, as I was closer to the pile.

The occasional person *was* walking by the gallery; I supposed if they pressed their little faces to the glass hard enough they'd see my middle-aged nakedness in the back, fumbling with two pairs of pants, fishing out phones.

The message was sent to both of us, a group-text thing, from Breezeann: "You might want to come back right away. Someone in a uniform just put up an auction notice on your front door."

* * *

We knew we had to get back right away, find out WTF this fresh hell was—though it was difficult, as the three of us were still naked, wet and intertwined, a situation that could not lend itself to speedy resolution.

Yet this was no 1970s European art film, and the longer we dallied, pleasurable as it was, the more I envisioned Ecology Partners, who collected our garbage in San Francisco, removing our belongings and rudely piling them on the breezy Noe Valley curb.

I was in one of those heightened postcoital states where either partner could not be out of immediate touching range. Realistically, it would be impossible to focus on Jake and our house business, even *foreclosure*, the word my brain did not want to process, if Tony was anywhere near.

Jake I was used to, Jake I could handle—despite his beauty, which hadn't tired me yet.

We were able to sit there and pretend not to be fascinated with the way Tony pulled on his minimal raspberry-colored briefs and then worked his jeans up and over his hairy thighs until they enclosed him in one perfect, seamless package.

There followed a closing group hug, and he kissed us both, back and forth, softly but deeply. It had to be quick; otherwise there was the danger of falling back into the makeshift bed and starting all over again.

We didn't. Tony slipped out the front door, much as he came in, yet so much had changed in the air during that short time in the gallery. It was as if the walls were a different color, a rosy peach, and actually glowed. The yarn sculptures looked . . . brilliant. Almost. Not to get carried away, but—

"Now, what happened at the furniture store?" Jake asked, once we were back in the car heading home. Funny, we were already ignoring the elephant in the room.

"We're racing back to save our house and you want to talk about *that*?"

"The house is a longer conversation," he said, not sounding quite convinced. "But there's got to be more about this firing than a simple management decision—this city is bursting at the seams."

I couldn't explain my surveillance of Darien and Mehrdad without sounding completely crazy, at least not in the short time it would take us to get home. "I think, when you get right down to it, an insurmountable personality conflict developed between Darien Unger and me," I said. "That's what happens when you were once the boss—somewhere, anywhere. You can't go back. I guess I found out the hard way."

He looked at me as if he was surprised I was being so sensible. "Keep your eyes on the road," I said. "The only reason I haven't puked is because we just had sex with that beautiful man. *What are we going to do about the house, Jake?*"

He was silent, tightening his grip on the steering wheel. "That was a good job for you. I know how much you liked working with Danny and being downtown every day."

He was successful at ignoring my attempts to talk about the house, but this was about to end as we pulled up right in front of it. "The Refuge job was never enough money, was it? This might be a blessing in disguise. I can find something better—at least under normal circumstances. Normal circumstances would mean you were still well-employed, selling art, and we wouldn't be panicked."

Breezeann leaned against the front doorframe, tapping her moccasin-clad toe as we climbed up the stairs. Typical—a frown and crossed arms over peasant blouse and vintage bell bottoms—which had somehow survived fifty years of laundering without massive structural failure.

She waved the papers at us, a taunt. "Naughty boys have not been paying the bank!"

I grabbed them from her, the tape still attached at both top and bottom, a few tiny chips of the still newish olive door paint clumsily stuck on. The words swam on the page, but it was clearly one of those "quit or pay up" notices. I'd have to read the fine print to figure out how far along this process was.

I marched past her into the house. It was cooler than normal; Breezeann must have left the front door open while she waited for us. In my periphery I noticed flickering in the living room corner, which could only mean Bernard was going to (maybe) manifest; not a surprise since we were in the midst of house drama, one of his touchstone concerns.

The giant, aging Dennis the Menace surfer-boy ghost would not distract me. I would read the notice. The headline read: "Notice of Foreclosure Sale."

Absorb this in small chunks: I would need to sit down.

My hands trembled; the paper shook. The gist of what I got from several quick attempts to read this frightening document was that this was the first in what would likely be a series of increasingly ominous threats.

Jake and Breezeann followed me in. He sat beside me, my partner in life and in this real estate venture, this *traitor*. Maybe that was too strong: this uncommunicative, reticent half of the collaboration.

I turned to him, letting the foreclosure notice fall to the floor. "How could you let it come to this?" If that sounded a bit histrionic, I couldn't let this perfect opportunity to dial up the drama go to waste.

He raised an eyebrow. "Like I said, it happened fast. I didn't mean to—one missing payment leads to another, then late fees, interest, delaying taxes—then on top of that, problems with the gallery, so there really was *no money* to even make partial payments." He looked out the window. "I'm so sorry, Ben."

If the ghost of Bernard had any powers to move things in our living world—which as far as I knew he did not—now would be a good time to smack Jake. As it was, he stayed in his corner and spun his arms in windmill fashion, which I did my best to ignore. There was no point in mentioning his presence to Jake, who couldn't see him, or in frightening Breezeann, who still might have to spend many hours alone in this house.

"So, basically—we're broke?"

He lowered his handsome face into his hands and whispered through them: "Yes."

I put my hand on his shoulder and squeezed. "This is a partnership—you could have told me about it."

"I know, I know," he said. "I always thought, it's right around the corner, I'll have the money to pay all the back bills. That didn't happen."

* * *

That was the beginning, maybe not the real beginning but the beginning for me, of our nightmare with the foreclosure. It was an endless cascade of paper, sometimes posted on the front door, sometimes sent by lawyers or other bank functionaries who were mostly faceless names behind impossible-to-contact corporations.

Truth was, Jake had gotten us in deep. We were months behind on the mortgage and there was no way now that I was out of a job and that his gallery was failing that we could catch up.

I began to think that the ghosts of Bernard and Connie had some sort of clue as to what was going on because I started seeing them much more often and they were agitated to a level I'd never witnessed before.

Bernard would now sometimes come out of his corners, and while I wouldn't say it frightened me, it was startling to see the tall dead surfer boy at the kitchen sink or lurking in the bathroom while I was on the throne reading, or standing—silent, almost accusatory—right inside the front door when I would come home.

Connie, for her part, would often pad into a room, sit down slowly then wag her ghostly tail and gaze up pleadingly.

I'd look down and say, "I'm sorry this is happening, dog. I wish I could fix it, but so far I haven't been able to figure out how."

We were going to have to move. Since the time that we became homeowners, rents in San Francisco had risen even crazier than usual, and it was no longer possible, especially for two marginally employed men, to rent anything within the city limits bigger than a charming Victorian claw-foot bathtub.

Transparent Connie would sit there, and I would throw out ideas. "How about the East Bay?" I would say. "What about Vallejo?" I would ask. "How about some other city entirely?"

It was good to have this quiet audience, because Jake and I barely spoke. At least at first. I got stuck on the idea of partnership— I thought, and perhaps I was mistaken, that we shared everything, even the less pleasant things, like, for instance, financial ruin.

He didn't have an answer that was acceptable.

Had he told Tony about his financial problems with the gallery? I assumed that all the unaccounted-for time he'd been spending at the gallery in the last few months was for this "dalliance" with Tony—which, I guess, I was now a part of so likely should not be so judgy. But it *was* possible he was avoiding me to not have to talk about the failure of Jake Brosseau Gallery.

Now that I thought about it, there had been other things. Not letting me see the mail. Taking his mobile calls out to the front porch. And, additionally, he'd lost a little weight. He said he'd given up those fatty salt-and-vinegar potato chips, a perennial favorite, but really, had it been stress?

Not that any of this mattered to our problem at hand. Which became urgent. It got to the level where cardboard boxes, the flat kind you had to put together, the kind that came when you got evicted, began arriving and were stacked in the front hallway.

And what an embarrassment it was.

Was it my imagination or did neighbors avert their eyes? Of course they knew; word got around. Both of us were home so much during the day, that red letter that someone's lost a job—or jobs.

They'd see Steve Ramos. He'd come back several times, that opportunistic real estate "person." He was not a man who had any shame when told to fuck off. He'd walk up and down the block, as if casing the area. Perhaps some of the reticence of my neighbors was from fear; if we got foreclosed on, what might happen to them?

He wouldn't wear me down. I'd do everything in my power to not have strident Steve be the salesman for our house. Yet the feeling I had, so often during this time, was that events cascaded around me and I had very little control over what happened next.

Jake, for his part, spent a lot of time in the garden out back. That was his baby, and wherever we ended up—the location of which we still didn't know—likely would not have a curated garden like this one on Elizabeth Street. His meditation. I caught him out there, on his knees, staring at the muddy earth, spade in hand, practically catatonic.

I still couldn't quite understand why he hadn't told me. I *could* have helped. Granted, I didn't make that much money at Refuge and I was overwhelmed with all of the Darien dramas, but I could have helped.

We were beyond that now. The process had accelerated to the point where auction dates came, were rescheduled, then came around again. We had just about exhausted all of the legal tricks we could find to stay in that house.

Open boxes then appeared in all the rooms. I may have put them there myself, but it would always surprise me to see them. Whenever I wrapped and put a treasured item into a box, I would notice Bernard flickering in my periphery, back in the corner. He didn't approve.

I turned to him. "What can I do? We're going to go and I expect you and Connie will come too."

What would come back from him was like a shudder, a dismissive groan. Another person might've confused it with the wind moving the century-old wood of the house. "I know you're sad," I told him. I didn't know what else to say. "We are too."

Even if we didn't know where we were going, I felt it was better to be ready, hence the initiative to pack. One day not long after, I was with Breezeann in the kitchen (she was now working for deferred compensation) when I heard someone come up the front steps. I was prepared to fight Steve Ramos.

It was Karen. She came alone, without my mother.

Breezeann brought us tea sans complaint. Peppermint, no caffeine, mismatched cups, as the good ones had already been packed up.

"It's from that hippie joint I go to in Nevada City," she said, and left.

Karen took a sip and brushed an errant strand of blond hair away from her face. "What good is it having rich friends if they can't do things for you?" she began. "I have a ton of room. Enough for you and for Jake and even for Logan."

It was true, she did. The reality was it was big enough so that I would never have to hear her and my mother together, which was a main consideration.

"Logan's back with Glenda," I said. "That won't change. Of course, she could always go back to South Africa, I suppose."

"Well—there's room, even if it's only for the weekend and he wants to come over. Buena Vista Park is my backyard."

I put the cracked cup down. "Karen—we're both unemployed."

"That won't always be the case. We can talk about rent or whatever when the situation changes."

"We were convinced we'd have to leave the City," I said. "Let me talk to Jake."

* * *

He didn't especially like the idea—but—it was practical; it made sense to accept Karen's largesse. It wasn't permanent. We could make decisions, but at our leisure. Or, if not at our leisure, at least we could dispense with panicking.

Karen's house was so big, there was also room to store everything we had, in her basement and her attic. In fact, it was on her third floor that we were ensconced. The storage room was on one end. In the front, there was a finished bedroom plus adjoining study and a full bathroom, which, if anything, had an even better view of the East Bay than the rooms below it.

As lucky as we were to have someone as generous as Karen in our lives, this was a sad time. It was as if Jake and I were in limbo— one house gone, the future one unknown. That, and we still had the dying art gallery to deal with.

Since we couldn't, for the first time in decades, "bring boys home" (though technically we probably could, but would we ever have that discussion with Karen, or, heaven forbid, Margaret? I don't think so), the now half-empty art gallery also served as our continued rendezvous point with Tony Ochoa.

Which could be counterproductive. Ostensibly, we were there to sell artwork at a discount. Those yarn pieces left over from B.J. Thompson, for instance. Maybe some of those wild landscapes from Rivers Sontag. B.J was easier, however, because she was still back in Oklahoma. Rivers was close, across the bay in Oakland, and seemingly had the ability to know whenever a piece of his was being bid on.

"Don't you *dare* sell one of my pieces for shit money!" he'd insist.

Truth is we didn't get many sales made when Tony was around. Luckily, Jake had paid for those "viewing couches" with cash so they hadn't been taken away. Our three-way or ménage à trois or polyamorous relationship or whatever you want to call it was becoming more and more the norm.

"Did you call Tony?"

"Did you text Tony?"

"Is Tony going to swing by?"

"I wonder what Tony's doing this afternoon."

It was like that. Insidious. Yet it didn't give off that slight dread like it might end with a negative, embarrassing outcome. I once caught Jake looking at me while we were in bed, a quizzical expression on his face. Tony was sleeping, his handsome face pressed into my arm.

"I love him too," I whispered—very slowly.

Back in the day-to-day at Karen's, it was Bernard and Connie who seemed to have a better handle on the future. They wouldn't come out of the storage room at the end of our hallway. I knew this because that was the only place I would ever see them, and of course they showed themselves only to me.

The simple fact that I'd find them perched on or next to boxes packed for a move to somewhere else indicated to me that they knew the stay at Karen's was temporary and they weren't going to be left behind.

Mom had been helpful, in her own way, assisting me by finding apartment rental sheets, both the printed kind and those online. Trouble was, we'd have to find jobs first to qualify.

She'd say things like, "The neighborhood I work in, Cole Valley, has lots of cute places in it!" or something even more unhelpful like, "Four adults in one house is pushing it, don't you think?"

Around this time Jake actually said something I'd been thinking about for quite a while, the *unthinkable*: "What if we left San Francisco?" he asked.

Really. What if we left? What if we went and pursued our adventure somewhere else?

The next day at Jake Brosseau was a good one for sales. After a lady from Tiburon left with two paintings by one of the locals, I mentioned the idea—leaving San Francisco—to Tony.

He put his arms around my neck and kissed my ear. "My company opened an office down in Santa Monica," he said. "They told me I could work from there if I wanted. Of course, on one side of my family there are lots of relatives in LA. What do you think? Maybe we could all go."

Maybe we could.

* * *

And yet, I couldn't imagine *not* living in San Francisco. It had literally informed my entire adult life. As the days of that week wore on, fewer pieces of art still hung in the gallery. On a day when Jake had a dentist appointment, I was there alone. As I played a half-hearted solo game of Gallery Runway, watching the few passersby on Utah Street, whom did I see but former guest star Wally.

I sat on a stool in the window (like an Amsterdam hooker) so he could not miss me. He headed for the door.

As always, Wally was nicely put together. A fitted suit, this one a dark tan, black shoes that looked like they'd just been polished. Slate gray flat cap with no brim, as befitted the cloudy day.

One of those guys who looked so good you wanted to squeeze him and never let go, so I tried. He kissed me, beard tickling, tongue gently probing, chocolatey espresso.

He wanted me to close up the place right then and there and come over to his condo. "I'm tempted," I began. "But—we have to liquidate this stuff; Jake's depending on me today. You know, Wally, I'm tired of letting him down."

That was more than I probably should have said. It tumbled out.

Wally squeezed my hand. "There's a cute young tech guy in here somewhere, isn't there?" My face must've given me away. "Don't worry," he said, "word gets around. Congratulations—to all *three* of you."

What a way to have an embarrassment of riches when you've been as materially poor as ever. Yet I didn't want him to leave right then.

"Maybe I could interest you in some artwork?" I hadn't forgotten that Walter had money. I took his hand to show him what we had left—though there wasn't much I thought up to his taste.

"Best stuff is gone," he said. "I should go—a conference call I need to jump on."

Time slowed, and I realized I could make a different decision—as the one I made by not giving in to Wally was likely permanent. But he was right about the tech guy being "in there, somewhere." Somewhere deep.

"Check out my GiveMeMoney-dot-com page for *Richmond Rack*," I yelled after him as he hurried down Utah toward SoMa. "Maybe you could invest there? Just a thought, of course."

He tipped his hat and winked.

* * *

That was the workday's high point. No one came in during the following hour, so I turned out the lights, locked up and still had half the afternoon left over. I'd take a leisurely walk through SoMa, as I had often done throughout my years in San Francisco. Perhaps, I'd happen by Refuge.

I had to admit I was curious. Had Danny been able to keep his new position as manager? Or had he succumbed to Darien Unger's evil plans himself?

Every time I made this walk it seemed like some new and mysterious business had popped up somewhere along the way. A tiny restaurant, maybe ten feet wide, that only served grilled cheese sandwiches with the ingredients strictly limited to California dairies. Or an emporium for young men that made sure that beards and mustaches—but not hair on any other part of the body—looked impeccable for the city's streets.

Enough of that. Sooner rather than later, I was a block away. At first glance the store looked dark, but was only midafternoon, the sun high and the fog still an hour from rolling back in.

From across the street I could tell the interior lights were off. The store windows were, in fact, empty. Then the strangest thing: Danny, dressed more for a house-cleaning (or porn-crew) Saturday than in his newly acquired business casual, stood in the window taping brown wrapping paper signs to the glass. One of them said "For Rent." The other said "Clearance Sale—Everything Must Go."

My initial feeling was to jump and revel in a glorious "I told you so" moment. But that would be childish and mean, would it not?

He shrugged, then beckoned me with a nod. I crossed the street. Inside the store, most of the furniture had been cleared out, the remainder clustered in groups along the walls.

"I guess you were right about Darien," Danny said, his voice echoing. "I mean, totally right. She made a deal with Refuge management to close this store and disappear in return for no formal charges against her."

It didn't seem right that she would walk away from this. Just like with Glenda, there were few consequences. "I'm sorry this happened, Danny. I know you were looking forward to being the boss."

"I was looking forward to the money."

We laughed, which felt good. I preferred Danny in his T-shirt and jeans, anyway. We hugged, which I don't think had ever happened before. At that moment, the back door opened and in walked Darien and Mehrdad.

Awkward with a capital *A*. She was dressed as I had never seen her before, something resembling mom jeans with a shapeless gray top one might wear to the laundromat.

Nobody moved.

Then, recognizing us—no doubt from our stakeout in Jack Early Park—Mehrdad scowled and leaned up against the doorframe. It was a shame he was a crook, because he really was kind of hot—I liked them swarthy that way—yet I digress.

Darien regained her composure and advanced, slowly.

"Now, this *is* a surprise," she said. To Danny: "My yoga clothes are in the bottom drawer of the desk. I forgot to take them the other day when I was kicked out of here."

The two of us backed up. Danny may have been in shock.

Darien went to the desk and knelt down in front of it. The bottom drawer creaked open. Her red hair bobbed up and down over the desktop.

"You won, Ben," she said. "I suppose that makes you happy."

I was going to laugh, but it came out as a cough. Various dark-colored spandex items landed on top of the desk.

"I'd be happier if you were doing time," I said. Danny sunk his fingers into my ribs.

Her face, now flushed to closely match her hair, rose above the desk. "But I'm not, am I? And I won't be."

"We should leave this place," Mehrdad said quietly.

"I'm almost finished." She stood up, her arms filled with her dirty clothes, looking quite diminished from her previous lofty perch as the boss.

Her eyes bored into mine, but her voice had more sadness than anger. "We had a good thing going here," she said. "Most importantly, we had a store and we had jobs for all of us. There's no store, no jobs and now I understand you have no house, either. So I ask you, Ben, what did this get you?"

She nodded to Mehrdad to open and hold the door. She stopped there, turned around and took it all in. The mostly empty store, us *traitors*, everything. To Danny: "I won't be back."

To me: "We're not done."

CHAPTER 14

I wouldn't dwell on Darien's threat. Danny and I embraced, made more jokes about my guest appearance on one of his porno sets—strictly in an observational capacity—and I left. Leaving Muni at Castro Station, I crossed over Market and started up the hill.

The last part of this new daily climb involved actual stairs, set into the concrete sidewalk, not a rarity in San Francisco. It was a workout and I needed it.

At our—meaning Karen's—block, Buena Vista Terrace, I stopped to catch my breath. Would I miss the wisps of fog that were even now coming over the treetops in the park above me? I thought I would—and how, then, could I ever leave?

When I got to the house, I couldn't have been more surprised to see Logan sitting there on the steps. The reliable sea breeze had turned the afternoon cool. He'd buttoned his jacket up to the neck, his arms crossed over his chest, hugging.

That feeling you get the pit of your stomach—what was it, exactly? Regret, guilt, longing? All those things, and more, the sum of which is greater than the parts? It was strong enough to stop me for a second.

I hoped he didn't notice—that he stopped me in my tracks. The nine-year-old.

"Logan," I said, "I'm surprised to see you. Nobody home?"

"I didn't check yet."

He must have just arrived. I couldn't imagine my mother not detecting an intruder of any size, unless she wasn't there. That was a distinct possibility; she had her own life, as she kept reminding me.

"Does *your* mother know you're here?"

He stood. "I walked over. I didn't tell her. She's at work today anyway."

I resisted the urge to inquire about about Brennan Reeves. Another of the casualties of not having Logan in my life on a daily basis was zero chance of interacting with Mr. Hot Assistant Principal.

But back to the situation at hand: "It's *nice* to see you, Logan."

He smiled. I heard a rustle behind him, something from inside one of the front rooms, someone in there, no doubt, looking out.

"Are there any kids my age on this block?"

I didn't know the answer to that. Kids like Tyler and Destiny, questionable as they were, lived at least two big hills away from us.

The door opened and my mother stuck her head out. Her white hair was wet, as if she'd just gotten out of the shower. "I heard all this noise out here," she said.

"We weren't being loud," I said.

"I was in the bathroom upstairs and I heard you." She sighed. "Do you want to come in, Logan? I'm not sure what I've got, but there may be some treats—unless Ben and Jake have eaten them all."

"Thank you, Margaret, but my mom doesn't allow that kind of processed sugar."

I laughed. "Let's go up to the park," I said. "It's a beautiful afternoon."

Logan jumped down the stairs.

Margaret whispered to me, "Is he staying for dinner?"

"I don't know," I stage-whispered back, and followed Logan up the block, where he'd turned the corner.

By this time in spring, the winter rains had stopped. Buena Vista Park, just one convenient block away, erupted in fragrance, plants in all shades of green and brown. Flowers bloomed everywhere, reminding me there was a payoff for putting up with such a high cost of living.

Logan had already started up the old stone stairs, which led to a number of pathways to the top of the hill. Between us was ghost dog Connie, which didn't surprise me a bit, as this park had been her favorite place in the entire world when she was alive. She zigzagged across the pathway, disappearing into the underbrush occasionally, then emerging close to Logan as he made his way up the hill.

I had great memories of this park. For years, its paths and bushes were the sites of epic debaucheries. Now I was mostly retired from that sort of fun but slutty activity (or maybe it was just more formally planned).

Also, it had become almost impossible to tell who was cruising and who was merely hiking. My gaydar was broken for the Millennial generation, which eliminated the majority of people still capable of hiking. Perhaps it was just as well—this would allow me to stay out of trouble with no active measures on my part.

All pathways eventually led to the top of the hill, where there was a clearing and a fantastic, 360-degree *buena vista* of San Francisco, the bay, the bridges and the ocean. Why wouldn't Logan want to see this? Over and over. He was a native. This was his kingdom.

He was standing on top of the picnic table at the very highest point in the clearing when I finally caught up to him.

"You're too fast for me," I said.

"Well. You're old, Uncle Benny."

"Someone better watch it if someone wants food later."

"Margaret will give me treats and she's even older than you."

This was, no doubt, a losing line of conversation I'd endeavor to change—I sat at the table while he paced back and forth checking every angle.

"How is it, being back at your mom's?"

"It's okay, she works a lot. I guess Harold's always around."

"Right. Harold."

"Sometimes, I miss you and Jake and Breezeann and Margaret and Tyler and even Destiny—though I see her at school."

I'm not exactly sure why it became clear to me at that point—maybe it was part inspiration from the view of the sun, lower in the sky, the possibility of it setting into the water. But all that natural beauty made honesty seem fitting.

"We miss you, too."

As soon as I opened my mouth I felt the heaviness lift. I sensed a furry creature just outside my periphery with a wagging tail; obviously Connie.

"Have they done the unit on human biology in your science class yet?"

Logan stood still, his eyes focused on the nearby tree line. "That dog I used to see at your house is here."

"I know. She can't hurt you; more importantly, that would be the last thing she would *ever* do."

"But why can I see her but nobody else can?"

"I'm *not* nobody!" I laughed. "It's because you're part of the family."

He scanned the bushes, squinting, searching for the elusive doxie. "About that biology unit—"

"I know all about fucking, Uncle Benny."

A young couple, pushing a stroller, passed us just as this nine-year-old dropped this bomb. They glanced at each other, then picked up their pace, obviously not wanting their infant to be tainted.

"That's good; it's good to know all about that."

"I think those people scared your dog away," he said.

"I know you know, your mother has never had a boyfriend or a husband since, of course, she's gay, but I'm not sure if you know that—the sperm donor, in your case—well, that was me."

He didn't move. Logan stared intensely at the bushes where he thought Connie had gone.

"Oh, I knew that," he said, finally. "I think she's right under that bush." He ran over to the trees about ten yards away and stood there, his back to me.

"She was never good about obeying commands even when she was alive, Logan." Trying to be helpful, or change the subject. Had I seriously miscalculated?

Eventually, he bent down, getting on his knees to peer under low-lying branches and leaves. "I don't see her," he said, almost too quiet to hear.

I sat on the picnic table until he was finally ready to come back. I thought he might have been crying, but his eyes weren't red, though he averted them. "I think I like cats better than dogs anyway; after all, my mom—who I *want* to live with—is a lesbian."

"So is mine. We have that in common."

As the sun lowered in the sky, growing its glint off the endless Pacific, we started back down the trail, the decision unspoken, following our feet and gravity.

"She—Margaret, my mother—is bound to have something you like," I said. "She may be, technically, your grandmother—though I think it would be a *mistake* to call her that."

He was a few steps ahead of me, kicking pebbles out of the way across the broken asphalt. Finally, he turned to look at me.

"You could take me to games, like the Giants."

"Seriously. You want to go to those?"

"Yeah, of course, why not?" he answered, to which I had no good response.

Thus flew my nascent idea of being a different kind of father, one who stressed museums and concert halls over muddy playing fields.

Maybe we could do both.

At Karen's house, as Logan bounded up the steps, no doubt anticipating treats, a text came in from Tony: *I've got to talk to you guys! It's about LA!*

* * *

The day we left was, cruelly, one of those perfect San Francisco days when there truly was no finer place to be found on the Earth. If it only could stay that way—low seventies, sunny, not windy, benign—but it never did. The kind of day where one could sit outside at the café across from Dolores Park and idly watch the world go by.

But, inevitably, the sea breeze would come, blow anything not tied down toward Oakland, make you scramble to throw on whatever sweater or jacket you brought—if you had the foresight to do that.

Over anticipating negative outcomes was a specialty, I admit. I resolved to not make this a feature in our new, supposedly warmer-all-the-time location in Southern California.

Karen lent us money for the U-Haul. Jake was apprehensive about the move, and so was I: One of her attic rooms stayed filled with boxes of our extra clothing, dishes and other housewares *just in case.*

With luck we'd send for it all in a year, maybe before. I didn't like goodbyes and came from a family that didn't like them either, so it was awkward with Mom.

To be honest, I wasn't over the fact that she had co-opted my best-friend status with Karen Kling. Becoming a lesbian at this late stage was one thing—not easy, either—but stealing my BFF was quite another. It was obvious she was going to stay—rich girlfriend, a job of her own, everything was so good here why in hell would she go back to that big drafty house overlooking Lake Michigan? (Though she did, at one point, offer it to us: "I have that empty place in Milwaukee. You could move there. That's not such a bad idea.")

Actually, it was a bad idea for so many reasons that could make

191

my head explode, not the least of which was the control issue. So, they—Margaret and Karen—stood together on the porch, arms locked, waving as Jake maneuvered our rental truck down the hill to Divisadero and eventually onto the Bay Bridge.

I watched the City recede in the side mirror—Twin Peaks and the Sutro Tower doing their best as landmarks of the enchanted land, getting smaller and smaller until they were gone.

We didn't say much until we had bested the Altamont Pass and Jake veered right onto I-5, which would take us to L.A.

He let out an exhale, which morphed into a whistle. "This truck is heavy," he said. "I notice it especially on hills."

"You want me to drive?"

He smiled. "I don't think that would be a good idea."

"That's probably a wise decision." I was secretly relieved; the manly pride could take the hit.

On one side of us there were endless green fields; on the other side endless brown hills. "That was kind of weird with Logan, huh?"

Glenda and the kid had stopped by briefly to say goodbye. It was awkward because of our most recent conversation, yes, but also strange because *nobody* wanted to talk to Glenda, who was still persona non grata.

I think Logan was better able to look directly at me *before* he knew I was his biological father. On the front porch, he looked down and off to the side. "Once we get settled, it'll be summer, you can come for a visit," I said. "They have the Dodgers, and I think we're going to be living pretty close to where they play."

He gave a little noncommittal shake of his head, but it was pretty anticlimactic. Glenda instructed him to "give your uncles a great big hug," which he did, and then they left.

"I don't think you have to act any different with him now that he knows," Jake said. "Just be you. Just be normal. That's what he likes."

Right. I guess I knew that. "Not sure why I bothered to even tell him."

Jake kept his eyes directly ahead of him on the road. "You wanted him to know you had his back, since his mother turned out to be crazy."

And what if she walks away again? A scary thought, especially since we'd no longer be right there to save the day.

With every mile farther south, the notion that we were making a terrible mistake got stronger. Jake seemed to pick up on that mood and squeezed my knee after what seemed like an interminable silence.

"This will be OK. It's natural to be nervous—but it's L.A. Every day will be sunny."

I wasn't sure if he was trying to convince me more or himself. While the Central Valley had gotten gradually hazy and then clouded over around Bakersfield, when we finally got that truck down off the Grapevine the sky was clear and a brilliant blue.

We were moving into something called a "bungalow court" in an area called Highland Park. It was a pity rental, scored by Jake from one of his regular collectors at the gallery. She owned several buildings in that neighborhood and happened to have a vacancy. She made him promise he'd open a gallery in the Arts District, once we got back on our feet.

Strange to be surrounded by money but not have any yourself! I had had that nice long run as head of marketing for Safe Harbor; then that had ended with the cancer and the best I could find was Refuge—but I was with Jake, who was doing great. We were a partnership where he was the main breadwinner. Now we were both starting over.

As we pulled off the freeway, I realized this neighborhood was like SF's Mission District, but with more hills. The houses had yards— cactus yards, but space. Two pluses, right off the bat. Murals with a distinctive Latin flavor, taco stands, botanicas. Would we be viewed as gentrifiers, when the truth was we lacked any capital (or any desire) to gentrify?

Jake wedged the truck in front of our new home—a double row of Spanish revival bungalows facing each other, a cracked plaster arch with the Avenue 58 address over a narrow walkway separating the buildings.

Certainly not Elizabeth Street. The price was right, most definitely, but would this portend our own slide out of middle-class comfort? I didn't even have both feet out of the truck when the black Prius slipped in silently behind us.

Jake also saw him in the side mirror. He let out a relieved sigh. "I'm glad he's here before we go in. We should go in together, the three of us." That I silently agreed was remarkable in itself.

Tony had followed us, driving our car all the way down. "We

could carry him over the threshold, I guess"—one of those nervous utterances that just come out that don't sound right two seconds later. "He is *younger*, that's what I mean. Lighter."

Jake smiled. "I know what you mean."

Tony was all smiles, the back of his T-shirt damp from the hot and long valley drive.

"You beat me!" he said.

The three of us embraced—group hug, then group kiss. Three men kissing in broad daylight in this new neighborhood we had no sense of. A flicker of that fear of violence that was always there, even after all these years, though buried deep.

The only complaint today came from a dog at the fence, a little Chihuahua with a showy personality. Behind it, in the mostly dirt and brown grass of a small house, were a couple of chickens, ignoring the barking but making their own noise.

And I'd been the one to celebrate the idea that in Los Angeles, there'd be *yards*.

Our embrace and my daydream were broken by the appearance of a short and sturdy middle-aged blonde at the top of the stairs, directly under the archway. Jake saw her at the same time I did: "You must be—"

"Marina Boyko. Yes, I am manager here, they told me all about you. Come up, I will show you apartment."

We followed her, single file. An aside: "That dog is dangerous. I would not get too close to that fence."

The "apartment" had a living room with a faux fireplace, a kitchen with an old and tiny built-in eating area, a hallway, two bedrooms and a bath. All had been painted a tasteful off-white. There was a small fenced patio outside a back door. I wondered if Marina was doing the mental math of "three men, two bedrooms" and what she was envisioning.

"I will let you get settled and we will sign papers tonight. That good?"

That *was* good. I wondered where she was from, Eastern Europe, possibly Russia? I guessed we would find out.

We didn't carry Tony across the threshold—it would need to be reenacted at some later time. However, once the main pieces of furniture had been carried up and in, in particular our bed, we knew the time had come to sanctify the new space, the new city, just for the three of us. Our *Benediction*, perhaps.

Tony: "I've been thinking about this for three hundred miles."

Me, too, actually, and I supposed it would finally be OK to admit it. Watching the two of them, Jake and Tony, fall into bed together, yet waiting for me and wanting me, I felt safe and desired, even if our present circumstances might be the very definition of vague (and decorator-less).

My shirt was off when the mobile rang. Jake groaned. When I saw who it was, I knew I had to answer.

"This will only take a minute, guys," I said, walking out into the living room, sitting on an unopened box of books. "Logan," I whispered, "you OK?"

"Hi, Uncle Benny! Are you at your new house yet?"

"We just got here. I think that you can call me 'Ben' now, or 'Benny,' if you want."

"I looked on the Internet. Dodger Stadium is close to the address you gave me."

I looked out the window. The noisy Chihuahua next door patrolled its fence, back and forth, forth and back, giving me *mal de ojo*.

"I think you're right, Logan. It *is* close by."

"We can go to games, then, when I come visit you and Uncle Jake."

"I guess we can. I guess we will."

"OK, I better go now. Mom's coming up the stairs, we have to make dinner." He hung up.

Outside, the Chihuahua stopped barking and stuck its nose through the chain-link opening, tail wagging. Connie had appeared on our side of the fence and was saying hello.

Laughter came from the new bedroom. "Ben, we're going to do this with or without you," Tony yelled. "Get in here!"

ABOUT THE AUTHOR

In addition to *Benefits,* Jim Arnold is the author of the novels *Benediction, The Forest Dark* and *Kept.*

Jim also directed the documentary short *Our Brothers, Our Sons,* about generational differences around HIV/AIDS in gay men, (nominated for Best Documentary at the 2002 Turin International Gay & Lesbian Film Festival).

He blogs at www.jimarnoldblog.com/blog.

www.ingramcontent.com/pod-product-compliance
Lightning Source LLC
Chambersburg PA
CBHW032132170626
46808CB00006B/2197